Spoiled Children

By

Elizabeth Sutherland

First published in Great Britain
by
For the Right Reasons
Tel: 01463 718844 or 07717457247
60 Grant Street, Inverness IV3 8BS
fortherightreasons@rocketmail.com
Changing lives through Enterprise

Cover design: Stewart

ISBN: 978-1-905787-12-8

Also by Elizabeth Sutherland

The Black Isle (nf): Lent Term (f) 1973: The Seer of Kintail (f) 1974:Hannah Hereafter (f) 1976: The Eye of God (f) 1977: The Prophecies of the Brahan Seer (edi0 (nf) 1977:The Weeping Tree (f) 1980: Ravens and Black Rain (nf) 1985: The Gold Key and the Green Life (edit) (nf) 1986: In Search of the Picts (nf) 1994: The Pictish Trail (nf) 1996:The Five Euphemias (nf) 1997: Lydia, Wife of Hugh Miller of Cromarty (b) 2002: The Bird of Truth (f) 2006: Boniface, Bishops and Bonfires (nf) 2010: Amendment of Life (f) 2010: Children of God (nf) 2010: One of the Good Guys (f) 2011: Columba and the Monstrous Wurrrm (c) 2012

Dedicated to my great grandchildren with much love

Part One

Ladymuir Farm

Bella

In the beginning a forest of tenements blotted out the sky. That winter ice fanned outwards from burst pipes and hung in glistening fringes from window-sills, turning the old buildings into glittering palaces.

That spring there were no flowers until the fire.

Bella stood in the black street bundled into a blanket that smelled of pee and smoke and watched the red flowers blossom in every window.

That was all she could remember of the beginning.

After the fire, there was Mr Gould, black-browed, fiery-faced with a temper as unpredictable as March. He lifted her off the bus. The sky was a great white eye and she, caught like a speck of dust, in its stare. She screamed and the sound spread over the flat Lanarkshire fields, uncontained.

Mr Gould lifted his hand and cuffed her across her cheek. His touch, like other punishing palms of the past, was reassuring. After a while when her feet grew tired of the stony lane and her right arm ached with the weight of the paper bag that contained an unwashed vest, a comb with some teeth missing and a pair of new pink knickers, she put her hand in his and held on to him. She expected no response, but after a while when she needed to wipe her nose, she found her hand imprisoned in his grasp. The snot ran in two streams down to her mouth, so she sucked it in.

He never spoke till they reached the farm. In the scullery he dropped her hand and pushed her into the kitchen. A tall, broad-bosomed woman with a great nest of straw-coloured hair caught up in a net and a face like a pale plate turned from the range and stared.

'She's a midget,' Big Lizzie declared. 'For why did you want to go bringing me a bairn like that?'

'She'll grow,' said Mr Gould. 'Sit in at the board, lass, and take your tea.'

Her nose was on a level with the kitchen table. There were two boys opposite with spiky red hair and faces all over freckles called James and Gordon. Twins. After a plate of mutton stew and tatties with tea as black as treacle, they took her to the barn and tossed her between them like a ball. Their breaking voices were raucous, their gawky bodies clumsy, but their hands, being used to lambs and new-born calves, were not ungentle.

She grew feverish with excitement, shrieking with fear and pleasure, but after a while they lost interest and disappeared on some ploy of their own. That was the first lesson she learned. There was no room for outsiders in their relationship.

Right from the start, Big Lizzie expected her to work. By her sixth birthday she could lay and clear the table, wash and dry the dishes, dust and polish the furniture. Outside she collected the eggs and washed them for the market. Before she was seven she could strip the cows and it was her daily task to deliver milk to the Hall in time for breakfast even on Sundays before she put on her best boots for the kirk.

Big Lizzie told her so often she was lucky that she believed it. 'When I was a bairn, orphans were left to rot in the workhouse. Count yourself fortunate that the fairmer brought you here.'

She always referred to Mr Gould as 'the fairmer'.

She had other stories about orphans turned out into the snow, bitten to death by rats, stolen by tinkers. 'Believe me, you're the lucky one. You're not here to enjoy yourself. You're here to work like the rest of us and don't you forget it.'

Big Lizzie set high standards and expected her to achieve them.

The milk cans were made of steel with close-fitting lids attached by a chain to the handle. The smell of milk lingered even after she had scoured them, sour but redolent of something sweet and sad. She put in her nose and sniffed.

Big Lizzie cuffed her, called her a dirty besom and made her wash them both again. Her swollen starfish fingers no longer felt the chill of the water in the tap.

At seven-thirty sharp, she set off for the Hall. In the January dark a white frost reflected steely stars. Each blade of grass was a sword. Mud ruts clanged against the bottom of the cans. Half way across the field she rested her arms. The stillness and the cold numbed her inside and out. She stood too long blowing smoke clouds with her breath. Even the chatty stream was subdued under layers of fretted ice.

She clambered across the style over the stone dyke first with one can and then the other. She shuffled through crisp mulches of dead leaves under the Spanish chestnuts, up the side of the pony paddock white as linen under the dawn moon, past the high garden wall where the door was kept shut to keep out the rabbits, beyond the tool shed where the gardener worked, beside a lid of green ice that covered the duck pond, up the slippery brae to the kitchen door.

She could not open it for the handles of the cans had frozen to her palms.

Saidie heard her call. Down the passage that smelled of candles and paraffin, she was swept into another world as bright and warm and full of bustle as a fine morning in a city street. The pain as her fingers and toes thawed made her cry. The cook bounced into the kitchen buttoning her apron. Her plump pink face was beautiful with concern. 'Och, the poor wee mite, the soul!'

She lifted her and cuddled her and blew warm breath on her fingers. She wiped her runny nose and kissed away her tears. Bella wanted to return her hug was she was too stiff and shy. Cook, used to instant cuddles from legions of siblings, was short of time. She sat her down on the edge of the table and sent Saidie up to the nursery to borrow a pair of Miss Heather's gloves.

They were red mitts with pink rabbits knitted on the backs in fluffy wool.

'Miss Heather says you're to keep them,' Saidie told her as she fitted them over the purple swollen fingers. They smelled of soap and sun.

Then Miss Heather herself came in. 'Is that the milk girl?' she asked in a cool clear voice, each sound as pure as a blackbird's note.

For a moment, before Saidie lifted her off the table, Bella was level with the tall thin girl. Her eyes were brown and anxious. Two half-grown front teeth seemed too big for her tender mouth. Her hair, scraped back from her brow, hung in two thick plaits down to her waist. Her wide gaze lowered as Saidie lifted Bella down to the floor.

'How old are you?'

'Six past,' she whispered looking down at her feet.

'Goodness aren't you small!' She said it admiringly. Heather Mowbray's relations were long, angular creatures with shoulders stooped from the strain of disguising their height. At seven, Heather was as tall as a ten year old. She had been conditioned from birth into believing that height was a disadvantage in a woman.

Bella kept her eyes downcast. Miss Heather was wearing brown buttoned shoes with green ankle socks over lisle stockings, and a kilt with a large silver safety pin. Her legs were long and as slim as the heron's stalks in the pond.

'Do the gloves fit?'

Bella looked down at her hands splendidly encased and nodded.

'You can have the tammy too, if you like.'

She pulled it down firmly over Bella's ears.

'The wee doll!' cried Cook, and Saidie lifted her to see her reflection in the mirror that hung between the windows.

The beret was too big. It covered her black clipped hair - Big Lizzie cropped it short for convenience - and flopped low on her brow. The pom-pom wobbled on the top of her head. It was the first time Bella had ever noticed herself. She saw huge black apprehensive eyes, frost-roughened crimson cheeks, cold sores around her mouth, but all she remembered was the beret.

'Well?' Saidie prompted. 'What do you say to Miss Heather?'

Words of gratitude jammed in her throat, none adequate to express how she felt about the hat, its smell, its touch, its colour.

'Cat got your tongue?' Saidie said sharply, but Cook had caught the glint in her lowered gaze.

'Let her alone,' she said, and Miss Heather asked, 'Can you come and play with me?'

When she got home Big Lizzie said, 'You're not here to play, you're here to work,' but she said nothing about the beret. She never noticed it, not even when Bella sat down at table still wearing it, not even when James and Gordon tried to pull it off and called her a puddock stool. Big Lizzie never said a word.

For weeks she wore it all the time and then one windless March day she left it lying in a corner of the scullery along with the boots and coats and crooks and creels. When she went back for it, she could not find it.

'Serve you right,' said Big Lizzie. '"Don't care" killed the cat.'

Frost had shrunk her mitts into felted rags. She hid them under her mattress in the attic. Sometimes she put them on in bed and clasped them between her thighs.

The bothy had a cobbled floor with the cracks filled up with sawdust. The corners were jammed with old machinery and tackle of another age. Great hoops of wire fencing and piles of stobs were stacked up to the rafters. It smelled of wood and earth and animal. Here Bella washed the eggs in a pail of water. Here also when the weather was too rough for outdoor work Mr Gould sawed tree trunks and chopped kindling. Bella gathered the sawdust into sacks for the ferrets.

'What's ferrets?' she asked him that winter of the beret as he came into the bothy with a bucket of bread and scraps.

9

He jerked his head towards a door in the inner wall and took down the key that hung on a nail outside. She followed him into a dark shed lit only by a skylight dimmed by dust and cobwebs, but bright enough to reveal a line of hutches on a level with her face. The feral smell was strong, sharp, not altogether unpleasant. As she stared, two furry yellowish creatures with long snouts reared up and chattered.

Some of the hutches were empty but she counted five fully grown beasts; two jills together, two hobs, and. furthest away, a great white creature with a gold ridge down his back poked his twitching nose through the wire mesh.

'Oh, the bonnie beastie!' she cried in delight. 'Can I get to clap him?'

Mr Gould lifted the lid of the hutch and with confident unhurried movements took out the animal, holding him firmly behind his forelegs and around his chest, cradling his hind legs in the crook of his arm. He opened his long mouth and Bella saw his teeth.

'When a poley bites, it's through to the bone,' Mr Gould warned her.

'I'm no' feared,' she said scornfully. She ran her fingers over the rich ermine coat.

'A ferret's not a pet for bairns, he's a working beast,' said Mr Gould putting the creature into a spare cage while he set about cleaning the hutch.

'Can I get to help?'

He told her to empty the tray of droppings in the midden, to rinse the feeding dishes at the pump. Carefully she arranged the food and set down the water and then while Mr Gould was busy with the jills, she lifted the lid of the spare cage and reached down for the big beast. He was heavier than she expected and his long sinuous body drooped down to the floor while his neat six-toed feet scrabbled for a hold.

Mr Gould spoke quietly. 'Put the beast down.'

She heaved with all her strength, but she was not tall enough to put him in the hutch.

'Do what you're told, ye wee besom. Put him down.'

Frustrated by the smell of food so tantalizingly near and the pinch of unfamiliar fingers, the line ferret twisted his head and nipped her thumb.

'Now maybe you'll take a telling,' Mr Gould shouted lifting the ferret firmly and putting him into the hutch.

Bella sucked her thumb. It was sore but not unbearable.

'He was just hungry,' she said swallowing her tears.

'The liney's no' for you, hen,' he said, no longer angry. 'He lives alone and he works on his own. He's pals with no-one. Maybe, just maybe, in the spring there'll be babbies.'

In March Mr Gould beckoned her into the shed. During the night one of the jills had given birth to seven tiny blind creatures that lay helpless and feeble in their nest. For the next few weeks, Bella was allowed to care for the mother. From the farmer she had learned just what the jill would permit and did not attempt to handle the mites, but as she watched them grow, her heart somersaulted with tenderness and pride.

Soon after their eyes had opened, the twins needed both jills for ratting in a neighbour's barn. 'A rare night it was,' so the boys said, with the ferrets as fierce as tigers in the ricks.

Next morning when Bella went to feed the mother, she could see seven little heads arranged neatly in a row. The bodies were missing.

'How could she be that hungry,' Bella wailed in anguish, 'with all those rats inside her?'

'I told you, hen, a ferret's not a kitty or a pup. Rights and wrongs don't matter when there's only the instinct to kill. Who kens what made her do it.'

But Bella, watching the restless bright-eyed jill had a moment of sharp comprehension. Maybe the babies were better back inside their mam. Tears came then, not for the ferrets who were safe, nor for the jill who had killed to keep them that way, but for herself, for the loneliness of being alive.

11

Lizzie

Tuesday evening was Guild night at the kirk. At seven prompt Lizzie Gould took off her pinny patterned with pink roses and washed herself. Bella filled the china basin in her room with warm water from the kettle and watched while Lizzie put on a lacy jumper crocheted in beige string. She hung over the tin box with King George and Queen Mary's picture on the lid and fiddled with the brooches and bangles.

'For why do ye no' wear these fancy beads?' She held up a necklace of yellow amber that had belonged, like everything else in the farmhouse, to Aunt Jess.

Lizzie slapped her hand.

'Put them down, ye besom. Have you nothing better to do than poke and pry?'

The words were Aunt Jess's, even the voice. Lizzie did not turn her head to see Bella creep crestfallen from the room. Part of her mind crowed at the manifestation of her power, part identified with the dejected child. She stared at the necklace lying on the dressing table. After a while she lifted it, rubbed the large central bead against the skin of her inner elbow and held it close to a piece of fluff. It clung to the amber. Then she fastened the clasp around her neck.

Involuntarily she turned her head, and, holding her breath, waited for some manifestation of Aunt Jess's wrath, the shadow of her raised stick against the wall. But there was nothing.

Aunt Jess had not gone, however. Lately it seemed that she had shifted from the watcher at her shoulder to a presence in her head and Bella had become the beaten bairn. With clumsy fingers she unclasped the beads and thrust them back into the tin.

But Bella was not broken. She was sitting at the kitchen table sticking twigs into conkers brought in by the twins.

'See ma wee hoose,' she called out contentedly as Lizzie, hair flattened under a brown felt cloche, came into the kitchen.

Lizzie looked contemptuously at the miniature make-believe furniture set in a cardboard shoe-box. Partly she was relieved that the harshness that had crucified her own childhood caused this bairn no pain. But also she felt cheated.

Bella

There was a small walled garden at the front of the farmhouse with two wooden gates, one at the side which opened out on to the yard, and other at the bottom which led from the front door to the lane. It was seldom used for everyone including Lady Mowbray and the postman came to the back door.

Lizzie's Aunt Jess who used to live at the farm and whose enlarged unsmiling photograph still hung in the parlour had grown roses and gooseberries and rasps and rhubarb in neat weeded beds. Lizzie who had feared Aunt Jess's punishing stick and pulverising tongue avoided it, and Mr Gould despised the size of the plot and the frivolity of its produce. The garden had grown into a wilderness.

One afternoon in early spring, Bella discovered it. She reached up to open the wooden gate with the rusty hinges and rotting spars and stepped inside. There, at her feet, under a veil of dead couch grass and shepherd's purse she saw mauve primroses.

Crouching down, she touched them first with her fingers and then with her face, laying her cheek against the tender petals. They were cold and fragrant, and, when she screwed up her eyes, they moved and magnified and breathed.

Listening with all her might she heard not just a courting blackbird's trill, not only the distant barking of a dog but also the sound of their individual pulses, a rustling urgent throb between her temple and the earth. She knew they were alive, not less than people or more than beasts but equal, though different.

It was a discovery that held her suspended out of time and when at last she lifted her head she was conscious of the immensity of the world of plants that had existed without her knowledge all along; flowers and grasses whose sighs and whispers were none the less a language for existing on the edge of her comprehension. She was spread all over with relief. Her body unclenched, opened out to the pale cool sun, her spirit lifted. At the same time, the importance of the farmhouse and its human occupants receded. Her sense of proportion shifted. The garden became the centre of her world. For company there were all these growing things.

With great daring, she tested her knowledge. She bent over the primroses and said out loud, 'Big Lizzie's got a fat bum.'

They all laughed with her. She watched them nod and wink through the water of joy in her eyes.

The wall round the Hall garden was nearly eight feet high. She knew it was a garden because of the fragrance that drifted over on summer mornings.

At seven-thirty, Mr Fraser finished raking the gravel round the house and unlocked the tool-shed. He was a jolly man, pink-faced with ginger stubble on his chin and a smile that curved round to the corners of his eyes. He called Bella 'Sunshine', which made her feel bright and welcome.

'Morning, Sunshine,' he called out from the dark hole of the tool-shed as she passed with the milk cans and his smile curved up to his eyes.

'I like gairdens,' she told him shyly one misty morning in June.

'Want to see mine?' he asked, taking the hint.

He opened the great wooden door just as the sun pushed away the mist and there was Eden the way the minister described 'full of every tree that is pleasant to the sight', so beautiful that her eyes ached in admiration.

The garden lay on a south-facing slope and was criss-crossed with neat dirt paths edged with box, catmint and lavender. Pinks and forget-me-nots spilled over rich dark soil. Lupins, foxtail lilies and sidalcea pushed spikes up to the sun, and, behind them, old lichened archways supported roses; Albertines, Bonnie Prince Charlies, Yorks and Lancs.

She walked on tiptoe while he told her their names and she remembered them as precisely as a good teacher will remember the names of the children in his class.

'I've got just a wee gairden,' she told him. 'There's a rose with pink petals and gold inside and there's yellow lilies and a tree all over blossom.'

'Flowers are like bairns,' he told her. 'They have their little ways. Good feeding's what they need. You get Archie Gould to put in a load of dung and they'll grow, don't you fret.'

'Flowers are my pals, ' she said, not looking at him. It was taking a risk giving so much away.

'You could do worse,' he said curving his wide mouth.

One morning he was waiting for her when she came running past under dripping trees clanking her empty cans. It was as wet as a waterfall.

'Hullo there, Sunshine,' he called out to her from the tool-shed. 'Come in out of the rain.'

Her hair, sleek as plums, dripped on to the shoulders of her coat and her face was as pink and shiny as a rose hip. Rain thrummed on the corrugated iron roof like drums and hung in curtains across the lintel.

'Tck, tck, you're as wet as a drookit cat.'

His earthy fingers fumbled with the buttons of her coat. She shook her wet hair like a puppy. On the bench among the seed boxes and pots there was a damp newspaper parcel tied up with string.

'That's for your gairden,' he told her, curving his mouth. 'There's lobelia and salvia and petunias all hardened off and ready to plant.'

She looked at him with delight, her eyes as bright as blackberries.

'Don't I get a kiss, then?'

His cheek was as rough as an old elm leaf and he smelled of soil and tarred twine. He squeezed her bottom through her dress.

Then he shut the tool-shed door and locked it and put the key beside the parcel. 'Would you like to meet my wee pal, then?' he asked and she sensed that his smile was crinkling up the corners of his eyes.

She knew what it was, of course. The twins peed in the midden, splaying their fingers over their cocks making arcs and sprays with their water, unconcerned by her presence in the yard. They whinnied and showed her what they could do and she had laughed and run away.

'Do you like my wee pal, then?' he kept asking her and she knew his smile was touching his eyebrows.

'Uh huh,' she answered, not wanting to hurt his feelings, for she would have preferred a puppy or a mouse. 'I'll need to get going now,' she said politely when it was over.

He unlocked the door and put the parcel into her hands. His face was red and sober and his mouth was straight. 'Mind you hold your tongue,' he said harshly.

She nodded, sensing he had taken a risk, but she was surprised he needed to ask.

Big Lizzie eyed the bundle of plants.

'You keep away from Bob Fraser, if you know what's good for you,' she warned. 'He's got a reputation.'

Next winter there was Malcy. He started off wrong and no one wanted him when he came.

The days had colours, cloudy shades, variants of grey, except for Fridays which were red. At dawn on Fridays Big Lizzie's frown could sour the cream. By dinner her tongue was as sharp as a bramble bush.

'Sticks and stones will break my bones but words they canna hurt me,' the twins chanted, but by tea time they were shifty and slunk out of the house sometimes taking the ferrets or the dogs. No one heard them come in. Mr Gould went down to the pub. Mostly he came home drunk.

Bella liked him drunk. His dourness sloughed off him like a skin. He made jokes with a loose wet mouth and his eyes were bright. Sometimes he caught her up in his arms and called her his bonny wee pet and gave her a penny for a bag of sweeties. Bella always laughed.

Big Lizzie did not like her to laugh. 'What's funny about a drunk man? He's a menace, so he is.'

One Friday night he came in steaming, his mouth loose, his cap at the back of his ruffled hair. He put a finger to his lips and cocked a thumb at Lizzie's rigid back. Bella clapped her hand over her mouth to hide her giggles till the tears ran down her cheeks.

Big Lizzie's disgust and frustration erupted. She grabbed Bella's arm and yanked her off the stool. 'See, gonna shut your mouth, ye ignorant midden. What's so funny, I'd like to know?'

Bella sprawled across the floor and hit her head on the leg of the table.

Mr Gould's good humour vanished. His face grew red as a turkey's wattle, his eyes glowed like hot coals. He flung away a chair that lay in his road and sent it crashing against the dresser. Three willow-pattern plates tumbled from their perch and smashed on the stone floor. The cups rattled on their hooks and the cat leapt for the window-sill and knocked over the Wandering Sailor. He raised his fist.

'Lift your hand to that bairn again and I'll stiffen ye.'

'Aye,' she replied with scorn, 'you do that, you great drunken gowk, but ye'll not smash up my china.'

"I'll do what I fucking please."

Challenging her with a leer, he dragged one hand along the shelf of plates and sent them tumbling to the floor.

She grabbed a poker from the fender and flew at him.

Even drunk he was a hard man, small, but strong as iron. He seized her arm and twisted it behind her back and prised open her hand. There was a distinct crack as her forefinger broke. The poker fell with a clatter, as he bore her screaming to the floor. He fell on top of her, forcing her legs apart with his knee, grinding the heel of his hand into her mouth.

'Get out!' he shouted at Bella and she fled.

That was how Malcy began. Big Lizzie made no secret of it.

Lizzie

Lizzie hated being in the family way. A black day it was when Gould walked into the farm, his boots wrapped round with rags, his chattels on his back.

'Scum,' pronounced Aunt Jess, peering through the scullery window. 'Muck off a Glasgow midden. Get rid of him.'

Lizzie, proud in the mantle of her aunt, stepped out into the yard. 'You've got to go,' she said, tall and haughty.

He eyed her from top to toe, his black eyes insolent. 'Who says so?'

'I say so,' she answered prickly under the probe of his eyes.

'Is that right?'

He went on looking at her but his expression changed. His eyes lingered on the broad hills of her bosom.

'Ye'd make a bonny handful on a dark night.'

Pink-faced, she told him, 'The mistress'll set the dogs on you,' but it sounded as if she was on his side. That was her first mistake.

He grinned and dropped his bundle at her feet.

'He'll no' budge,' she complained back in the kitchen.

'Tchk,' said Aunt Jess seizing her stick. 'We'll soon see about that.'

She flew into the yard scattering the hens. Lizzie followed, head high and virtuous.

He took off his bonnet and stood up straight. 'I want to be a fairmer,' he told her bold as a bull calf.

She laughed at that. 'A fairmer, eh? And what do you ken about fairming, ye big-mouthed tinker brat?'

'I can learn.'

'Not on my fairm, ye can't.'

18

'Not on my fairm, ye can't.'

He stood his ground. 'I'm cheap,' he said slyly, taking the fast route to her mercenary mind.

Being short of a labourer, Aunt Jess thought fast. Maybe she could get twice the work out of him for half the wage so she hired him. He slept in the bothy and worked all God's hours till he was lean and sharp as a two-pronged grape. On pay days he stood in the kitchen, cap in hand, while she counted out the shillings.

'What you need with all this siller beats me,' she grumbled.

'What I get here would na keep a moose in rats.'

Aunt Jess laughed. 'Give the fairmer here a cup of tea, seeing he's so hard done by,' she told Lizzie, her voice larded with irony.

But there were other ways of becoming a farmer than digging tatties and hoeing neeps with a bothy for a bed, which Lizzie, in the days of her innocence, never suspected. He courted her crudely, nipping her bum as she bent over the hen boxes, hoisting her milk-stool till she had to dance for it, tweaking the tail of her hair. She responded predictably, slapping off his hands, sticking her nose in the air, giving him the edge of her tongue.

It was a courtship nevertheless and one November afternoon as she ran across the yard to the privy in the midden, he caught her. It was pelting and he ran to fetch a sack for her head. The rain plastered his black hair to his scalp making him look young and harmless. He guided her to the bothy.

'Gi'e us a cuddle, lass. That's all I'm asking.'

He smelled of hay and horse and sweat. Rain glistened on the red skin of his cheeks and the black stubble of his unshaven chin.

'Just a cuddle, hen. I wouldna lie wi' you. I'd never do that,' but, even as he spoke, he had her pressed to the wall and was pushing up her skirt.

His excitement was fast and uncontrolled. While still protesting the innocence of his purpose he was thrusting between the flesh of her thighs. Within seconds it was over.

'You animal, you beast!' she cried.

'You'll be back for more,' he grinned at her, cocksure.

And she was. He had her in the byre with the new milk cooling in the pail. Behind hedges. On his straw mattress and once, daringly, on the horsehair settee in the parlour. Until she got caught with the twins.

Aunt Jess took her stick to her for the last time. 'Fool!' she cried. 'It was not you he was after.'

To Gould she said, not without admiration. 'You got what you wanted,' but she was not talking about a bride.

For appearance's sake, she paid for the wedding.

Bella

Sundays were purple and began when the chores were done. Bella changed into clean combinations and black wool stockings that itched her thighs. She had a bottle green dress made for growth but it was worn out before she grew into it. Big Lizzie took off her pinny and emerged in mauve rayon with white polka dots which Bella admired. Mr Gould wore a black suit and attached a collar to his shirt. His chin was still smooth from his Saturday night shave. He sat at the end of the pew with folded arms, a cut above the miners and their families behind. Between him and Big Lizzie, the twins fidgeted, their red heads slicked with Brylcreme. Bella sat squashed between the plaster wall and Big Lizzie. If Mrs Urquhart tilted her maroon felt to the right and Miss Mary Urquhart cocked her beige straw to the left, she could see the minister in the pulpit. He had a pink face and glasses and sometimes he shouted up at God and sometimes he shouted down to the congregation.

Occasionally Mrs Urquhart gave her a sweetie to suck in the sermon, smuggling it into her palm as they walked up the aisle.

Big Lizzie noticed but she did not forbid her to eat it. Mrs Urquhart was the minister's mother.

Apart from the Urquhart hats, all she could see were the family feet. Big Lizzie's brown lacing shoes bulged over her bunions, the boys' boots were scuffed already from the road to the kirk. Mr Gould's feet were small and unfamiliar in black shoes honed to a mirror shine.

Then one Sunday in September in the middle of harvest the feet all disappeared behind the mound of Lizzie's belly. The mauve dress was strained and as Bella stared, it rippled and twitched as if there was something inside. That was Malcolm.

His birth, coming when Lizzie was forty and the twins seventeen, was protracted and difficult. The district nurse came into the kitchen when it was over and Bella made her a cup of tea.

'You've got a fine wee brother, lassie,' she said, elbows on the table, hands clasped around the cup. There was blood in her fingernails.

A brother? Bella had not thought of the baby in relationship to herself. A brother indeed!

He looked like a baby ferret, blind with a pale fuzz of hair on his pink head. She was careful not to touch him.

Three days later, Big Lizzie came downstairs. She was tetchy and dispirited. Her orders no longer rang with authority and her tongue lacked the spice of malice. The baby girned in his crib in a corner of the kitchen, but Big Lizzie would not pick him up.

'I'll no' have a spoiled wean in my house. He'll take his feed when I'm good and ready to give it to him,' she grumbled.

There were plenty of visitors. Mrs Urquhart and her daughter brought a pram set, hand-knitted in lemon in case the baby had been a girl.

'What a lucky wee girlie to have a baby brother,' Mrs Urquhart gushed to her as she gazed into the cradle. Her breath smelled of violet cachous.

'Gosh, I envy you,' Miss Heather said while Nanny and Big Lizzie put their heads together. 'I'd swop my pony for a brother.'

After they had gone, the kitchen ticked and simmered while Bella peeled tatties for the tea and Big Lizzie dozed, whey-faced, in the basket-chair. Then Malcy began to yell.

Bella hovered in an agony of anxiety. Big Lizzie opened her eyes and caught the girl's unguarded expression. 'What's the bairn to you?' she taunted, exasperated. 'It's no' as if he was your brother. Bloody kids.'

The infant's wails grew louder. Big Lizzie rose stiffly from the chair and with resentful hands picked him up. Slowly she unbuttoned her cardigan and then her dress. Her right breast, swollen with milk, blue-veined, brown tipped, hung over the baby's head tantalizingly out of reach as he mewed and butted as frantically as a lamb. At last she lifted him and with a twist of his small head he fasted on to her nipple.

Suddenly she yelled, and, tearing the child from her breast, flung him across the hearth. 'The little bugger bit me,' she cried in outrage and pain.

Bella, frozen with horror, saw blood on her blue-veined breast.

The child, still wrapped in his shawl was seemingly unhurt. His head had fallen against the soft flank of the aged sleeping collie, but he was screaming with fright.

Bella flew to him. She sat on the hearth and pulled him across her knees, awkwardly, afraid he might break. His eyes were wide open, as blue and dry as a thrush's egg.

'Don't bring him near me,' Lizzie cried covering her breast protectively. 'You get yourself straight down to the chemist and buy him a bottle. He'll take that powdered stuff or starve.'

Bella ran all the way to Ladymuir and back again. Later, when she coaxed the rubber teat into his mouth she saw that Malcy had been born with two well-developed lower teeth.

Gradually Malcy became hers to feed and clothe and wash. Mr Gould protested occasionally and Lizzie drew herself out of depression for long enough to tell him to find someone else to mind his freak. He turned his black frown on Bella. Although her short stout legs dangled inches from the floor and her arms were only just long enough to encircle the wean, she handled him liked a woman. Her short hair fell forward in wings. All he could see of her face as she bent over the bairn was the wide bridge of her nose, but her confidence was reassuring. The wee craw could manage fine.

When Malcy was six months old, Lady Mowbray called. She sat on the horse-hair couch in the parlour and accepted a glass of port which she did not drink.

'I would like to see the gel,' she told Big Lizzie.

Bella washed the smell of onions off her hands and fixed the grips either side of her parting and stood shyly at the door.

Lady Mowbray was very tall and thin with a face like crushed tissue paper under her silver hair. She wore an oatmeal tweed coat and skirt and brogues with leather fringed flaps and she carried a walking stick. Her hands were raw and twisted like tree roots with arthritis. She was Miss Heather's grandmother.

'Come here,' she commanded, 'and let me have a proper look at you.'

Big Lizzie propelled her forwards.

'How old are you, Bella?'

Before she could answer, Lizzie was speaking. 'Coming up for six, your Ladyship.'

Bella flushed at the insult. She knew she was eight because last harvest she had received a card from Miss Urquhart who kept the Children's Register at the kirk. It had been cut out in the shape of an eight and Gordon had read it to her. Big Lizzie had bought her a pair of Sunday boots and Mr Gould had given her a bar of Duncan's Hazelnut Chocolate and the twins had bashed her shoulders eight times, so she knew; but she said nothing, not with Big Lizzie's face as sour as a cherry plum.

Lady Mowbray looked from one to the other, aware of the lie. 'She should be at school, Lizzie.'

Big Lizzie clicked her tongue and shook her head. 'How can I send the likes of her to the school?'

Lady Mowbray rose. Five foot eleven and a half of aristocratic backbone. Her smile stretched thinly across her lined face.

'She may be small for her age but that is no reason to suppose she is half-witted. I must insist that you see to it, please.'

'Bloody interfering bitch,' Big Lizzie muttered as they watched her stride across the yard.

'I'd like fine to go to the school if I could take wee Malcy,' Bella said.

'Well, you can't,' she snapped.

At school Bella's head, cushioned on her forearms, lay in a pool of sunlight on her desk. She drifted down into the golden warmth of sleep.

'Wake up, Bella Gould,' the teacher snapped. 'Hold out your hand.'

Her palm was as rough as a working man's, the immature lines already etched with grime. Her nails were as tough as little claws. She scarcely felt the sting of the strap.

'There's something the matter with that child,' Miss Dunlop complained to the head teacher at break. 'She's either absent or asleep. Can it be something to do with her size, do you suppose? Glands?'

'More likely her background. She's a typical product of the slums, bow-legged with rickets, lethargic from lack of proper food and insufficient rest.' Mr Mackenzie had trained at Jordanhilll and worked in a school in Govan. 'Make allowances. Her potential is nil.'

'I'm not so sure,' said Miss Dunlop who was keen and optimistic. 'She's almost literate and numerate which is more than could be said for the Gould twins at her age.'

24

'A flash in the pan,' said Mr Mackenzie dismissively. 'I know these children. Their reading seldom progresses beyond the headlines in the *Record* and their counting is circumscribed by their pay packets.'

Miss Dunlop shook her head ambiguously.

In fact Bella liked school. Forming letters in her copybook, puzzling over the shapes of words and figures was pleasurable and while she was thus occupied, there was no time to be anxious, but when she had to sit still and listen, farm life, as huge as a January shadow, reached out to darken her mind. Sometimes she escaped in sleep but Malcy was always there even in her dreams, a grizzling, snot-nosed waif waiting for her return.

One day when she came back from school he was not hanging about the lane, nor was he squatting filthy in the yard steering a stick between the islands of cobblestones. She could not find him in the house where Big Lizzie was lining curtains with black-out material. Her foot punched the treadle sewing machine like Miss Dunlop's fingers on the blackboard, impatiently.

'Where's wee Malcy?' Bella shouted over the whirr and clatter.

Lizzie decided to hear her after the third time of asking. 'He had it coming to him,' she said, her mouth tight as if full of pins. 'You mind and leave him be.'

She knew where he was.

The old privy was a noisome shed that backed on to the midden. A plank had been nailed across the hole in the seat since one of the twins had fallen in. Seepage from the midden kept the dirt floor sodden with slime even in summer, and with the door latched it was just light enough to see the cobwebs looped across the roof.

It was Big Lizzie's most effective punishment. The threat was sufficient to quieten tantrums and to quell high spirits. Bella had been put there for spilling a pail of milk, until the farmer, hearing her greet, had lifted the latch and taken her with him to the cattle mart. She had sat in the big hired truck, squashed between him and the driver while the beasts lowed in the back. He had bought her a cornet and a bag of wine gums. Bella knew that Mr Gould would not interfere with Malcy's punishment.

The latch was almost too high for her to reach and it was clogged with rust. The door had warped and was stiff to open. Malcy had stopped screaming but she could hear his long shuddering sighs.

He was filthy and he stank because he had soiled his sodden nappy and slipped on the floor.

That put paid to school.

Miss Heather called at the back door one hot July morning.

'Can Bella come for a picnic?' she asked.

Big Lizzie eyed the wicker basket packed with orange squash and banana sandwiches.

'Some folk have work to do.'

Miss Heather cocked her head to one side and turned on her charm. 'Please, Mrs Gould, please say yes.'

Bella was mangling from one tub to another in the washhouse. She stood on an egg-box to reach the handle. Malcy sat in his pushchair sucking a strap. The leather dye tanned his mouth and ran down his chin, his yellow hair gleamed like buttercups in a ray of sunlight.

'Let me have a go,' said Miss Heather, seizing the handle, but her thin arms had no strength in them. 'Hurry up,' she said, 'we're going for a picnic up the river.'

'Did she say I could get?'

'She didn't say you couldn't.'

Bella piled the flattened clothes into a basket and dragged it on to the drying green. Miss Heather flopped down on the grass between mats of clover and eyebright. Through half-closed eyes she could see Bella, her mouth full of pegs, pinning the clothes to the line in regimental order, nappies, semmits, shirts and dungarees.

26

'Do be quick,' she said yawning. 'I'm absolutely boiling.'

Bella pulled the strap out of Malcy's mouth and scrubbed his chin with the corner of her cotton dress. He girned and twisted away from her touch.

'Do we have to take the brat?'

Babies like dolls in cradles were all very well, but toddlers who whined were boring.

'Why can't she keep him?'

'Because she can't,' Bella answered testily, an echo of Big Lizzie herself.

The lane was hedged with beech trees and the ditches overgrown with hemlock and cow-parsley. Bella trundled the pushchair over the stony road and Malcolm hummed a tuneless note which throbbed and wobbled in his throat over the rough track.

It was a long way round to the river but the short cut over the fields was impossible for the pram with the corn grown into tall green spears. The time passed in a dream as Miss Heather unravelled one of her plays.

'Once upon a time there lived a king and queen who had only one child called Una and they all lived happily till one day a dragon swooped down out of the sky and took away her parents. She decided to find them with the help of the Red Cross Knight. You can be Una. I'm the knight…'

The road turned into forest track and the pram was a milk-white ass. A ruined cottage became a gloomy cavern and Malcy the scaly monster that lurked inside.

'You, Lady Una, remain here while I make sure no fierce or loathsome beast lurks in yonder cavern,' cried Heather in a knight's voice. 'And you must say, "Fly, fly for in this den there dwells a vile monster hated by God and man".'

So she did, while Heather flailed the air and feinted at Malcy with a stick. 'I'm fighting valiantly, but I've never met a monster before like this. Its tail is round my throat. Aarch! I'm done for.'

'Strangle it, kill it, cut off its head,' cried Bella who was now Una.

The knight obeyed with a flourish and Malcy began to grizzle.

'Now the knight is enchanted by a witch and meets a lion.   I am the lion.'

Heather bared her large teeth and roared and prepared to spring.   'At the sight of your tender beauty, my fierce heart melts.'   She grovelled and purred and pretended to lick Bella's hand and lolloped beside her along the road.

Thus the play continued with Heather acting all the best parts and Malcy being the monsters, but Bella was always Una on her milk-white ass until the end when the knight defeated the dragon in a stunning climax, and Una - now played by Heather - was reunited to her parents.

'Can we get to do it again?' she asked eagerly, but Heather was silent, her lips pressed together over her teeth giving her a stern and unfamiliar appearance.

'Do you suppose,' she asked after a while, 'that if I had not lost my parents I would be different?'

Bella stared at her.   'Are you an orphan then?'

'Of course.   Didn't you know?   I lost my parents when I was three.'

Bella drew in her breath.   'Orphan' was another word for dwarfie, crawface, drudge.

'You couldn't tell,' she said admiringly.

They left the push-chair by the side of a narrow, hump-backed bridge, and swung Malcy between them upstream to a pool formed by a bend in the river under a grassy bank overhung by a leafy oak.

Miss Heather was wearing a bathing suit under her cotton dress.

'Ouch!   It's freezing,' she cried, testing the shallow end. 'Come on in.'

Bella looked at the pool.   The water was brown threaded with gold.   Damosels darted over the surface and midges hung in clouds beneath the trees.

28

'I'm not allowed.'

'Do you always do what you're told?' Heather asked her scornfully.

'I'm needing a costume.'

'Have mine,' cried Heather, peeling off her black wool suit and flinging it up on the bank. There she stood, laughing, without a stitch. Bella was shocked.

Malcy sat on the shingle beach close to where the water trickled over smooth round stones. He began to girn for he was uncomfortable and hot. Bella took off his nappy and washed his fiery bottom. He staggered towards the edge of the river and squealed as the water touched his toes. Losing his balance he sat down hard and when he had got over the shock he did it all over again, challenging Bella to be cross.

'Don't fuss. It's good for him,' said Miss Heather in her grandmother's voice, so Bella took off all his clothes and laid them to dry on a whin bush.

The water sparkled deliciously. Miss Heather splashed and shrieked and shivered like a puppy. Malcy sat on a wet flat stone and threw pebbles. Bella could wait no longer. She took off her boots and sweaty socks, her dress and underskirt and vest, then, after some deliberation, her knickers too. She did not fancy getting them wet.

Her body unaccustomed to nakedness, felt light and vulnerable, aware of every breeze and leafy shadow. Her skin was ringed and ridged with garter and knicker elastic. She clutched her shoulders undecidedly.

'Come on,' cried Heather. 'What are you waiting for?'

The shock of the water took her breath away. The stones hurt her feet, but after a while with the river up to her thighs and her body numb, she no longer felt cold.

'I'll teach you to swim, if you like,' said Miss Heather, lying on her back in the water and kicking her feet.

Chance or instinct made her turn her head. Malcy had staggered from the safety of the shallows towards deeper water. As she watched, he fell face forwards and submerged.

Now, the water which had seemed so light and frothy turned to treacle. Her legs moved with nightmare slowness through the morass. She could not reach him. It was Miss Heather who picked him up and carried him to the bank. His body was cold and slippery as a fish. He spluttered and coughed and tried to cry.

'He's got cramp,' said Miss Heather knowledgeably and began to run his body with her towel. Bella, shivering, her fingers numb and clumsy, forced on his clothes. When he stopped spluttering, Heather popped a chocolate biscuit into his mouth. After a while he fell asleep, his little body curled into a ball in the shade of a broom bush.

When the girls were dressed and sitting, heavy-limbed and lethargic, chewing sandwiches, Bella spoke aloud the words that had been running like water through her head.

'Jings, what if he had drowned?'

'Do you suppose,' Miss Heather said after a sober pause, 'that they would have cared?'

Bella did no answer. That was the worst of it. She knew that no one would have really minded, not even herself That was the shaming truth.

The knowledge was too heavy to contain in conscious thought. It sank down into the depths of her mind. She stood up and gathering a handful of stones, threw them one by one into the centre of the deep brown pool.

Big Lizzie was not herself. Her plump goose-pimpled arms shrank to sticks. Her round pale face turned sallow and full of hollows and her creamy hair became wispy and dry as last year's hay.

Some mornings she did not rise till late, and, though the twins did the milking, coming in with their shoulders all over cow hair where they had dozed against the beasts' flanks, there were all the other chores and there was Malcolm.

When Lizzie came downstairs the broth had to be simmering in the pot, the kitchen clean and Malcy fed and quiet and playing on the mat. She took the cup of tea Bella prepared for her without comment. Some days she could not drink it. Her hands would grip the pock marked porcelain sink for a while and then she would pour it away. She did not like Bella to stare.

'One day the wind'll change and you'll be stuck with that face. Away you and feed the hens.'

Lizzie loved her hens. 'Ma bonnie bairns,' she cried them. 'Tookie. tookie. took.' At the sound of her voice, they would coming running on stiff frantic legs from all over the yard and gather round her, clucking and scratching and scrambling for corn. 'Great greedy gowks,' Big Lizzie would grumble, but her eyes were soft.

Bella knew there was something far the matter when she was sent to feed the hens.

Malcy did not like them. The first time she took him into the hen house to collect the eggs he screamed himself purple. The birds fluffed out their feathers and squawked and scattered the straw.

He did not like the ferrets either, crinkled his nose at their smell and refused to go into the shed even when his father was there. He disliked the farm dogs and the calves, the pet lambs that buffooned about the yard, even the week-old chicks Lizzie reared in pens down the side of the back-field.

At first Bella thought he was afraid of the beasts and she coaxed him to fondle them, but he pulled away, disgust in his face not fear.

One of the chickens in the coup was sick. It crouched in a corner, a ball of drooping fluff, its eyes dull slits under half-closed lids. She removed it and put it under an upturned bucket until she had fed the rest. When she had finished, Malcy and the chick had gone. She found him behind the coup plucking at its fluff. He poked it and it cheeped, gaped and excreted on his hand. He twisted its neck right round. When he saw her he held out his fingers.

'Nasty, dirty, dead,' he told her with disgust.

'You made it dead,' she accused him.

'Serves it right,' he shouted defiantly, rubbing his hands frantically on the grass.

She picked up the little corpse. Its cooling looseness, its unspeakable loneliness reached down to her tender core. She lifted it, making a cradle of her hands. She thought of the young ferrets safe in their mother's gut. She would have liked to put the chicken back in its shell.

'We'll bury it,' she said.

There was a sycamore that bent heavy branches over the dyke. Underneath, the earth was rich and mulchy. She scraped out a little hole and laid the creature in a shroud of leaves.

They were both absorbed in the burial but they were not together, for while, sadly, she sought to tuck the corpse away in the safe dark belly of the earth, he was excited, intrigued, pleased with himself.

He often played there alone.

Lizzie

When the twins ran off to enlist, Lizzie gave up trying to conceal her sickness.

The doctor's consulting room needed a new coat of paint. His jacket was crumpled as if he had slept in it.

'How are the family, Mrs Gould? I hear those twins of yours have joined up. You must be proud of them.'

Lizzie fixed her gaze on the eye chart on the wall. The doctor's bronchitic breath sawed in and out like the farmer in the woodshed. 'They never needed to go to the war,' she said bitterly.

Right from the start they had been her bairns. She had suckled and nurtured them, chided and guided their coltish growth. She blamed the farmer for driving them off with his vicious ways. Yet the farmer too was proud of his sons. They saw eye to eye over that, if nothing else. Maybe it was God's punishment on her for her harshness to the wean. But that was not her blame.

'You should have come sooner, Mrs Gould,' the doctor was saying studiedly non-committal.' How long has this been troubling you?'

'The bairn bit me in the breast.'

Logic told her it was not the bairn's fault that he had been born with two well-developed teeth and Aunt Jess's pale blue eyes, but she could not forgive him.

After her marriage, Aunt Jess had put away the stick and sharpened her tongue. Grudgingly she had come to admire Gould, likened him to her own father who had been a hard worker, a whisky drinker with a punishing fist. For Lizzie, the two of them together had become a conspiracy. She stood it till the twins were born.

One autumn morning when the mist was so thick that she had to feel her way across the yard, she came in from the dairy to find the old woman in her bedroom where the babes lay girning, fretful for a feed. It was not fear that the old woman would harm them but rather terror that she might possess them that turned Lizzie into a tigress. She flew across the room, seized her by the shoulders and spun her out of the room.

'Leave ma bairns alane, ye auld witch!'

Cringing alarm spread like grease across her aunt's face, unforgettably obscene.

'Dinna hurt me, Lizzie. I'm an auld woman.'

Now it was not fear of dispossession that maddened Lizzie but the knowledge that she had been conned all these years, scared by a straw image, beaten by a fraud. She thrust the old woman out on to the landing and shoved her hard. 'Git oot ma sight or I'll batter ye.'

'No Lizzie, I'm begging you - '

They were the last words she spoke. The force of the thrust sent her flying backwards down the steep staircase. She died instantly from a broken neck.

Though Gould said nothing, he guessed what Lizzie had done. She saw reluctant respect in his eyes. Their relationship shifted. For a while it seemed Aunt Jess had gone, but not for long. She had been born again in her own bairn.

The doctor was writing. 'The district nurse will call to dress the wound. This prescription will ease the pain.'

She took the piece of paper listlessly, stared at it unseeingly in her hands. Aunt Jess accompanied her on that weary homeward walk. From then on she seldom left her side. 'Did you really think,' she cackled in her ear, 'that you'd get off scot-free?'

Bella

Bella did not understand the change in Big Lizzie. Stern and stiff though Lizzie had been, she had also been a prop, a framework to her life as secure as four walls and a roof. Without it, she was adrift. Big Lizzie's harsh tongue and high standards were preferable to this amorphous freedom.

At first she tried to rouse the sick woman by inviting her interest. Each time she completed a task, she pushed open the bedroom door to report. 'I scrubbed the scullery, Mistress Gould,' or, 'I blacked the range.' She was not looking for praise - Lizzie was always miserly with that - but for comment. 'Did you mind and scour the outside of the pots?' or, 'Did you cardinal the back step?'

But Lizzie was not interested. The extra tasks went unregarded and when Bella grew tired and careless nobody noticed. The less she worked, the less she felt inclined to do, so that the garden sprouted weeds and Malcy's clothes went unchanged and unwashed. Mr Gould, busy in the fields, cared only that his dinner was on the table when he was ready for it.

It was Danny who put her wise.

She was swinging on a gate, pushing off with her feet fast till the gate came to a juddering halt against the hinge. Malcy was girning, wanting up beside her, but she hardly heard him. His whines merged into the background like the sound of the tractor

34

in the field or the hens in the yard. She was not even dreaming. She was in a dwam, mindless, like a cow chewing cud.

Danny was old and dour. His face was a mass of wrinkles, his old bones held together by his clothes. His deafness isolated him from companionship and he seldom spoke. He had come out of retirement as an obligation to Mr Gould while the twins were at war. He had a way with the beasts, especially the sheep and his closest companion was his dog, a snappish collie as much a loner as himself.

Danny looked at Bella swinging on the gate. 'Hiv ye nae wark to dae, lassie?'

Bella stared at him. Apart from grunts and jerks of his head, he had never communicated with her directly. His voice was gutteral, loud, so that he could hear himself. His faded blue eyes were lively with contempt.

'Yon puir wife's dyin' ben the hoose and here's you actin' Lady Muck like you was born to it. If I were the maister, I'd skelp yer bum.'

Bella stood on the gate a long time while it swung erratically to Malcy's push. Danny's rebuke was normal, familiar, even welcome. Big Lizzie dying was different. Death was seven ferrets in their mother's gut, a chicken in a mulch of leaves, a safe home in the cemetery. All the best people were dead. She had never thought of Lizzie as one of the elite. She had never considered her to be in danger of that.

Such thoughts were too heavy for her to hold. All that remained was a need to make amends. When the kitchen was gleaming and smelling sweet, with the mounted buffalo horns on the mantelpiece sponged against the coal reek from the range, the china vases washed and sparkling on the dresser, the dirty clothes collected in the wash-house, her and Malcy's bedroom aired and tidied, she set a tray and made Lizzie a cup of tea.

Usually she put it down on the commode cupboard by the big double bed where it cooled and the creamy milk congealed in patterns on the surface. Today she waited.

'Your tea's cooling,' she said shyly.

Though drugged and drowsy, Lizzie heard her. She opened her eyes and saw not the sturdy black-eyed orphan holding a cup of tea, but Aunt Jess dressed in her best black curly lamb, tapping an impatient stick and beckoning her to get up.

'Ye auld bitch,' she sighed, and, stepping out of her skin, followed the old woman who had been both her cradle and her cross. At the door she turned, looked back and saw Bella standing by her bed.

'Mind and remember to turn the mattress,' she said distinctly in her normal voice. For a moment, Bella was fooled.

Meanwhile Malcy had gone outside. He was pulling the heads off all the marigolds...

On the night of the burial Mr Gould got drunk. He sat in the basket chair and drank the whisky left by the mourners after the funeral tea. He did not get steaming or clownish the way that made her laugh, but teary and sentimental.

'Poor Lizzie. She was a fine woman, so she was. The best in the world. She was a good wife and a good mother to the laddies,' he repeated over and over again.

Bella knew it was the drink talking, that he would not say these things when he was sober, but she understood his loss. Lizzie had been the pivot round whom they had all danced a variation of steps. As she washed and put away the best china, she had solemn thoughts. Mrs Urquhart and the other women had told her she must learn to take Lizzie's place, that she had been spared for a purpose. With so many telling her, she thought it must be true. It might not be so bad. She and Mr Gould had always got along fine. Meanwhile she was tired. It had been the longest day of her life.

She took off her apron and hung it on a peg.

'Ye're no' going' to leave me on ma lane? No' the nicht.'

'I'm away to ma bed, and it's time you were and all with the cows to milk in the mornin'.'

She could hear Lizzie's voice in her mouth.

'Ye'll tak' a swallow first, just for her sake.' He was maudlin. 'Just one wee taste?'

She was not yet as strong as Lizzie. She saw his wretchedness, his need for company. She crossed the room, but, instead of taking the drink he offered, she knelt down to loosen the laces of his boots. Then she eased his slippers over his feet.

'Ye're a good lass, Bella. It was the best day's work I ever did bringing you to the fairm. Now there's just the two of us, we'll get along grand.'

The three of us, she thought, remembering Malcy, but all she said was, 'I'm away to ma bed, Mr Gould, and I'd advise you to do the same.'

He let her go.

Hours later she heard his stumbling steps on the attic stair. He fumbled with the door and stood there in the moonlight in his woollen underwear. His eyes were swollen not just with the drink.

'I canna sleep doon there on ma lane, hen.'

'Dinna wake the bairn,' she whispered easing Malcy closer to the wall in the bed they had shared since he had outgrown the cradle.

He wrapped his arms around her. 'Gi'e us a cuddle, hen,' he said and fell instantly asleep.

That night Malcy wet the bed.

'It's time he was out of here,' Mr Gould grumbled in the morning. 'You'll need to put him in the twins' room, hen.'

There was a war on but apart from the planes that hounded the night sky, you couldn't tell for the siren could only be heard when the wind was from the north. But there was no cream to spare for the Hall as it had to go to the depot, and, once a week a man came for the eggs and checked their number against the hens. She usually managed to save a few extra for Miss Heather in the holidays.

The twins were overseas, too far away to get compassionate leave for the funeral. Gordon wrote sometimes, short notes that gave away nothing except that they were still together and the weather was hot.

Mr Gould grew thin and tired and black-tempered working in the fields all of God's daylight hours, wrestling with the tractor that needed unobtainable parts. He took his spite out on Malcy, cuffing his ears, bruising his arms. If Bella interfered he would fall into a dour mood and go down the pub and drink all he could get. Mostly he was too tired or drunk for more than a cuddle but sometimes when he had supped just enough whisky to put the life back into him, he hurt her. All the time he did it he groaned and repudiated himself; sometimes afterwards he wept.

Once she lied to comfort him, 'I don't mind. Honest.'

That displeased him more.

'You should mind,' he snarled. 'You should stop me. You lead me into sin. You make a hoo-er of yourself.'

She wept at that and tried to leave the bed but he held her back. 'It's too fucking late now. We're both for the fiery pit, so forget it.' He turned over and fell asleep.

When Malcy was five he was sent to school. Bella took him one late August morning when the corn was ripe and they kept her too. The head lectured her for truanting and she sat at the back of the class and worried about Mr Gould's dinner. At break, the other girls crowded round her full of questions and personal remarks. They were all at least a head taller than she was and some of them had breasts. She laughed at everything they said and some of them pointed to their heads and raised their brows and whispered, 'Wee Bella's daft, so she is.'

At dinner-time she ran home and took strong tea and wedges of spam sandwiches out to the fields where Mr Gould was cutting the oats while Danny with some women from the village stooked the sheaves. Mr Gould was hot and surly.

'What kept ye?' he asked.

'The school.'

38

He didn't answer. He didn't speak to her all night.

Next day she took Malcy to the end of the school lane and ran back through the fields to bake scones and layer them with jelly. The head teacher noted her absence with no more than a resigned sigh and went to look in on the infants. He noticed Malcy's neat yellow head, his watchful blue eyes, his firm closed mouth and thought, 'Now there's a child with potential.'

Sometimes Miss Heather helped with the harvest. She wore grey pleated shorts and an aertex shirt and her long thin brown legs got scratched with the thistles. She was put on the cart with Bella to load the sheaves and when it was piled high they led the horse back to the stack-yard.

She chattered all the time, even when they were pitching the sheaves over to Mr Gould who was building the stack. He answered occasionally with a grunt.

'He's the strong silent type, your father,' she said as they rode back to the fields, their legs dangling over the back of the cart.

'He's no' my faither,' Bella replied, surprised. Only strangers made that mistake.

'Come off it, Bella,' she answered, amused. 'You don't have to pretend with me.'

'He's not my faither,' she insisted stubbornly, her eyes fixed on the dusty road that flowed like a river below her feet.

'Of course he's your father,' Miss Heather said in her poshest voice. 'You're as alike as two peas. Everyone says he's your father.'

Bella shook her head. 'I'm an orphan,' she insisted stubbornly, as near to anger as she had ever been.

Miss Heather held up her hands in mock protection. 'Okay, okay, have it your own way. You should know.'

But the seed had been sown. 'He would have said,' she argued. 'He would have told me.'

'Did you ever ask?' Miss Heather suggested, sounding bored.

For the rest of the day Bella burned with doubt under the hot sun. She wanted to reject the idea for privately she believed her father had been a football player, the hero of his team, who had died at the hour of triumph after scoring Rangers' winning goal. There was a glimmer of reason behind this fantasy for she had a dream-like recollection of riding tall on the shoulders of a man with curly black hair while the fans surged around them. Secretly she was relieved that he was dead so he need never be ashamed of the way she had turned out.

Because the idea of Mr Gould as her father was so unwelcome she began to believe that it must be true, yet she did not know how to ask him.

He came in at the back of ten when the dew was beginning to fall, hungry and wanting his tea. She watched him wolf a plate of mince and tatties and swallow a pint of tea.

'Are you my faither, then?' The words erupted out of her, graceless, beyond her control.

He reached out and slapped her face.

'For Chrissake what sort of a fucking question is that?' Tears of surprise and pain started out of her eyes as her cheek flared. She ran out of the room and up to the attic where she was too hot and unhappy to sleep.

The harvest was gathered and the threshing done before he forgave her. He'd been at the beer for the first time since the corn was cut. It had been a fair harvest - he would admit to no more - and he had heard he was getting two Italian prisoners-of-war for the tattie howking.

He came in with a belated birthday gift, a brush and comb set and a box of Black Magic from his sweetie ration.

When she thanked him he took a piece of paper from his inside pocket.

'Here, hen, take a look at that.'

The paper was folded several times and the creases stained as if it had lain in a pocket for some time. The writing was so thick and heavy that it had come through the back of the paper. She opened it out, mystified by the long words and bold script.

'It's your birth certificate,' he told her, avoiding her eyes.

She pondered over the words for a long time to get them right. Her mother had been called Isabella Gould. 'Isabella' - that was nice. Better than plain Bella.

'It does nae say who ma faither was,' she ventured at last.

He avoided the implied question.

'Isa was my sister, God rest her soul. You're the spitting image of your ma, so you are.'

'Then I'm an orphan right enough?'

He shrugged. 'All I ken is that you're illegitimate, hen, and that's no an uncommon complaint hereaboots.'

Bella bowed her head. Bastard was even worse than orphan.

The knowledge sank like a stone down to the depths of her mind.

Once a week Bella turned out the twins' room. Though Malcy had slept there since his banishment from her bed, it had an unused air. His room was almost as sparsely furnished as her own but she had imprinted something of herself on her attic surroundings with a jam jar of pansies or roses on her window-sill, a faded red velvet pincushion with her name spelled out in rusty pins on her chest of drawers, and H.J.Ford's illustration of Una and the Lion torn from Miss Heather's book and tacked to the wall over her bed. There was nothing much of Malcy in the room where he slept. Even the cardboard box full of battered motors and the Hornby train set had belonged to the twins.

The few toys that were his remained in their original wrappings stowed away in the press.

She thought he didn't care for them until one day she took out Lady Mowbray's last Christmas gift, a Noah's Ark, and unwrapped each pair of animals from their tissued folds and arranged them for her own amusement. Malcy was outraged. His complexion whitened, his eyes iced over.

'It's spoiled now,' he cried. 'You've ruined it.'

'How?'

'It's not new anymore.'

41

He was obsessed with newness. As good as new, like a pair of grey school shorts handed in by the district nurse who could vouch for the cleanliness of the previous owner, would not do. He suffered the twins' cast-offs only because he had no choice. Any gift, however small, would be packed up in its original parcel and put away. It was enough for Malcy to possess it.

At school he kept his pencil and copybook in pristine order. His backward sloping writing contained few mistakes. He was neat and tidy in his habits. He could not abide to soil his person or his possessions.

'He'll never make a fairmer, yon,' Mr Gould grumbled, though he had known this since Malcy had been a toddler. It didn't matter for he had the twins, but Mr Gould despised this finicky son.

Although the child's peculiarities made less work for Bella, she thought them disturbing. As he grew from bairn to schoolboy she found he seldom needed a second telling. He could not sit down to a meal with dirt on his hands and his boots shone from the shine he gave them. Looking back, she realised that his obsession with cleanliness dated from that day in the privy.

His hatred of dirt and darkness extended to a loathing for the creatures that lived in these conditions. She found a shoebox under his bed. Curious to see what it contained she carried it to the window, sat it down on the scarred table where he did his homework and eased off the lid.

What she found scared her for she disliked insects, but she was also sickened by what he had done to them.

Two earwigs, three beetles of different sizes, a ladybird and a reddish centipede had been impaled by pins taken from her heart-shaped pincushion to a piece of cardboard cut out to fit inside the box. Each specimen was labelled with the date of its capture. Each from its twisted appearance, had been pinned to the board alive.

When he came in from school she set on him. 'You wee horror, you wee tyke. What made you do such a thing?'

For a moment he was defiant. 'They're dirty. They live in the dirt. I've seen you kill wee beasties. My mammie killed spiders. I saw her.'

'They're creatures,' she argued. 'Living creatures, like you and they wee flowers in the gairden and the chickens in the coup.'

'So?' he answered scornfully, then he saw her face. 'Keep your hair on.' But he was not sorry.

'Burn it,' she commanded and opened the top of the range.

He stuffed the cardboard through the round hole and into the flames. The flare lit up his face. His expression was concentrated, absorbed.

'Don't you care about the wee beasties?' she asked curiously. 'Don't you mind that you hurt them?'

He looked at her with genuine surprise.

'You're daft, so you are,' he said. 'Dafty Crawface.' He grinned at her cheekily.

'Sticks and stones,' she answered automatically, but she was no longer angry.

Dimly she realised that his hateful words and deeds were more hurtful to himself than they could ever be to her, but he would never know it. She was weighted down with pity.

The Eyeties arrived in time for the tattie howking.

Mario made rings out of silver sixpences with initials carved on them. He had black wavy hair on his head and even more on his chest. He flirted with all the women and he was rather plump.

Niccolo was a clown. He laughed and gesticulated and sang soulful arias in a throbbing tenor.

They arrived each morning under guard in the back of a three-toner full of POWs and were picked up again in the evening, but no one considered that they might want to escape. If Mario could be said to have an ambition it was to make all the women from grandmas to wee girls fall in love with him. Niccolo aimed to get through the day on a minimum of labour.

43

The children gawped as Mr Gould's voice grew louder and slower in an attempt to make himself understood. The women eased their backs and sneaked sly previews of the enemy.

Within a couple of days Mario had promised rings to all the women in the fields and Niccolo had the bairns wetting themselves at his antics. Especially Malcy.

Bella had never met men who made it so plain that they liked children. Of all the bairns who helped to howk tatties, the Eyeties admired Malcy most. They were ecstatic in admiration of his golden hair. Though no one knew the half of what they were jabbering about, there was no mistaking '*bellissimo*'.

Niccolo crept up behind him dawdling in his row, seized him and swung him up on to his shoulders and pretended to run off with him. Malcy's bright hair flopped up and down as he bounced on the Eyetie's back. Bella stared. Malcy did not like to be touched or cuddled or messed about. Since he was three years old he had not allowed her to hold his hand and he would dodge if she attempted to straighten his collar or brush his hair. But here he was on Niccolo's back, his hands clutched round the swarthy neck. She watched his expression change from outraged dignity to cautious delight.

Niccolo galloped with him across the field and pretended to ditch him, '*Uno, duo, tres,*' into a clump of nettles by the burn. They sauntered back hand in hand.

From then on Niccolo had a shadow that waited at the foot of the lane for the truck to arrive each morning, who sat beside him in the dinner break, who trotted behind him up the tattie drills.

Bella watched the tight bud of Malcy's nature begin to put out shoots. He became a proper bairn and before a month was up he was chattering away in Italian to the genuine delight of the Eyeties.

When the tatties were lifted, the prisoners were kept on to help Danny and Mr Gould to expand the farm for the war effort. More cattle, more pigs and sheep were bought at the market and another horse to help Prancer pull the plough over the strips of unclaimed land.

Malcy would not go to school until the Eyeties had arrived. Sometimes he ran home at dinnertime to eat his piece beside them in the bothy.

Mr Gould would not have them in the house. They were the enemy and not to be trusted, foreigners and therefore inferior, Catholics and thus idolaters. He tolerated them on his land as a necessary evil. He regarded Malcy's passion for them as further evidence of his son's ill-nature. He believed the lad deliberately cultivated their friendship to spite himself. He grew harsher to the boy which further alienated the prisoners to whom child abuse was abhorrent. In return they worked as little as they could get away with and Mr Gould added 'bone idleness' to his long list of complaints.

Bella was caught in the middle. She too enjoyed the company of the Eyeties. Mario's flirtatious manner made her feel grown-up. Niccolo's good nature was comforting. She would have liked to take her dinner in the bothy too and slip a buttered pancake to the prisoners like the other women did, but she stayed away. 'He'd kill me,' she told herself.

Instinctively she understood Mr Gould's antagonism. These two 'layabouts', as he called them, were responsible, however indirectly, for the absence of his older sons. Though he never said so, he missed the twins, looked for their letters, anguished over their safety, remembering his own experiences in the Great War trenches. He was inclined to blame the prisoners, too, for the deliberate alienation of Malcy's loyalty. Knowing this to be unjust only made him harsher. He needed her to be on his side.

She also knew that Malcy needed his new friends as her garden needed the sun. She could not blight those tender shoots of affection with the frost of her disapproval, so she giggled and kept her distance from the wops as she walked the uneasy tightrope of peace.

She spent more time in her garden.

Mr Fraser was 'digging for victory'. It was unpatriotic to grow flowers in war-time so the big garden flourished with sprouts

45

and caulies in the dahlia beds, and Ailsa Craig tomatoes instead of cyclamen and melons in the greenhouse. Clumps of parsley hedged the rose borders and runner beans replaced the rows of sweet peas.

Damp newspaper parcels full of cabbage and lettuce thinnings were left for her instead of polyanthus plants and begonia tubers. She did not go into the tool-shed again. Sometimes when Mr Fraser's grin stretched right round his cheeks she knew he would like her to go inside, but, instinctively, she understood that his wanting her was not so important as his need for her to refuse.

Afterwards when her breasts began to grow there was a change. He no longer called her Sunshine, grinning inanely all round his face. Instead he used her name and taught her all he knew of garden lore. She was a willing apprentice and tested out her knowledge in her own small plot.

Sometimes he pushed his cap back on his head and scratched his bald scalp. 'Jings, Bella, who'd think to look at you, ye hae sic a strength in your airms.' There was an admiration in his tone which pleased her. 'Mind you,' he added, 'you've no' sae far to bend as the rest o' us.'

Though her breasts grew round and her bowed legs grew stout and sturdy, they did not lengthen. She knew this by the marks on a tree, a tall straight beech with a skin as smooth and grey as an elephant's trunk. When she was sure no one was watching, she would measure herself against a previous notch. Sometimes she would cheat a little by lifting her heels, but she could not fool herself. In the last year she had grown less than half an inch.

'You look as if someone had taken a hammer and dunted you,' Malcy told her and it was true. She was all squashed down like a figure in a distorting mirror. Not much brow, no neck to speak of and the rest of her as dumpy as a Disney dwarf. Grumpy, Malcy called her, or Dopey, but secretly in her dreams she inclined to Snow White with her sleek black hair and her rosy cheeks. She was still hopeful of growing tall when she grew up. She had no fixed notion of when this was likely to happen. The division between adulthood and childhood still loomed ahead of her like a chasm. She had no idea that the rift was a mirage, maturity an illusion.

There were changes at the Hall too. Cook had gone into the munitions and Saidie was married with bairns of her own. Lady Mowbray managed with the help of Nanny who grumbled at Bella for not bringing more cream and eggs. Miss Heather was at boarding school and only home in the holidays. Sometime she wrote to Bella.

The best thing about the war is the siren. If the air-raid lasts after midnight we get an extra hour in bed. Our house-mistress goes with Poles. Will you get Mario to make me a ring?

Bella treasured her letters. She kept them in the black tea-caddy decorated with gold dragons. Sometimes on winter Sundays when Mr Gould snoozed in the chair she took them out and read them all from the beginning like a book. When, rarely, she replied, her letters were painstakingly constructed with every word checked in the dictionary bought for a penny at the kirk Jumble Sale.

Mario and Niccolo are driving turnips for the sheep. Mr Gould and Danny are ploughing the whinny brae and carting away the stones. Malcolm got a star for his writing at the school. Mario will need a sixpence for the ring. Mr Fraser gave me two doz strawbs for the garden. It's likely Malcy will eat them all like he pinched the rasps last year.

One night Mr Gould came up to the attic with beer on his breath. He stared at her breasts pushing out of one of Lizzie's old cut-down night-gowns, then he asked, 'Are you a woman, hen?'

She did not understand him. Surely he knew her age. She was not a child certainly, but a woman was twenty at least.

'I'm rising fifteen,' she said offended.

'Don't act dumb, Bella. You ken what I'm talking about.'
She had no idea so she giggled and turned her head into the
pillow.

He was angry. 'Don't play games with me, bitch,' he said
rising above her and yanking her head round by her hair. 'I
don't want any more bastards in the family.'

Her black eyes were scared and ignorant in the moonlight. He
let her go.

'Forget it, hen. You're still a bairn.'

That offended her even more.

The telegraph boy came to the front door. He propped his bike
against the garden wall, wrestled with the rusty latch and
whistled his way tunelessly between the rows of sprouting
broccoli and beds of well-dug, newly mulched soil.

Spring was beginning to break through winter cracks,
dandelions appeared in the yard, hedges were greening and hens
on the lay. The fields were harrowed, the oats sown and the
lambing started. Sparrows nested in the gutter. One of the jills
was pregnant.

Bella knew the telegraph boy who helped with the tattie-
howking and was about to check him for coming to the front
door when she saw the orange telegram.

'It's for the fairmer,' he said.

He kicked a stone on the path and slammed the gate behind
him. Though he did not know for sure what was in the
telegram, he could guess.

Mr Gould came in for his dinner at noon. He opened the
envelope with his back to her. For a timeless moment he stood
with his head bowed over the scrap of paper, then he crushed it
and jabbed it between the bars of the range. It flared briefly and
was gone.

'Take your dinner,' she said, but her voice was no louder than
a sigh. He did not hear her.

By the back door, he paused long enough to choose from the
stack of crooks and sticks and implements, an ancient horse-

whip. The leather thong was black with age. He strode across the yard towards the bothy, anger boiling in his blood.

Malcy sat between the Eyeties outside the bothy door playing cards. They looked up expecting Bella with a pot of tea to take with their dinner pieces. Their eyes were bright, their voices full of laughter. That picture glimpsed for less than a second before Mr Gould raised his whip, stayed for a long time in Bella's mind.

What he said made no sense to her then. He stood in the doorway, his hand clenched on the whip while the rage churned in his head.

'Cassino,' he spat.

Niccolo looked up comprehending. 'Casino? *Si...si.* Casino nice-a-place...' His voice tailed off as the farmer struck.

'Murderers!' he shouted. 'Filthy fucking murderers! You scrounge off my land and murder my sons.'

Before the Italian knew what was happening the whip slashed savagely across his face and twice again streaking his bare protective arm with blood. When Mario tried to stop him, the farmer dropped the whip, grabbed him by the throat and hammered his head against the wall till he fell unconscious on the cobbles. Mario tried to crawl away, but the farmer set on him with his boots, kicking him in the gut and kidney until he vomited blood.

Malcy flew at his father, kicking his shins, his face white, his eyes glittering, but Mr Gould sent him sprawling across the yard.

'Get out of my sight, you effing fraterniser. You're not fit to lick your brothers' boots.'

Bella ran for Danny.

It was all hushed up. Danny told Bella to say she had been in the house and the police were told that the Eyeties had fought each other over a hand of cards. The camp commandant was not satisfied. He insisted on further inquiries.

Malcy disappeared.

Mr Gould went straight to the store of liquor he was saving for the twins' return. He took two bottles of whisky to his room and drank himself stupid. On the second day he allowed Bella in with a cup of tea. The closed room stank and the farmer lay across the bed still in his working clothes. Maudlin drunk he grabbed her hand as she put the cup on the commode chest by his bed.

'I did a stupid thing, hen, a wicked thing.'

When she did not answer he let go of her hand.

'I'm packing it in, hen. There's no future here with the laddies gone. Lady Muck kens what she can do with her bloody fairm.' Tears of self-pity oozed under his swollen lids. 'I could do with a wee refreshment, pet.'

The neighbours were considerate coming with gifts of food and a treasured bottle of malt. They fed the beasts and milked the cows and Danny coped with the lambing. Bella looked everywhere for Malcy but he did not come home.

'He'll be fine,' Danny reassured her. 'He kens how to look after number one.'

She could not sleep for worry. Putting on her coat over her nightgown she went out to look for him.

It was bright with a bombers' moon as she searched the bothy, byre and barns. She even went as far as the Hall calling his name in a low urgent voice that roused night creatures and startled sleeping birds. She was in the back field when she heard the distant wail of the siren and almost simultaneously the drone of a plane overhead. There it was, a single black beetle scuttling over the sky. She could tell it was in trouble by the way it stuttered and stalled. Then she saw the bombs, a stick of incendiaries that fell like black stars out of the sky and blazed into life when they hit the farm. Byre, bothy, barns and beasts exploded into a garden of scarlet flowers that thrust up through the soil of the night to diminish the paling moon.

It was like the beginning all over again. But this time there was no Mr Gould to find her.

50

Malcy was hiding near the Eyetie camp. He saw the bomber creep towards the farm. It seemed to him that it had materialised from deep inside his head, that it dropped its cargo at his express command.

Next day he was removed to statutory care, an orphanage in the south end of Glasgow.

Bella went to work at the Hall.

Part Two

Ladymuir Hall

Heather

The train journey from Edinburgh to Ladymuir was like a bridge linking two lives. Though it lasted just about an hour, it crossed a chasm. Heather found it harder, strangely enough, to go home, to fold her busy wings and shrink back into the grub.

The process began the previous night in the dormitory manifesting itself in lunatic activity and a sleepless night. Her restlessness had been induced not just by a mug of Eno's Fruit Salts, a handful of Allenbury's Throat Pastilles (still un-rationed) and several spoonfuls of tinned blackcurrant puree, but also by the imminent break-up of the group.

School was her family where every member was interdependent, a close community where individuality was not encouraged. Heather liked to conform. She thrived on the ordered existence, protected by rules, competitive within bounds. In such an atmosphere she was contented, committed, safe.

Her school report reflected her satisfaction. *Heather usually maintains the high standards she sets herself,* the head-mistress had written. *She is a responsible and responsive member of school.* In such a community Heather found the freedom she needed to excel physically in sport, passably in class and socially in the common room. Her house-mistress had already earmarked her for a position of authority.

At Ladymuir none of this was important. Life without timetables, study and sport was uncomfortable, without companionship and gossip, lonely. Time took on a new dimension. Disturbing shadows crept out of the closet of her mind. Old fears returned.

She hugged her arms, chilled not just by the draughts in the unheated train, but by a sinking sense of loss. It was not just

52

that she was afraid of exploring her own individuality, not merely that she needed to see herself through the eyes of her peer group, but more a yearning, both mental and physical, which she could not properly understand, but which was as painful as home-sickness.

Now, as the train approached the station, Ladymuir - not just the concept but the fact - loomed menacingly. The shadow became substance, while the school she had left so recently dwindled and wavered with the quality of a dream. She saw herself as she had been in the dormitory, lively, laughing, like a snapshot so unfamiliar that she exclaimed inwardly, 'was that really me?' She had become the gawky, unconfident adolescent wondering if the strap which opened the train window would stick which sometimes happened so that she couldn't open the door and what she would do if it did.

A soldier with a kit bag opened it for her from the outside. He caught her eye and winked. She blushed and fumbled with her case and filed the episode away to ponder later on. (There was that Heather too.)

Lady Mowbray was talking to the station-master.

'There you are, my dear. Macdonald was just saying that the train was up to time.'

The uniformed official nodded at her. 'Back for the holidays, then?' She did not have time to answer. 'Lucky for some,' he added and pulled out his pocket watch. He always said 'lucky for some' making it plain he was not among the favoured few.

'Come along, Heather. We mustn't keep Mr Macdonald from his work,' Lady Mowbray said sharply, as if Heather had been somehow to blame.

'Having a word' with the station-master was an unvarying ritual. Her grandmother would no more have thought of avoiding it than of gossiping with the porter. Heather followed her up the covered ramp to the car park. Two elderly Sealyhams called Honour and Bright barked and pawed at the windows of the Morris Cowley.

'Shut up, you stupid beasts,' said Lady Mowbray affectionately. 'Young Missie's home.'

She drove straight and fast down the centre of the road. Once, long ago, she had been told by a chauffeur that she could keep to a perfect line. She had taken this as a high compliment and had driven that way ever since, her chin thrust forward, her hands clamped at a quarter to three on the steering wheel, straight down the middle of the road. If anyone attempted to pass she held on to her position unflinchingly and remarked, 'Silly arse. No one can drive these days.'

She parked three feet from the kerb loosely opposite the grocer. Before the war, the Torry brothers would give Heather a boiled sweet from the tall jar on the counter and Mr Parker, the chemist, would find Gibbs Ivory Castle competitions for her to colour-in. The shop-keepers were still friendly, but there were no sweets to hand out even when the monthly account was settled, and no way of avoiding the queues. Lady Mowbray had taken to telephoning her order and honking the horn to announce she was ready to receive it. She waited for two minutes exhorting the panting dogs to be patient and then commanded Heather to hurry them up. 'What on earth can they be doing in there?'

Must I? Need I? Heather protested inwardly, but those were words she used only to Nanny. Confident, eager-to-please Heather of the fifth form would have sprung out of the car to oblige her house-mistress. Here, she dragged her feet.

There was a queue in Torry's that curled like a conga round the shop. A consignment of oranges had come in. The Torry brothers, pencils behind ears, cut out coupons, measured ounces of butter and distributed the fruit, one per ration book. She hovered near the door. Housewives in headscarves and darned stockings stared at her lilac uniform and purple felt hat with the school ribbon twisted round the brim. She took it off and fiddled with it uneasily. If she waited too long, Grandmother might honk again.

So she spoke. 'Mr Torry?' Her voice came out high and posh. Everyone turned.

Sam Torry looked up. 'Her Ladyship's order? I'll be with you in two ticks.'

He carried out the box. 'I've put in an extra orange,' he told her as he stowed it in the boot. 'I've put in an extra orange for Miss Heather,' he repeated to Lady Mowbray through the window, touching his forelock.

Her grandmother accepted it as if it were no more than her due.

The car roared along in low gear and swung through the lodge gates. Lady Mowbray talked about the dogs; 'I'm sure Honour has fleas'; the depot where she packed parcels for prisoners of war; 'You'd better come with me. It'll give you something to do in the holidays'; the iniquities of Fraser who was too busy digging for victory to weed the flower-beds in the front.

'Oh, by the bye,' she added as they bumped up the avenue. 'Did I tell you? I've engaged Bella Gould to help in the kitchen. Poor Nanny gets so dreadfully overdone.'

Bella... Between rhododendrons, Heather caught her first glimpse of the Hall. The forsythia was like sunshine on the walls. Daffodils edged the mossy croquet lawn, but, behind the mild façade of spring, the house was unchanged. The open windows - Lady Mowbray believed in fresh air - gaped like mouths. Upstairs, the blinds half drawn against the sun were like heavy lids. She was reluctant to get out of the car.

'Which room is she to have, Bella, I mean?'

Lady Mowbray was surprised. 'I've no idea. Nanny made all the arrangements. Does it matter?'

It mattered a great deal, but Heather shrugged and asked if she could put the car away.

Allowing her grand-daughter to drive was another of Lady Mowbray's idiosyncrasies. She had judged her capable at twelve so she permitted it. She got out and called to the dogs who heaved themselves off the back seat. Honour started biting and scratching her flank.

55

'Stop it, darling,' she said as Heather slid into the driving seat. She drove round to the garage at the back and took in the groceries.   She preferred to sneak into the old house unobserved. There were no shadows in the kitchen.

Nanny was waiting for her. She rose from the table where she was knitting khaki socks and clasped her to her bosom. Heather hugged her back like Wendy's Nana, without reserve. Nanny was dear, of course, but, like Nanny Darling, not exactly human. Then she perched on the kitchen table and answered every question twice.   Nanny's deafness was a trap.   She said 'Pardon?' automatically, but if Heather changed the question she always knew.

'How do you think your Granny's looking?' she asked in her loud English voice. Forty years in Scotland with the family had not altered her Hampshire accent.

'All right,' said Heather. 'Okay.'

Nanny shook her head and narrowed her lips. She had new very white false teeth.

'She's failing. It's all this gadding about, packing up parcels and handing round tea. She's a glutton for punishment.'

Heather laughed. 'She says the same about you.'

'Pardon?'

Heather caught sight of Bella at the scullery door. 'Fancy seeing you here,' she said swinging her long legs and staring at the short broad figure in the cut down green overall.

Bella giggled.

Bella being here might make a difference.

Architecturally, the Hall was divided like a sandwich into three distinct sections. The front, a Victorian addition, consisted of large drawing- and dining rooms, a spacious hall with a mosaic tiled floor and a gracious curving staircase which swept up to four fine south-facing bedrooms where Heather and Lady Mowbray slept.

The back, an Edwardian extension, consisted of a large kitchen, servants' hall, scullery, bootroom, laundry and lavatory

56

with a neat row of servants' bedrooms on the floor above where Nanny slept for choice over the range where it was always warm, with Bella next door for convenience.

The middle section was the original Hall built in the late 17h century, a jumble of low-ceilinged, oak-panelled rooms with small infrequent windows and passages that sloped and twisted, linked by unexpected steps. The three floors included a library full of mildewing copies of the Strand and the Waverley edition of Scott's novels, a billiard room, and the tennis room where sagging rackets and rusting croquet hoops were stored. Upstairs there were innumerable dank bedrooms, and, above them, the attics.

The kitchen quarters were linked to the front rooms by a long dark passage where cockroaches lurked. Halfway up the front stairs a narrow arch led into the old bedrooms.

When the war started, Lady Mowbray magnanimously suggested eating in the servants' hall to cut down labour, but Nanny disapproved and now there were Bella's legs to keep up the old standards.

Heather was afraid of the old dark rooms. Their furnishings were clouded with mould. Rust pock-marked the curtains and white crocheted counterpanes. Mushrooms grew on the Indian carpets. The stench of damp was like unmade beds. Something inhabited the old hall, a presence that haunted the cupboards and concealed itself behind the wooden panels and shutters. It fed on darkness and at night it came out with the shadows and invaded the whole house.

At school she was able to look at her fears objectively and try to analyse the causes. Sometimes she was even able to speak of them.

'My home is haunted,' she confided to a friend as they walked to church, amazed at how easily the words slid off her tongue.

'Lucky you. I'd adore to see a ghost. Tell me more.'

When it came to that point of the conversation there was nothing much to tell.

'What! No headless knight, no grey lady, no coffins and clanking chains? You're neurotic,' teased her friend and they both laughed.

At school she could throw open a closed door and go into a dark room without the chill of fear. Some houses were even welcoming. She tested them like a dog with a twitching nose and sensed if they were light or clouded.

During that first day of the holidays when her school persona still clung to her like her Chilprufe vest, she teased Nanny affectionately, listened to the local gossip and strode through the dark passage from kitchen to dining room hoping that she had outgrown what she believed to be childish nonsense. As the day wore on she could not stop herself listening, clenching her mind, holding her breath at the approach of darkness and she knew that nothing had changed.

The dogs had been walked till they flopped, the black-out curtains drawn, three hands of piquet played with her grandmother under the painted eyes of five generations of dead Mowbrays on the wall. The cards were put away by the time Nanny came in for the nine o-clock news. She tried to concentrate on Alvar Lidell as he announced tragedies and triumphs for the Allies as they marched through Europe and felt guilty because she found such momentous events a bore. Her mind darted bat-like, frantic, over the episodes of the long day in an effort to postpone the time of trial. Yet, over all, like a superimposed photograph, she saw the bend in the stairs, the arch, which she would have to pass on her way to bed.

Bella brought in the night-tray, a glass of hot water with a dash of whisky for Lady Mowbray, a tumbler of cold milk for Heather, tea for Nanny and herself. When they had finished, Nanny assisted Lady Mowbray upstairs followed by the dogs liberally dusted with flea powder.

'Would you like a game?' Heather suggested indicating the cards.

'I wouldn't mind,' said Bella, giggling.

58

In Bella's company she retained a remnant of Heather of the Fifth.

Over the Easter holidays she taught her bezique, poker patience and several board games. Bella liked *Knight's Quest* best. Six paths led through dragons' dens, enchanted swamps, and witch-infested woods to a princess who lay on a couch surrounded by a thicket of roses. Her short thick fingers rattled the dice box and her huge black eyes were delightedly absorbed in the exotic adventures of her Knight.

'Come up with me?' Heather said casually that first night when neither of them could contain their yawns.

So Bella stumped up the staircase beside her that night and every subsequent night so that Heather did not have to tread the corridors and pass the dark archway alone. Safe in her room, she imagined Bella walking back through those secretive passages, passing half-closed doors and trembled. As she pulled the quilt over her head she was filled with guilt that she could so easily endanger the innocent Bella, for she had no doubt that the presence was there, watchful, waiting, evil. Before the night was over she was right back to where she had been for as long as she could remember, enmeshed in chains of fear.

All her life Heather had taken it for granted that she was the hub round which the household revolved. While she was at school, the people at home existed like a pack of cards in the drawing-room cupboard, unused, waiting for her to take them out and deal. She had never thought of Lady Mowbray in any context other than that of grandmother, or of Nanny, who had been born Miss Edith Maddox, as having had any life other than that of nursemaid.

Watching Bella at work, it occurred to her that she - Heather - was not the pivot at all and no more necessary to existence at the Hall than a vase of flowers on the mantelpiece. Her importance to her grandmother was minimal. The old lady's life was anchored in habit. Tea, milkless with a dry biscuit, at seven-thirty which Bella took up to her; the dogs walked at

59

eight-thirty by Bella wet or shine; breakfast at nine in the dining room served and cleared by Bella. Small household duties like arranging flowers were now performed by Bella, allowing Lady Mowbray the freedom to enjoy her war-work. Little treats such as tea in the summer-house on a mild April afternoon were made possible by Bella.

In the kitchen, Nanny's domain, Bella was equally indispensable. She peeled potatoes, cut up vegetables, blacked the range, cleaned Lady Mowbray's brown brogues and Nanny's black wide-fitting courts. Once a week she scrubbed all the back premises. When she had time, she weeded the front beds and pruned the roses.

Heather was relieved. She enjoyed the freedom from distasteful chores and the demands of two old ladies, yet, coming from a school whose motto was 'Service before Self', she could not help being aware that Bella was being 'put upon'. On the third day of the holidays she protested.

'Grandmother,' she began as they ate luncheon in the daffodil-filled dining-room. 'Don't you think Bella has too much to do?'

Lady Mowbray looked at her sharply. 'She's a good gel. Don't put silly ideas into her head.'

To Bella, she was more cautious. 'You don't have to work in the garden, do you?'

'I like it,' she answered, surprised.

'You can't like old Fraser.'

Bella looked away. She does, thought Heather. She likes that smarmy old man with his sleazy smile and greasy trousers. She has no sense of judgement.

'Do you like working here?' she probed. 'Is it better than the farm?'

'I like it fine.'

'You cant like everything and everyone,' Heather said with a hint of impatience. 'It isn't sensible.'

Bella giggled. Laughter was her refuge Heather realised. Like that Japanese gardener at a nearby estate who sang when he was sad, Bella laughed too much.

'I hate Hitler,' she offered as an afterthought, but Heather was unconvinced.

She was not so insensitive as to believe that Bella had been born without normal emotions, only that she had learned to hide them. Bella was like an egg, hard-shelled with the inner parts protected and unseen whereas she - Heather - was the fledgling naked in the nest. Yet, of the two, she believed Bella might be the more vulnerable. She walked through the dim and musty passages of the Hall careless of danger. Surely it was wiser to be aware.

'Be honest, Bella, don't you sometimes - just occasionally - hate it here?' she probed later when they were playing Halma on the kitchen table.

'Nope,' said Bella firmly shaking her short dark head.

'Are you never afraid?'

Bella looked up. 'What's there to fear?'

'Oh, you know. The war, the future, things like that…this old house?' Her voice was studiedly casual as she played her turn.

Bella was silent for a while, then she said, 'Her Ladyship says Malcy can come for a week in the summer.'

It was a clue but Heather missed it. She should not have mentioned fear and the house, not with the presence hovering outside the door, slithering along those passages in the dark. She forced herself to concentrate on the game.

When it was over, Bella filled her hot water bottle and carried it along the passage to the front of the house and up the stairs. Heather trod hard on her heels, jostling her, forcing her into a race, making her giggle, clowning her way to bed, but the presence had never before seemed so close.

Bella

From her window near to the angle between the kitchen extension and the old house, Bella could see part of the walled garden and the lawns with the great round pink rhododendrons and the rose beds she helped to keep trim. All was orderly and as close to perfection as Fraser and wartime permitted, matching her life in the Hall, which was disciplined, busy and pleasant. Though accustomed to hard work, she was not used to being thanked, the extra hours noted and herself appreciated.

'How nicely you do the flowers, Bella,' her Ladyship would remark, pausing to tweak a branch of pussy willow or pick up a fallen petal.

Nanny would slip her an occasional sixpence to make an extra journey to the village to buy a corn plaster or a bag of sweeties. It seemed to her that her life was as cherished and safe and as circumscribed as a plant in the great walled garden.

When she leaned out on her sill and looked under her window the view was very different. There, between the concealing beech hedge and the iron-barred windows of the kitchen offices was a wilderness of mare's tail, dock and nettle that grew rank and profuse fed by a network of ancient drains.

That first summer she had forced her way into the narrow triangular patch and attacked the growth, but the mat of roots intertwined with those of the hedge and were deeper than she could reach, their urge to sprout too strong for her. Within a fortnight the weeds had all returned, the more profusely for their pruning.

It didn't matter, she told herself. No one could see the mess, not even Nanny who secretly delighted in keeping her window closed now that she no longer had to set an example to Miss Heather. Yet, the fact of its presence cast a small shadow. It made her think of Malcy.

She had taken her time to visit him and she had only been the once. In the city she had got off the tram at the wrong stop and when she'd asked the way, the polis had taken her to the Home mistaking her for an orphan. That had given her a red face. The matron with her untidy bun of greying hair and mauve hand-knitted cardigan had had a right good laugh.

'We'll keep you, no bother,' she joked as she led the way through a large shabby playroom that smelt of cabbage and carbolic soap into her office.

The children were having their dinner. 'Your Malcolm is a quiet wee laddie,' she remarked lighting herself a fag. 'Never know what he's thinking. Still waters run deep is what I always say.'

Soon there was a tap at the door and Malcy stood there. He looked small and nipped in as if he wanted to share nothing of himself. His yellow hair was very short, parted at the side and slicked down with water. His grey shorts were threadbare and his shoes scuffed in need of a good polish.

'Here's my wee skinny-malinks,' said the matron drawing him close with a large woolly arm. He submitted to her hug without raising his eyes from the floor. 'Hold your head up, sonny, and let your sister take a good look at you.'

He spoke but without lifting his head. 'She's no' my sister.'

The matron's voice sharpened. 'She's as near to a sister as you're likely to get, my laddie, and you're lucky to have a visitor.'

He looked up for long enough to shoot Bella a swift accusing glance.

'Be sure and have him back by five. There's a nice walk in the park.'

He said nothing until they were in the middle of a wide sea of emerald grass which darkened as the clouds bowled overhead. Then he turned on her. 'I'm no' going back. You can't make me. It's like the jail in there. It's murder.'

She let him talk. After months of holding his tongue, nothing she could say would stop the flood.

'...they're rotten, all of them, dirty, stinking scum. It's your fault I'm stuck in there.'

In a way it was her fault for she had done nothing to prevent him going into care. She hadn't raised a finger.

The rain started, slanting through the windy park. She sat in an empty shelter that had seats facing four ways, dangling her short legs, while he marched round and round, muttering misery and abuse.

'...you don't want me near you. You never did. You'd be glad if I was dead.'

Grinding down the rank thoughts that sprang from the pit of her mind, she stood up, caught him by the wrist and dragged him close. Then she smacked him hard across the face. 'Sticks and stones,' she cried. 'Sticks and stones.'

His left cheek flushed scarlet. It was a long time since she had smacked him and she was as surprised as he was. For a moment she thought he was going to cry.

'I'll tell the matron on you,' he whined, 'ye auld Crawface.'

She took him into a café where he wolfed down a plate of chips and a glass of ginger. Then she bought him the Beano and the Dandy and gave him the rest of her sweet ration. While the assistant was weighing out toffees, he stole an ink rubber from the tray on the counter. She watched him do it, saw the challenge in his eyes, but she did nothing, knowing that it was almost five and that the worst she could do to him was to take him back.

That night Lady Mowbray questioned her. 'Did you enjoy your visit? How did you find Malcolm?'

It would have been so easy to say 'fine', but, just as Bella felt forced to control the unseemly growth beneath her window, so she was compelled to deal with the imperfections within herself.

'He'll never settle, not in a month of Sundays.'

Lady Mowbray nodded.

Heather

Malcy was brought to the Hall by bus one hot morning in late July by a welfare officer in a shiny city suit. Lady Mowbray saw him alone in the dining-room where he waited for as long as it took him to drink two cups of tea. He did not stay to say good-bye to the boy. When he had gone Lady Mowbray rang for Malcy.

The welfare officer warned her to put a mackintosh sheet on his bed, not to leave money lying about and that if he caused trouble to contact the orphanage immediately. It was an inauspicious start, but Lady Mowbray who had a sense of humour was aware of this and prepared to give the child a chance. She did not, however, expect to be charmed. Malcy was respectful and he was also beautiful; his clipped short hair was layered in shades of gold, his blue eyes seemed anxious and his skin was too white.

She got Fraser to hang the old canvas hammock between two elms at the far end of the lawn. She unearthed a set of rusty clock-golf numerals and suggested to Heather that she put up the croquet hoops. She remembered she liked small boys. Her own dead son had been a nice child too, what she could remember of his short pre-prep school childhood.

Nanny took him to her heart. He was clean and punctual and tidy and he did not answer back. He was given the run of the grounds, and, apart from the front rooms, the freedom of the house. Except at meal times, he was seldom seen.

'You wouldn't know there was a child in the house,' Nanny said as if this was a matter for congratulation.

Heather knew that he spend most of his time in the old Hall and in particular the billiard room. She had seen him disappear down the dark passages.

'What does he do in there?' she asked Bella anxiously as she was clearing the table after lunch.

Bella was no help. 'Where's the harm in it?' she said defensively.

'But he ought to be out in the sun,' Heather insisted.

'Wee Malcy was never one for the fairm or the gairden.'

'I don't like him in there,' she complained. 'It's an unhealthy room.' She was going to have said 'evil' but changed her mind. Her horror of the old part of the Hall had not lessened but she was no longer convinced it was rational. Since the start of the summer holidays, she had come to believe that the source of her fear must lie within herself, dating it back to an afternoon, when, as a very young child, she had got lost in the old rooms. She remembered searching in vain from room to room, presumably for a way out of the maze, but her memory was hazy. It might have been a dream. She had an impression of heaving walls closing in on her, sucking the breath out of her lungs, stifling her screams. Believing that this must surely be the source of her fears alleviated them to a certain extent. Lying awake in the long light mornings, she was able to look straight at the shadows, examine the physical manifestations of terror, the palpitations of her heart, the sweats and clench of muscle. Mentally at least she had stopped running, but Malcy's long periods of isolation in the billiard room disturbed her. She tried to elicit her grandmother's support but without success.

'It's good for the old rooms to be used. I remember your father loved them. Besides Malcolm is not a destructive child. What possible harm can he do?'

She knew he went there when the household was in bed. She sensed him there and when she saw him in the morning eating his porridge at the kitchen table, his hair damped and sleek, his face shining clean, goose pimples - for no good reason - stippled her brown arms.

She found him hard to talk to, could not be spontaneous with him, so that her every remark sounded silly or patronizing as it hung unanswered in the silence. He gave her no help. Not often at a loss for words, ridiculously with Malcy, she was shy.

He spoke to Bella though. Behind the closed kitchen door she could hear his childish treble set against her contralto. Often she wondered what they said to each other. Towards the end of his stay, she caught them arguing.

She had come through to the kitchen after Nanny and Lady Mowbray had gone to bed, bringing the Ludo board. Malcy liked Ludo, not so much to win but to catch the other counters and send them bouncing back to base. Bella made no attempt to dodge his pieces, but Heather did and was ashamed of herself for pitting her wits against a nine-year old child.

She heard their raised voices and broke in on the argument. 'Well, what's it all about this time?' she asked lightly. 'Little birds in their nests should agree.'

Surprisingly it was Malcy who answered. 'I'm no' going back to that dump. She can't make me.'

Heather looked at Bella but her head was bent while Malcy stared at her with wide challenging eyes. It took her a moment to realise that she was expected to be the referee. Bella was waiting for her to say, 'Of course, you must go back,' while Malcy was willing her to say, 'you can stay.' She shied from the responsibility.

'Let's play Ludo, shall we?' she said brightly. 'You can be red, Malcy, if you like.'

Bella helped her to set up the board.

'I'm no' playing,' he said sullenly, tilting back his chair.

'Come on, Malcy, you start,' Bella placated.

'If Malcy doesn't want to play, we can manage quite well without him,' Heather said, an echo of Lady Mowbray, displeased. She turned her back on him and rattled the dice.

Bella threw a six and took out a man. She threw another. Her face brightened. She looked up at Heather to share her pleasure and then suddenly the board, counters, dice and shaker flew across the room.

'Malcolm!' Heather turned in anger and saw his blazing eyes. 'How dare you?'

'You can just get down on your knees and pick up all they pieces,' Bella, equally outraged, retorted.

'I'm the Magician,' he cried triumphantly. 'I can do anything I like.'

'I'm warning you, 'said Bella. 'Pick up they pieces or go to your bed.'

'Pick them up yourself,' he shouted, kicking the shaker under the dresser as he banged out of the room.

Bella scuttled about the floor finding the counters. 'He's a right bad bairn when he wants to be.'

Heather was immediately contrite. 'Perhaps we were rather mean. After all, he's only got two days left.' The force of that sweeping hand had frightened her, prickled her scalp, chilled her bare arms.

At breakfast Lady Mowbray looked up from the *Times*. 'I think we might ask Malcolm to stay on for another week.'

It was not a question, it was a statement. Without thinking, Heather replied, 'No.'

Her grandmother rustled the paper disapprovingly. 'My dear, aren't you behaving rather selfishly? I thought he might enjoy the raspberries. Fraser expects a heavy crop this year, and he could help to pick them.'

Nothing more was said, but two days later the welfare man returned in a battered Ford and took Malcy away. Heather gave him a packet of Rowntree's Fruit Clear Gums from her own sweet ration. She was ashamed.

That night she had a bad dream. She was carrying armfuls of tinned peaches and packets of tea from the POW parcel-packing depot towards the billiard room. Light glimmered under the closed door. She did not want to go in but it opened as she approached. Closing her eyes in terror, she realised she could see without them. The room was hot and full of movement, lit by a fire in the grate. Gradually, like dust, the shadows settled and she could make out the shape of a large serpent on the hearth. It held wrapped within its coils, from neck to knee, a body she did not recognise. As the serpent turned its big flat

68

head to look at her she threw the tins of peaches at it and turned to run, but inevitably she was drawn back until she found that she herself was that body clenched and choked by the scaly coils. It opened its wide mouth to swallow her and she was engulfed in a stench of sulphur and feral beast. This, she realised was the presence she had feared, this the cause of many haunted nights. Just before she awoke, she saw that it had Malcy's watchful eyes.

For a long time, she lay, reliving every detail, clenched in the familiar grip of terror, not daring so much as to change her position under the sheet.

For a year Malcy continued to spend part of the school holidays at the Hall. Heather learned that he was coming to stay for good that first Christmas morning after the war. Lady Mowbray called Bella into the dining room and gave her an envelope.

Bella, believing it to contain her Christmas box would have pushed it into her apron pocket if Lady Mowbray had not told her to open it. The old lady's wrinkled lips twitched with amusement, but she did not catch Heather's eye.

Bella stared at the envelope which was addressed to her employer and had already been opened. She took out the letter and gazed at the typed contents.

'Well?' said Lady Mowbray expectantly, but Bella did not lift her eyes from the sheet. 'Do you realise what it means?'

After a while Bella shook her head, but Heather had the impression that she understood.

'It means,' said Lady Mowbray triumphantly, 'that when Malcolm comes for New Year he will not be going back to the home. He will attend school in the village and live here at the Hall. He will, of course, be expected to take a share in the chores and to help Fraser with the garden.'

Bella's face flooded with colour.

'I thought you would be pleased,' said Lady Mowbray complacently.

Bella folded the letter, put it back into the envelope and laid it on the table by her employer's elbow. 'Excuse me, your Ladyship, but wee Malcy does na like the gairden.'

'Nonsense,' said Lady Mowbray, somewhat taken aback. 'He's far too young to have likes and dislikes.'

After Bella had gone, she said, 'Strange gel. I thought she would have been more enthusiastic.' When Heather made no comment, she added irritably, 'Don't sulk. It does not become you.'

'I'm not sulking,' she protested, 'I'm just surprised.'

'Why should you be? Is it so rare for me to act out of charity? Am I such an ogre that I may not take pity on an orphaned child?'

'Of course not, Grandmother. I only thought you might have consulted Bella first.'

'But I did it for Bella. She's a good gel. I want to keep her. Besides, Fraser needs help in the garden. It will work very well.'

Heather wanted to smile. The old lady's motives were so transparent. She was not good at guile.

'Nanny approves,' she continued. 'Believe it or not, she and I like the boy. It's pleasant to have a well-behaved child about the place.'

Heather sensed that she needed to be reassured, that she was not entirely at ease with her decision. For a moment she saw herself as the stronger, the wiser of the two. She stood behind the old woman's chair and put a hand on her shoulder, feeling the frailty of flesh and bone. Then she leaned down and kissed the papery cheek.

'Happy Christmas, Grandmama.'

Lady Mowbray's mouth pursed with pleasure at the unexpected embrace. 'I have done the right thing, haven't I?' she asked, but Heather could not give her reassurance she sought.

'I hope so,' she said still unable to commit herself.

Later she discovered the letters. Thirty-two sheets taken from an exercise book, folded and stored in an oblong manilla envelope. The writing was childish but neat, unmarred by spelling mistakes, written with a sharp pointed pencil that made small holes in the flimsy paper. She pulled out one at random and read:

Dear Lady Mowbray
I hope you are well. I like the Hall. I would like to live in it all the time. I hate the Home. There is a man who beats me called Mr Donaldson. One of the boys is to be boarded out on a farm. I would like to be boarded out but not on a farm.
Hoping this finds you as it leaves me, Malcolm Gould.

She opened the next in the bundle. It was dated the following week.

Dear Lady Mowbray
I am writing to ask you to send me a picture of the Hall. It is a nice house. I wish I could stay in it all the time. This Home is a horrible smelly old place. I wish Hitler had bombed it like he did the farm. I am glad he did not bomb the Hall.
Cheers for now, Malcolm Gould.

She sorted through the rest of the letters. They were all alike. Each contained a hint as broad as a beam. Malcy had discovered that Lady Mowbray's social conscience was her Achilles heel and he gnawed away at it until he had gained his ends.

Malcolm

In the Home there were too many bodies squashed together like tatties in a pot, aggressive, noisy, with indistinguishable personalities and predictable behaviour.

At the Hall there were too few who swam round each other like small fish in a cloudy pool. Malcy made a discovery.

71

People had more sides than a dice cube. The way they acted towards servants, to superiors, to contemporaries, to children, to strangers, to intimates and by themselves, were all different. He was curious about the inhabitants of the Hall.

From the arch half-way up the stairs he could watch the upper landing, and, below, where the dining- and drawing-rooms led into the Hall. Lady Muck, for instance, was querulous with Nanny, indulgent to Heather, opinionated with her friends and daft by herself. First signs of madness; wrinkled stockings and talking to yourself. She did it all the time. Came bustling out of the drawing-room to stand dithering in the hall. 'Now what did I want, dash it , dash it, dash it, what on earth am I looking for, oh yes, the secateurs. Where did I put them? Bella will know.' Boring stuff like that, but sometimes there were gems. 'I like the boy. Whatever you may say, I like the boy. I know having him here is risky but every step one takes across the road is potentially dangerous and there are times when one just has to trust ones instincts.' Gratifying, but who was she trying to convince?

He supposed that the sum of the different parts must make up the whole. Yet, that was not always obvious. Lady Muck's attitude to him was dependent upon his behaviour to her. By being 'obliging', as she called it, he could get her to nod and smile like the china mandarin on the drawing-room mantelpiece.

If Lady Muck was clay, Nanny was plasticine. Nanny, who took out her teeth and sucked sweets when she thought she was alone, liked respect with a hint of cheek. He hooted inwardly when she tipped him two-pence to fetch her glasses or hold her wool.

Most of the time he liked to watch Miss Snooty. Once he was sure she had seen him lurking in the archway for she had stared into the shadows with wide and whitened eyes as he cowered back expecting her to accuse him, but when he ventured out she had gone, leaping up the rest of the stairs, two at a time as if the devil were at her heels. He liked to see her scared. Sometimes he put his eye to her keyhole when she was preparing for bed.

72

He never saw much for the door was too thick and the keyhole too narrow, but he could hear the wireless crooning soppy music and once he had caught her dancing, a swift blur of pink nightgown and streaming hair that had filled him with an incomprehensible yearning that caught at his heart like a stitch.

He found he could not cultivate Miss Snooty like the others for his own feelings continually obtruded. There were times when he hated her for her power to move him, so he sulked, and there were times when he ached to please her, so he showed off. He longed to be indifferent to her so that he could manipulate her by his charm or servility. Above all, he needed her to notice him. Mostly he ended up by annoying her.

Heather

That Christmas, Heather fell in love. She had been trying for months. At school everyone was in love.

She met him at a cocktail party and felt in her breast the sweet sharp pierce of Cupid's shaft. That was the way she described it to a friend, ringed round with inverted commas and exclamation marks. He was forty-two, sallow, gaunt with a brown mole on his cheek and thin brown hair. No beauty, she told herself with idiotic pride, but his eyes were large and green, dark-circled, poet's eyes. His name was Piers Wood-Johnston and he was a captain recently demobbed from the Gurkhas.

It was said that he had had a bad war.

He stood with his back to the wall drinking gin-and-It and talking to other men, but, as she circulated, she was aware of him as if he held her on a leash.

At home she took him into her fantasies, and, as she walked the dogs through drab winter lanes, she nursed him through jungle fever, listened with tears to his tales of suffering, rescued him from every conceivable danger, and always he would reward her with long silent looks, a clasp of the hand and sometimes with a kiss. Her body swooned, her limbs grew heavy and her breasts tender as she thought about that kiss.

She met him again at a dinner party on New Year's Eve. He sat across the table and watched her with his poet's eyes as she sparkled and scintillated like crystal in candlelight. She overheard her host, a gentleman farmer whose land marched with the Hall, remark to Lady Mowbray that she had a beauty on her hands. She wanted to be beautiful for Piers.

He spoke to her once after dinner to ask where she lived. She blushed and her eyes shone as she replied. The sound of his voice and the nature of his question fed her imagination so that at any hour of the next day she expected him to call.

After New Year, Lady Mowbray invited him among others to a tea-party. Bella made scones and a cake and brought in the silver teapot on a tray. Heather could think of nothing to say to him. Everything important had already been said over and over again in her imagination. It seemed ridiculous to remark on the weather or the Labour government to someone she had kissed in her imagination and to whom she had confided her secrets. So she was quiet and watched his fingers yellow with nicotine and feathered with silky black hairs. When he offered her a cigarette, she took it and puffed out smoke from time to time with the insouciance of a sophisticate.

That night she danced around the kitchen. 'Well?' she demanded. ''What did you think of him? Isn't he dreamy? Isn't he the bees knees? Totally divine? Oh, Bella, have you ever been in love?'

Bella watched her with admiration in her huge black eyes and laughed. 'Who, me? No fears.'

Malcy said, 'He's got diarrhoea.'

'What do you mean?' both girls cried indignantly.

'I heard him in the lavvy. What a pong.'

Bella giggled but Heather said coldly, 'What a little beast you are.'

He met her eyes triumphantly. He knew exactly what he had done.

74

Piers went back to his rubber plantation in Malaya, but there were others to take his place. Falling in love was delightfully easy, she found. Sometimes it was possible to be in love with two or even three men at the same time like James Mason and Barry Skene who was the brother of a school friend with whom she exchanged long chaste letters posted clandestinely in an pillar box outside the school gates, and Mr Russell.

Brian Russell lived with his mother in a charmingly converted miner's cottage in the village and commuted daily to the city where he was a master in a small private school. During the Easter holidays Lady Mowbray engaged him to come up to the Hall three times a week to coach Heather in Latin for her school certificate. He was a studious young man with wiry black hair and exceedingly good teeth. Behind thick glasses his small grey eyes were unexpectedly hot.

Heather had never been taught by a man before. Nor had she ever spent so much time in male company. While they worked side by side in the dining-room, she fell ardently in love.

Brian had never taught girls before and was not inclined to take seriously her academic ambitions. He could not, however, resist her pretty admiring eyes fixed on his, the scent of her long clean hair. He drew down the blinds against the strong spring sunshine, took off his glasses and kissed her moist pink mouth.

Those kisses…a butterfly touch of closed lips, a gentle friction that grew firmer, until with wide open mouths their tongues touched. Ten minutes of Latin, fifty minutes of kissing but it was the Latin that seemed too long.

Once she opened her eyes and saw Malcy staring at her through the gap between window-sill and blind. He did not move when she caught his eye, but stayed there expressionless, immobile. Now I'm for it, she thought. That little beast will tell tales, but she did not break from the embrace and he did not run away. For the time being, for reasons she could not interpret, she allowed him to watch, as if his presence added another dimension to the kiss.

Malcolm said nothing and nor did she. There was no point. The four weeks of holiday were over. Two days later she put on her school uniform and departed. Kissing Mr Russell had been pleasant but it was even more delightful to boast about it in the dormitory during the long May dusks.

In June Lady Mowbray wrote to tell her that he had become engaged to another teacher and was moving permanently to Edinburgh.

'She caught him on the rebound,' her friends consoled her, suitably amazed.

Barry Skene's sister asked her to stay for half-term. 'He's dying to meet you,' she enthused.

That hot summer of 1947 Nanny got ill, shut away from the light with shingles in her face. Heather visited her nearly every day. She breezed into the shaded room, with gold glints in her long brown hair. Sometimes Malcy went with her, his skin glowing with health, his hair bleached white.

'You're a pair,' said Nanny admiringly as she covered her eyes against their brightness. 'You'll be darkies before the summer's out.'

Bella stayed to bathe her eyes and change her linen and listen patiently to her long complaints.

Malcy had taken to following Heather about, as if, by holding his tongue at Easter, he had earned the right. A year ago, it would have annoyed her, but, lately, popular Heather of the Sixth and nervy Heather of the Hall had merged into attractive Heather of the World. The holidays flew past in a round of tennis parties, dances and picnics in the company of boys.

She loved them all, their hard bodies, their hairiness, the smell of their sweat, the mystique of their maleness. It was as if she had spent her whole life up till now shut up like Rapunzel in a tower, surrounded by women with her back to the window that looked out on the male world. It had taken her sixteen years to let down her hair.

76

Although that clasp of uneasiness still clutched at her throat as she passed through the old Hall, the night terrors had receded. Instead of crouching, muscles clenched, under the eiderdown, she swooned with the wireless crooning love songs into her pillow. In the privacy of her room, she danced with veils and dreamed of sheiks and Laurence Olivier. She was intoxicated by the world she had discovered, and Malcy, being male, was in a small way part of it. So when she visited Nanny or practised tennis strokes against the stable door or sun-bathed in the canvas hammock under the elms, she let him watch. Although she gave him so sign that she knew he was there, she was content to let him worship at her shrine.

He gave her presents; a bottle of Californian Poppy scent and a brown wooden bangle which she liked and pushed half way up her tanned brown arm.

'Where did you get that?' Lady Mowbray asked.

'Malcy gave it to me. Wasn't it sweet of him?'

'Where does he get the money,' her grandmother said. It was more of an exclamation than a question, but it made Heather curious enough to ask.

'I earn it,' he told her, his wide eyes neither guilty nor innocent, but unblinking, without expression. 'In the gairden,' he added popping an aniseed ball into his mouth.

That was a surprise for he hated to get his hands dirty and would go to any lengths to avoid outdoor work. Bella usually covered up for his deficiencies in that department. Heather was touched.

It was not in the garden however that Malcy earned money for presents and sweeties.

One hot August afternoon, Lady Mowbray asked her to find him to pick raspberries for an old friend in Ladymuir. She went out to look for him. The garden was fragrant and humming with worker bees, but there was no sign of Malcy, or of Fraser for that matter.

Having nothing better to do, she decided to pick the fruit herself. It was cool and pleasant between the tall hedges of

77

leafy canes. She went to the tool-shed for a punnet, intending to line it with cabbage leaves. Without thinking she pushed open the door. To her surprise Malcy and Fraser were both there shut away from the summer sun.

'What on earth are you doing inside on a day like this?' she asked lightly, without suspicion.

Fraser had his back to her, but as her eyes adjusted to the gloom it was evident that he was fumbling with his buttons. Malcy, expressionless, took a gobstopper out of his pocket and plugged it into his mouth, rolling it around his tongue.

And immediately she knew.

The flush started low down on her stomach and spread hotly throughout her body, making her tremble. With an expression of disgust, she ran out into the cool clean air, feeling sick.

Mr Fraser

Lady Mowbray had a horror of wasps. She flapped at them fanatically and screamed at the suspicion of a buzz. When Heather squashed five of them against the dining-room window at luncheon, her grandmother summoned Fraser to find the bike.

He located it high up in the eaves of the west wall in the groove between the old Hall and the front extension. Pushing his cap back on his head, he whistled. 'Take some shifting, this. Best to attack it at dusk when the buggers are drowsy,' he told Bella. 'Keep them all away.'

Fraser shared Lady Mowbray's hatred of wasps, like ruddy Jap soldiers they were, bayonets fixed. Every year he outwitted battalions of the yellow bastards with strategy, cyanide and smoke. He had been looking forward to the attack and was plotting his method when Sunny Jim had come to the tool-shed with his hand held out.

As he set the ladder fully extended some six feet to the left of the bike, Malcy was still on his mind. Maybe he'd come down too hard on the lad, taken his own fears out on him, for Miss Heather coming in like that had scared him shitless. He'd let the lad have his bob tomorrow, show him there were no hard feelings. As he returned from the tool-shed carrying a sack impregnated with paraffin attached to an eight-foot pole, he thought he caught a flash of the bairn's pale hair in the rhodies.

'That you, Sunny Jim?' he called out, but, apart from the dusk noises, drowsy rooks and whining midges, he heard nothing. 'Best keep away if you don't want stung,' he warned.

Lighting the sodden sack which burst into flames he gripped the end of the pole and slowly ascended. The ground was spongy and he felt the ladder shift and settle under his weight.

As he climbed nearer he saw that it was a huge bike. Already he could hear the buzz of the creatures hovering round its mouth. His first strike would have to be hard and accurate if he didn't want the buggers swarming all over him.

Bracing his shins against the second highest rung, he lunged sideways with the flaming pole attached to the now thickly smoking bundle. At the same time the ladder shifted, tilting him off balance. He fell with the bike and the pole in a swarm of angry, stinging insects.

The crows rose from the rookery in a black cloud cawing and croaking, drowning the gardener's cry. Next morning the wasps were still crawling over him when he was found dead from a broken neck.

Malcy was stung twice just under his eye. His face swelled up painfully and he was loud in complaint.

'What a fuss,' Bella chided him as she dabbed the stings with baking soda. 'I thought you were told to keep well away.'

He fidgeted and writhed away from her fingers.

'I never touched the ladder,' he insisted.

She paused for a moment, the cotton wool in her hand. The lid to the deep well of her mind lifted for an instant, and as quickly closed again.

'I never said you did.'

Lady Mowbray was shocked by Fraser's death and even wept a little, but Heather, not just because she had never liked the man, could not mourn. Now she could forget about what she

79

had seen in the tool-shed. Yet her relief was accompanied by guilt that she could be so selfish as to regard a man's agonising death as a means of getting her out of an awkward situation.

Heather

Heather had a first cousin-once-removed called Eva. She was an angular, energetic, country woman like Lady Mowbray who wore tweeds and lipstick usually chewed off at breakfast. She had inherited, through her husband, a place in Hampshire which had been commandeered by the army during the war.

It had taken her three strenuous years to restore Nightingales after the ravages of the army. Her only son, Miles, a widower, spent most of his time in his London flat. She needed something useful to do, and, after a week's visit to Ladymuir, found it in Heather.

'It's time that gel came out. It's not as if you need her here as long as you have Nanny and Bella.'

Heather held her breath. It seemed that all her life she had been waiting for the opportunity to escape from the Hall. Her grandmother could refuse her nothing, so she left school with five credits and a pass in Latin, in tears, promising eternal affection for her friends, and set off full of anticipation for Nightingales and the season.

Lady Mowbray drove her to the station in the Morris, puttering and spurting gravel down the drive. Bella and Nanny waved from the front door, but Malcy was not with them. She caught a glimpse of him lurking behind a tree by the Lodge. He did not return her wave.

Malcy

Malcy waited for the Glasgow bus. He wore long trousers, dark grey flannels with a knife crease and his navy school blazer, carefully pressed. His black shoes shone and his short gold hair was slicked into a cow's lick on his brow. He drew in his lips and held them together at a supercilious angle cultivated in front of the kitchen mirror, and stood with his heels together, not exactly at attention, but with his body poised and straight, showing no sign of cold or impatience this chilly November Saturday of his fifteenth birthday.

His wallet contained a Bank of Scotland five pound note presented to him that morning by Lady Mowbray in an envelope with his name scrawled all over it in her large untidy hand.

After a while he pulled out of his pocket a silver watch with Roman numerals, consulted it and decided that the bus was three minutes late. Anger stiffened his stance. If they knew who he really was, they would not dare to be late.

Malcy had worked out at an early age that his birth had been in error. He should never have gone to the Goulds, endured such an upbringing; nor was it his intention to skivvy for that querulous old bag a day longer than necessary.

It was not that his body was wrong. Far from it. He approved of his physical appearance, particularly now that he had given up sweeties and the acne spots on his chin had more or less disappeared. He had once been cast as Gabriel in the nativity play at the orphanage. He had enjoyed posing in wings and halo and hearing the audience's complimentary remarks. To be thought 'angelic' on account of his looks exactly matched the image he chose, for the moment, to portray.

Nor was there anything wrong with his brain. He approved of his shrewd mind always a step and a half ahead of everyone else. His mind and body worked in harmony. Only the environment was wrong. His creator had mistakenly dumped him in the wrong womb, placed him accidentally or out of spite into the wrong life.

God was a bungler. Look at the mess he had made of nature, the dirt, the waste, the stench; capricious too. Told men to love and forgive each other and then, contrary to his own commands, dumped them into sulphuric pits out of sheer revenge. Where was the forgiveness there? Kidded on he was like a father. Malcy knew all about fucking fathers. But God was not smarter than Malcy. At an early age he worked out who he really was. Hitler's son. *Javohl.*

When the knowledge first knocked the breath out of him, he thought that the Fuhrer might have smuggled him into Britain, a sort of secret weapon who would grow up to destroy the fairmer, the English and the rich in that order. Look how he had sent that solitary bomber to obliterate the farm. As he had grown older, common-sense had told him that Hitler would never have placed him with morons like the Goulds. Another discarded theory was that he had been kidnapped from his cradle by spies, dumped in an orphanage and then fostered out like Crawface to the farm. But Miss Snooty swore she had seen him when he was a day old and she was too dumb to lie.

The truth was far more subtle. God had bungled and instead of overshadowing Eva Braun, he had got hold of Lizzie Gould.

Unforgivable of God, and yet, bearing in mind who he really was, the error was not insuperable. As he climbed on to the bus, it occurred to him that it might have been planned that way to give him the chance to prove himself. Better still, that the Magician, like the fairy godmother in one of Miss Snooty's tales, had decreed, that, though he could do nothing about his messed-up birth, he could dish out looks and brains and the ability to overcome the disadvantages.

He took a seat near the front of the bus to avoid the smoke of fags which hovered lethally over the passengers in the back and paid the conductress for a half-return. He turned his head and saw his reflection in the grimy window, still, against the kaleidoscope of the passing world. It was a symbolic image, one that he would not forget. '*Achtung, achtung, achtung.* I'll make my mark,' he assured himself. 'Men will remember me. *Javohl.*'

As the bus approached the suburbs it filled with passengers. A woman carrying a basket, her purse only half-hidden under a mackintosh, with a folded push-chair and three young children climbed in and looked around for an empty seat. Immediately he stood up and with an old-fashioned gesture of his hand and head, indicated his. He did not look at her but he was aware of her approval. He thought, she will tell her old man about the handsome lad who gave up his seat. Inside, he was laughing so hard he had to bite the inside of his cheeks.

At the bus station, he lifted out the push-chair and set it up for her. He accepted her thanks gravely, touched his forelock the way Fraser used to do when Lady Muck came into the garden, then with a dazzling smile disappeared into the crowd.

He crossed to the Gents and locked himself into a cubicle. There was £9 and a half crown and some coppers in the purse. Taking off his shoe he stuffed the notes under the insole and dropped the coins into his trouser pocket. The he wiped the purse with his handkerchief and standing up on the seat pushed it into the cistern.

That was only the start.

He visited a bookshop and bought a new biography of Hitler, ate a pie and chips at Woolworth's and queued to see *Stick-up* at the Regal. It was full of dozing housewives with shopping baskets. He changed his seat twice.

'I hope you have had a successful day, 'Lady Muck asked him that evening when he presented her with a quarter-pound box of Black Magic chocolates.

When he took off his shoes in the privacy of his bedroom, he counted twenty-two pound notes. There were still well over three pounds left in his pocket and his wallet. *Javohl.* It had been quite a successful day.

He kept the money in a bible. Lady Muck had given it to him for his twelfth birthday. Not what he had ever wanted for it was shabby and smelt musty; very old though, published in London by Robert Barker, printer to the Kings Most Excellent Majesty in 1606. It had a heavy cardboard cover bound in hide and it was six inches thick. Someone had added a flap and a lock which still worked with a rusty key. There were some illegible notes written on the fly-leaf in a spidery hand and his name added below in bright blue ink. *Malcolm Gould, from Janet Wedderburn Mowbray.*

Though it had taken him hours to cut out the centre, it made a smashing cash-box. Who else but a genius would think of using a bible to store his filthy lucre? He kept the key inside the brass nob on his hollow bedstead with the string wound round the base.

Inside the bible he counted ninety-two pounds.

At school Malcy cultivated anonymity. He did not go to football matches or kick a ball around the playground. He did not join in the furtive groups behind the toilets to smoke and exchange tales of sexual exploits. He did not stand at street corners or hoot at girls nor did he belong to a gang. At the same time he managed to give the impression that he acted like everyone else.

On Monday morning he arrived as usual early, but not first. He took his place at assembly without exchanging a greeting. His algebra exercise had been calculated to reach the middle of the pile. Once he had written an essay entitled *After the War* and lost himself in a fantasy of how Hitler had escaped from the Berlin bunker, come to Scotland, raised a small but dedicated army and overthrown the English and the toffs. It had caused a sensation in the staff room and thereafter he had been watched. Being noticed as the Archangel Gabriel in an elementary school play was all right because it had no connection to reality. Being noticed as a protagonist of Nazism could be unwise.

In the dinner hour a group of boys huddled on the hot pipes when Malcy went to the toilets. No one paid him a blind bit of notice which was how he liked it. The toilets were as usual mucky so he stopped briefly to rinse his hands.

'Malcy,' cried one of the coarser lads, ' is it right you showed it to Jeannie Bain behind the lassies' cludgie?'

'Ask Jeannie Bain,' he replied a shade too cheekily, flashing his brilliant smile.

'We 're asking you,' said another older boy, a bully. 'Go on, tell us, Malcy - son.'

Malcy looked at their stupid pimply faces, the heat in their pig eyes. He thought of the hoard in the bible, remembered whose son he was. How dared they? How bloody dared they!

'Go fuck yourselves,' he said contemptuously and turned on his heel.

Their raucous laughter hooted after him, but they left him alone.

Sex was too important to be dirtied by sniggering louts. It had nothing to do with Jeannie Bain. Sex was Miss Heather Snooty Bell.

All over the Hall he had hides so he could watch her when she was at home. He dreamed of her drifting down the staircase with her long brown hair floating over her shoulders, down into his arms, begging for it and someday he was going to give it to her just as a favour to herself.

At Christmas Heather came home. Lady Muck ordered a car to meet her at the station and she arrived at tea-time with her hair in a sleek page-boy, her neck as long and slender as a swan's. He waited in the background and watched her kiss her grandmother, hug Crawface and ask for Nanny who was in bed with a cold. Then she looked around and said, 'Where's Malcy?' She asked for him.

He stepped forward, flashed her his brilliant smile and took her suitcase.

He was drunk on her presence in the house. On Christmas Eve Lady Muck had friends in for cocktails. He and Crawface handed round trays of canapés and G and Ts and all the time he was aware of her as if there was no one else in the room, her poshness, her scent, the clean shine of her sleek brown hair. After a while he put down the tray, left the drawing room and climbed the front stairs to her room.

He noted her untidiness, pink silk cami-knickers on the floor, stockings like brown mice on the carpet, a drift of expensive face-powder on her dressing table, her brush thick with dark strands. He clicked his tongue and automatically began to tidy up.

He picked up the blue silk blouse she had been wearing earlier in the day, remembering the curves of her body beneath its sheer texture, and, for the first time in his life he was stirred, not just with sex, but with tenderness. It was a strange sensation, almost painful, full of a yearning ache he could not understand. He turned off the light and pulling back the lace counterpane lay down on her quilt and pushed his head into her pillow pressing his mouth into its softness. For the first time since he had been a small boy he felt the sting and heat of tears.

Then she came in. The door opened slowly enough to allow him to spring off the bed and on to his feet. She was surprised to find the light on and did not see him immediately. When she noticed him standing there and caught her expression he was amazed. She was scared shitless. He could see the whites of her eyes.

'What are you doing here?' she asked but the question was tentative rather than accusing.

He had his answers ready and rolled them smoothly off his tongue. 'Turning down your bed, Miss Heather. I noticed the bulb in your bedside lamp had popped. I was changing it.'

He pretended to fiddle with the lamp under the shade and switched it on. 'There you are,' he said flashing her his smile. 'As good as new.'

He thought he had convinced her, though it sounded as phoney as hell with no dud bulb to show her. He was even expecting her thanks but she was looking beyond him at the bed. The mark of his body was obvious, the blouse lay rumpled on the quilt.

'Little twerp,' she said contemptuously, all fear of him gone. 'You have no business to be in here. Please go. I don't like you in my room. In fact I don't like you anywhere.'

She shouldn't have said that. One day she would be sorry.

He went straight to his own room, put on both bars of the electric fire and opened his bible. His loot amounted to £157 and a ten shillings note.

The gas chambers were too good for her. *Javohl.*

Nanny was failing fast. She was no longer able to leave her room. Crawface was kept busy running up and down the back stairs with tablets and chamber pots and hot water bottles. The doctor called three times a week. He wanted to put her in hospital but she would not budge.

'She always was a stubborn old so-and-so,' he said.

'I can manage,' said Bella.

Sometimes Malcy took her a cup of tea. She lay back on her pillows, skeletal, yellowish, dozing or querulous. Pain exhausted her. Deafness isolated her. When there was more than one person in the room she thought they were talking about her.

'I can hear every word you say,' she would mutter crossly.

One afternoon in February, Malcy found her asleep. Her head lay turned to one side. Her mouth hung open and she snored. He gagged at the sour smell of sickness in the room.

'Wakey, wakey, rise and shine, come and get it,' he said, flashing his smile, setting the tray down on her bedside cabinet.

She did not respond. The drawer in the pedestal beside her bed was open sufficiently to reveal her handbag, a worn leather envelope with a brass catch. He glanced at the old woman. Though her head was turned towards him, her eyes were shut. With a flick of his quick neat fingers he drew out the bag, opened the flap and found the purse. There were three notes and some silver in change. Before he could take them, he felt her hand on his wrist, clammy as a fish. She was wide awake, her eyes malevolent, her strength undiminished.

'Thief!' she cried triumphantly. 'I always knew you were too good to be true.'

It was the lie he resented. She had been the first at the Hall to fall for his charm.

87

'Let go, ye auld bitch,' he said coarsely. 'What would I want with your rotten siller?'

With a twist of his wrist he freed his hand.

'Don't you think you'll get away with it.' She jabbed at him with her forefinger. 'I've worked long enough with children to tell a bad one when I see him. Lady Mowbray will know what to do with you.' Her voice weakened. 'She'll put you back where you belong.'

He reached for her pillow and jerked it sideways from under her head.

'Don't threaten me, fart face.'

She did not hear him. She saw only the pillow in his two hands, too close to her face. She tried to raise her head. Suddenly her heart leapt right out of her body or so it seemed. It lay there gasping on the counterpane and then it stopped. She died with a streak of terror in her eyes.

It was obvious immediately that she was dead. He was astonished. He had not thought that a human being, though old and sick, could be so vulnerable. He had only removed the pillow...he had only touched the ladder.

He poked her hand feeling with curiosity the papery mottled flesh move over the brittle bones. Then, because he had seen it done in the movies, he closed her eyes with his thumbs. She looked younger in death, smoothed out, as if she was sleeping. Like Fraser, only he hadn't been able to get close enough to see him properly because of the wasps.

Remembering Fraser, he felt again the sense of awe, of respect for himself, that he had had the nerve, the ability, the courage to end a life. He badly wanted to pee.

After a while he lifted her head and replaced the pillow neatly. He arranged her hands, crossing them piously on her pink bed-jacket. Then he covered her head with the fold of the sheet. He took two pounds out of the three in her purse and left the small change.

Then he went to the lavatory.

That spring Lady Muck sent for him. She was sitting in the drawing-room in the sun with one of the dogs on her lap, the other wrapped around her feet. Her face was white like crushed tissue paper. Her arthritic hand, enmeshed in the dog's scruff, trembled a little.

'It's time we had a talk about your future,' she said, and added, nodding at the sofa, 'sit down.'

He perched deferentially on the edge and leaning forwards folded his hands between his thighs. She's going to put me away, he thought with a flash of fear.

'What would you like to do with your life?' she asked. 'Have you given it any thought?'

Petals from a spray of orange blossom dripped on to an occasional table at his side. He had a strong urge to tidy them up.

'I shan't be here forever, you know,' she added humorously, as if she didn't quite believe it.

He was shocked, not by her remark but by his own lack of forethought. He was nowhere near ready for her to pop off.

Watching his expression, she was pleased. 'However, I don't intend to go quite yet. Nobody dies of arthritis or so I'm told.'

The dog on her lap fidgeted. Malcy caught her expression of pain, and, anticipating her request, rose to remove the animal.

'You are a born servant, Malcolm,' she said meaning it as a compliment.

His hand tightened on the dog's scruff making it yelp. He had never thought of himself as a servant. The son of the Fuhrer was one of the master race.

'With proper training,' she continued, 'you could go far, rise to be butler in an important establishment.' When he did not answer immediately, she added querulously, 'Nobody wants to be a servant since the war. I can't think why. It's an honourable profession. Perhaps you have something else in mind?'

He looked her in the eye. 'I'm suited here. Don't send me away,' he added cracking his voice appealingly.

That pleased her. 'My dear child, I have no intention of sending you away. You're much too useful to me. There's a home for you here as long as you like. I'm relieved to find you content. It's an unusual quality these days. On the other hand we have to be sensible. You have your whole life before you and it's important to make plans.'

'What you said, then,' he muttered, purposefully inarticulate. He could not bring himself to say 'servant'.

She beamed on him. 'I do think you are being entirely sensible. We'll talk again when you've left school.'

Although he still slept in the bleak north-facing room next to Bella on the servants' landing, Malcy had long ago commandeered the billiard room in the old part of the Hall. There, under the table, he would read and dream and scheme. No one interrupted him.

On the day he left school he suggested with cautious deference to Lady Muck that he take over responsibility for the old Hall. Bella had enough to do with the cooking and all. He wanted to take a greater share of the burden. Waiting at table, running errands, attending to fires, left him with time on his hands.

Her Ladyship approved, commended him, gave him the appropriate keys, and, at his request, told Bella that the old part of the house would henceforth be his concern.

Bella was not as grateful as she might have been. 'It's no' like you to be looking for work,' she said suspiciously.

He asked for paint. Six weeks later he took her on a tour of the rooms, now glossy and aired and fresh and her suspicions were quietened. She was, she confessed, thankful to be shut of the work. Just to be on the safe side he kept most of the doors locked. He told Lady Muck you couldn't be too careful these days with thieves and vandals on the loose. She commended him for his thoughtfulness.

Inside one of the old attic rooms he had discovered chests and boxes stuffed with silver and porcelain, trinkets and *objets d'art*.

There were Spode vases and Chelsea figurines, jade dragons and ebony elephants. Treasures from every age and country.

Inside the bible with the loot, there was a list of antique dealers, silver-smiths and second-hand traders compiled from telephone directories and from his Saturday afternoon wanderings in the city. Against some of them there was a date, an item and a sum.

He was never greedy or over-ambitious. One, possibly two pieces at a time, and he seldom visited the same dealer twice. He was content to accept low prices for the sake of anonymity. Sometimes the dealer would eye him curiously, until he put on his posh voice, widened his blue eyes and spoke of a war-widowed mother.

Malcy had four voices. Posh reserved for Lady Muck, the drawing-room and the antique trade. Corny American for peers and school acquaintances, coarse for Bella and the kitchen, German for himself. '*Javohl, mein herr. Achtung! Seig heil. Kaput.*' The clipped precise expressionless voice commented continually in his head.

The notes in the bible amounted to £472.

Crawface had a boyfriend. Hard to believe and for a while Malcy refused to credit the fact until it jumped up and hit him in the eye.

The old range had been exchanged at Miss Snooty's suggestion for a gleaming white Esse that ate up the anthracite. The driver of the coal lorry was called Ginger, an ex-corporal in the HLI with enormous freckled biceps streaked with dirt and a greasy black cap which hid his tight red curls. Clean, he looked younger than his twenty-eight years with round naïve china blue eyes. He had lost one wife to a military policeman from Ealing during the war. He was looking for another.

Wee Bella with her smile and buttery scones appealed to his homing instincts and the coal lorry was to be found parked at the back of the Hall most evenings. The kitchen was full of the stink of Woodbines as he sat back in the basket chair and boasted about what he did to Jerry in the war.

Malcy hated him. He did everything - short of putting weed-killer into his tea - to be shut of him. But cunningly. *Javohl.*

Ginger had a knife, taken from a dead German, or so he claimed. Malcy wanted it.

'Say, Big Shot,' he drawled in his pseudo Yankee, ' how come you got away with it? It's one hell-of-a cutter. I'd just admire to have one like it.'

Ginger laughed. With one eye on Bella, he leaned forward and handed it over. 'It's yours, mate. Keep it.'

'Gee, man. You're one swell guy.'

He weighed it in his hand grinning and wanting to plunge it into the coalman's gut.

Later when Bella was seeing Lady Muck to bed, he poured Ginger another beer and changed his voice to intimate and coarse. 'You're a gentleman, so you are. Who else'd be nice to poor wee Bella? Ye ken she had nae faither?' and so the water dripped slowly, drop by drop, on to the flesh of Ginger's heart.

'Who else but a pal would look at yon wee dwarfie twice?'

And to Bella when the coal lorry had gone 'He's no' playing straight with you. He's got a lassie in the village. He's only here for what he can get.'

Bella said giggling, 'Och, Ginger's all right. There's no hairm in him. He's nice, so he is.'

Once he caught her sitting on his knee, their heads together, necking. Inside, he jumped and exploded like a firecracker. He jerked the simmering kettle off the hot plate and scalded his hand so that she was forced to rise.

Lady Muck noticed. 'I do hope we are not going to lose Bella,' she asked him anxiously. 'Is there anything behind this affair with the coalman?'

'No,' he replied too sharply, and added, 'he's got a girl-friend in the village.'

She looked at him with raised brows but said no more. He knew he had not convinced her anymore than he could fool himself. He would not let it happen. Nothing was impossible. He only had to want it enough.

There was always the Magician.

When Malcy had first gone to the Hall, he began unconsciously to search for somewhere safe, a nest, a private place to unpack the furniture of his teeming mind. He found it under the billiard table in the library. Fungus had been growing on the carpet and the room had smelt dark and mouldy, but hidden under the heavy-sided table he felt secure. Over the years he had cleaned the carpet and aired the place meticulously and made it home.

The room was full of mysteries, old Strand magazines with picture of murderers and shrieking women and dripping blood. There were also the Tarot cards.

Intrigued by the pictures of the Major Arcana, he laid them out in a wheel as the rules advised. In each of them he saw signs and images that related to himself. The Skeleton with the scythe reminded him of the fairmer, dead. Lady Muck was the Queen all dolled up in pearls, sitting on a throne. Crawface was the wee lassie watering the ground from a jug. Miss Snooty was the tall woman with long hair and a needle-sharp sword in her hand. When he gazed down at them all, it seemed to him that they were dancing around him, imprisoning him, suffocating the life out of him so that he could not breathe.

The moment of terror passed and he saw that he still held one card in his hand. The Magician. Fair-haired with a sweet smile, the figure was a boy much like himself. He placed it at the centre of the wheel. Immediately the perspective changed. The Magician was in charge, moving, manipulating, controlling the others. He was filled with a sense of power.

That was the night the Ludo counters had been swept off the board across the room. The Magician had done it. The Magician inside himself.

The cards were still in the drawer in the billiard room. He tried to shuffle them but they were damp and soft and stuck to each other. When he had cut them, he spread them out in a circle with the Magician in the centre. He had no idea how to interpret them but he knew they contained truths.

Yet as he gazed from the Magician outwards to the other cards he could make no sense of the patterns and the symbols. After a while he picked up the Magician and found that another card was stuck to the back of it so closely that he had to prise them apart with his nail. He held the Devil in his hand.

The Devil and the Magician. He looked from one to the other and saw that there were likenesses between them. Each held up one hand while the other pointed below. Both carried a torch, but while the Magician held his light aloft, the Devil thrust his down in flames towards a man and woman chained at his feet. Malcy was filled with awe and understanding. The Magician was the Devil in reverse. Halves of a whole; together they represented power.

He lifted the Magician in his right hand and recognised, once again, the outward appearance of himself, young and blonde and superior. Then he gazed for a long time at the dark-winged, fierce-eyed Devil in his left hand. Suddenly he clicked his tongue, shook his head and whistled with amazement through his teeth. *Vunderbar. Javohl.* He understood. This too was himself, his inner self, the way he wanted secretly to be with lesser mortals in his power.

Suddenly he shivered. The room was bloody cold.

Three days later, he carried Lady Muck's morning coffee with the Times neatly folded on the silver tray into the drawing-room. She did not move when he approached.

When he saw her he froze with fright. Her head was thrown back against the back of the chair, her mouth was grossly distorted and she was breathing raggedly. He thought she was dying.

He put the tray down and inwardly railed against God, the devil and the Tarot cards. This was the last thing he wanted. Then he saw her eyes, scared, beseeching, alive.

'You're going to be fine,' he told her fiercely. 'I'll not let you die. I swear it.'

He knew that she had heard him, that she understood.

She had suffered a stroke, the doctor said. He would send in a nurse. With care she might recover some of her powers. Meanwhile her granddaughter should be informed.

Miss Snooty arrived home by the next train.

'What am I to do?' she confided in Bella in the kitchen, spreading her elegant hands. 'I can't be in two places at once. I'm needed at Nightingales too. Cousin Eva has cancer and I may as well tell you, though we haven't announced it yet, that I'm going to marry her son, my cousin Miles. Nightingales is open to the public at weekends. I have to be there. I suppose Grandmother could move south, but she would simply hate that…'

Malcy answered from the shadows. 'Lady Mowbray's been good to us. We'll not let her down, will we Bella?' and again insistently, 'will we, Bella?'

Bella paused before replying, then she shook her head and fixed her black eyes steadfastly on Miss Snooty. 'We'll no' leave as long as your gran needs us.'

He let out all the air in his lungs in one long quiet exhalation of relief.

Miss Snooty gazed at Bella with tearful eyes. 'You can't imagine how thankful I am to hear you say that. Being so far away, I need someone here I can trust and one hears such dreadful things these days…My grandmother is so fond of you both. I'll see if Mrs Bain at the Lodge would come in a few more hours in the week to help with the rough work. Anything you need you only have to ask.'

It was Malcy who replied. 'We can manage,' he said firmly. 'We've managed so far, haven't we?'

She looked properly at him then and he could see her thinking, 'Malcy's improved.'

He lathered his voice with sincerity. 'Lady Mowbray's all we've got. The Hall is our home. Where else would we go? What else would we do?' It was the simple truth.

She nodded. 'All the same, I can't thank you both enough.'

Not a word about Ginger. It was doubtful if Miss Snooty had even heard of him. It was true, however, that he had a second string to his bow in the village. He married her within six months.

After the nurse left, Malcy took over the care of Lady Muck. Under his domination she recovered sufficiently to shuffle short distances on sticks, to feed and wash herself with difficulty, but not to speak. The syllables got twisted around in her head. Nor could she write. Painstakingly he taught her to sign the housekeeping cheques. She understood every word he said.

He took to wearing black. He wore black drainpipes, a black polo-necked sweater, black pointed shoes, and, in winter, a black jacket. With his gold hair and clear skin he looked stunning. Lady Muck's callers ogled him and talked glowingly about his devotion. He always appeared in time to serve tea and to see guests into their coats.

He could do what he liked with her.

He took her for drives in the Morris steering the old car sedately down country lanes. He pushed her in a wheel chair out in the sun. He changed his day off from Saturday to Friday. On Friday he handed her over to Bella. Fridays were sacrosanct. On Fridays he continued to visit the dealers. Sometimes he went into cafes for coffee and the juke boxes. Half-envious, half-contemptuous, he watched other teenagers rock and roll, but felt no part of them. Often he went to the flicks and ate liquorice all-sorts in the dark.

The bible could no longer contain his loot so he opened a Post Office Savings account in the city under the name of Malcolm Mowbray. The sum stood at £884.

Lady Muck did not like him to leave her, not even on Fridays. There were always a few tears. It would be easy to rob her ragged. Her rings were fat with diamonds. Her brooches burgeoned with emeralds and sapphires. She would have given him anything he wanted. But Malcy was wise. *Javohl*. He knew about killing the golden goose, and there was Crawface always on the watch.

'You do anything to harm that poor old lady and you're for it,' she once warned him when he had boasted that the old cow was like putty in his hands.

'As if I would!' he protested, all injured innocence. 'I'm partial to the old bag.'

And in a way he was. She was his property, his creation, his puppet, his meal ticket and his future. All he had to do was keep her contented and to keep her alive.

Television was the answer.

Before her stroke, she had insisted that telly was vulgar and would not have it in the house. However, Malcy, who found her constant demands tedious, asked Miss Snotty to have it installed in the drawing-room. He chose the set himself, a cabinet model with a twenty-inch screen. Contrary to expectations, Lady Muck was enthralled. She could understand the programmes without having to comment or communicate herself. The set remained permanently switched on. Miss Snooty gave him and Bella a smaller edition for the kitchen.

Two events occurred in the summer of '53. He put his fist through a panel in the billiard room and found it soft. Further investigation revealed that the old Hall was rotten to the core. Flamboyant black and white mushrooms flourished behind the wainscots and the shutters. It was only a matter of time before the builders would have to be called in to gut the place. Then his call-up papers arrived. Within three months he would be square-bashing on National Service.

Arrows of anxiety needled his mind. He shut himself up in the billiard room and took out the Tarot pack. Choosing seven cards at random he fanned them out on the floor, and there, between the Devil and the Magician, was the Burning Tower. As he lifted it he heard the old house sigh.

On the evening of September 25th the electricity failed. Nothing unusual in that. The Hall had needed rewiring for

97

years. The electrician in Ladymuir had urged that this be done. Miss Snooty who was now Mrs Henry Percy-hyphen-Drake had put it off knowing how the upset would affect her grandmother.

Malcy rang through to the electrician and gave him dog's abuse when he said he could not come out till morning. He reminded him that Lady Muck was an invalid, a good customer and gentry. The electrician, infuriated by the lecture, was not likely to forget that call. On his work sheet he stabbed out 8 30 am and substituted 2 pm with a question mark.

Malcy replaced the receiver and asked Bella to look out the paraffin lamps. He set one down at Lady Muck's elbow, tilting it slightly under the leg of her television spectacles. The purple fuel swilled in the glass container.

'Be careful,' he warned her as he picked up her supper tray. 'You don't want to knock that lamp over.'

Concentrating on choosing a post-prandial chocolate, she did not turn her head.

Back in the kitchen, he and Crawface sat down to their evening meal. Liver and bacon, garden potatoes and runner beans.

'I'll miss the old bag...when I get called up,' he said unexpectedly.

'Not half as much as she'll miss you,' Bella replied gathering up their plates.

He switched on the kitchen telly. He could not settle to watching the Brains Trust. 'What a load of crap.' He found a pack of playing cards in the dresser drawer. 'Give us a game of knock-out whist.'

The telly blared as he picked up his hand.

At twenty minutes to ten, Bella laid down her cards. It was time to take the old lady up to bed. She opened the kitchen door. Smoke billowed in.

'Jesus wept!' exclaimed Malcy.

He almost suffocated trying to get through. By the time the Fire Brigade arrived it was too late. The old house with all its contents burned like toast. The fire had started in Lady

Mowbray's drawing room, the experts said. Probably she had upset the lamp. If only the electrician had called that evening as he had been asked to do. The electrician said he was sick and tired of warning her Ladyship. According to him, the Hall had been a fire hazard for months. Miss Snooty wept and blamed herself.

Arson was not suspected.

Heather

The church in Ladymuir was full of men with known faces in unfamiliar frames. Two distinguished-looking gentlemen in black ties turned out to be grocers, the Torry brothers. Bain, the gardener, looked like a tanned diplomat. Of the women present, most were drab and elderly except for a bosomy blonde who later turned out to have been Cook now married to an Italian café owner.

The congregation sang *O God of Bethel* like a male voice choir and Mr Urquhart, the minister, raised a mountain of prayer, referring to the deceased as 'that most sweet and patient lady'.

Heather's mouth twisted in an exact imitation of Lady Mowbray's characteristic moue of amusement. She felt a strong affinity to her grandmother as if part of the old woman had settled within herself. This then, she thought, is resurrection; my parents, my grandmother, my ancestors in me. When I die I shall live on in my child. Her gloved hands moved protectively to encircle the mound of her womb. She was five months pregnant.

At the graveside eight men stepped forward to take a cord from the coffin before it was lowered into the ground, Miles first, Malcolm last. Watching him, she thought, how frightening not to know one's heritage, to have no platform from which to dive into the pool of life. Where, for instance, did Malcolm get his looks? Certainly not from the Goulds.

From whom did he inherit his fastidious habits? Not from farmers. She had read somewhere that most Scots were genealogically descended from the four sons of Malcolm Canmore, the uncouth vandal king and Margaret, his beautiful civilised English queen. Outwardly Malcy was serene, controlled, obedient, but she never quite knew what lay beneath. How strange to be Malcy, not to know the progenitor of his urges and impulses. How odd to be Bella who did not even know the name of her father.

As Heather watched the coffin as it was lowered, shockingly light (not even she knew how scant were the remains), her eyes turned with relief to Miles. She knew his antecedents as well as she knew her own. Their portraits hung in gilded frames down the length of the gallery at Nightingales, gentlemen and generals until the First World War, bankers thereafter. Their names featured in history books. Their money maintained the estate.

This was, she supposed, the main reason why she had married Cousin Eva's son, a safe bonding of ancestry, a linking of past to present with an eye on the future. Although he was fourteen years her senior and had already buried a wife, she knew from the first time they met that they would marry. Looking at him now as he stood erect by the open grave, his thinning hair dishevelled slightly by the wind, she did not regret her marriage. She was aware of his faults, his moods of withdrawal, outbursts of impatience, his boredom with domestic matters, his lack of interest in sex, without feeling compelled to change him. Nor did he presume to criticise or comment on her mistakes, though she knew there were times when she irritated him intensely

One school friend had remarked shrewdly at the time of their engagement that she had probably seen in Miles a reflection of the father she had never known, and another had exclaimed, 'You can't be serious! He's old enough to be your father.'

There might have been some truth in the remarks but she could not see that it mattered. Miles and Nightingales were like school, a place hedged in with habit and routine, a haven where she felt safe. She could not regret the loss of the Hall with its warren of shadowed rooms. She refused to examine the site, could not even visit the pile of blackened stones.

'Let me remember it the way it was,' she told her husband. That too was a lie. Let me forget.

Forcing her attention back to the funeral, she was inevitably aware of the ancestors beneath her feet, seeing them as godparents at a christening feast, parading their gifts before her unborn child. A mathematical bent from one, a sense of humour from another, a good eye from a sporting grandfather, and, inevitably, her long angular bones. A touch of originality maybe from an eccentric ancestor, but nothing unpleasant, nothing that could not be accounted for. Her child was safe.

The family plot was headed by a wide curved stone built into the outer wall of the cemetery enclosed within wrought-iron railings. She used to come here with her grandmother clutching a jar of wild flowers to put on her parents' grave. (Grandmother had a horror of flowers without water.) God was never mentioned. No need. His presence was assumed. *In God's Keeping*, the stone proclaimed and Heather never doubted it.

She saw God as a Blake illustration, an old man with hair as white and plentiful as clouds and eyes that pierced the skin of her soul. 'Please God, don't let it hurt,' she used to pray before a visit to the dentist. 'Please God, protect me in the dark.' She knew he wouldn't, not because he couldn't, but because, to indulge her would not be good for her. God was no sudden deliverer, no Santa Claus with a sack of goodies, no gentle Jesus meek and mild. He was the male equivalent of Mrs Be-done-by-as-you-did. Religion was not a crutch but an aspiration and a goad.

Duty, high standards, leadership were qualities she had been taught to respect and look for not in others but in herself. God did not exist to help her out of holes. He was there for the unfortunates, the disadvantaged and the weak. She had been educated to know right from wrong and when she fell short of these standards she did not expect to be excused. She saw herself born into the high tower of privilege, one to which much had been given and therefore from whom much was to be expected. She had already begun to play the role of do-gooder at Nightingales. Being useful made her feel safe. 'Look at me, Nanny. I'm a good girl. I did my jobbies and I tidied my toys.'

But her self-esteem was as precarious as a paper parasol. Looking up from her grandmother's grave, she saw Bella and was drenched in guilt. She looked dreadful. The borrowed black swagger coat with padded shoulders and cobbled up hem took away the short neck she already had. The black crocheted beret exaggerated her broad nose. Stout lacing shoes, the sort sold to schoolboys, broadened her feet. Malcolm's cruel nickname had never seemed so apt. She looked exactly like a crow with its plumage plumped.

Yet Bella was not fat. Years of manual labour and a healthy appetite had broadened her shoulders, toughened and solidified her short frame. As far as Heather knew, she had never had more than a day's illness in her life. Nor, apart from her stout bowed legs, was Bella ugly. Her brilliant skin, scarlet-cheeked, gypsy-brown after a hot summer would make a mockery of cosmetics. Her eyes expressed benignity while betraying nothing of emotion or intellect or anything that might lie deeper. Yet Bella was no fool. As Heather had good cause to know, Bella was filled with common sense, good humour and real kindness.

I owe her, Heather thought. She could never look at Bella without guilt. Her fragile self-confidence withered in Bella's presence. Those black uncritical eyes should have knifed her with accusation for Heather had known about Ginger. He had told her himself, blushing under the mask of coal dust in the High Street in Ladymuir, and Bella knew that she had been told. Heather was in no doubt that Bella had stayed with Lady Mowbray not so much for the old lady's sake, but so that she, Heather, might escape, and she, Heather, had allowed it to happen, taken away Bella's chance of happiness to cement her own.

102

Because of that and the guilt she felt towards her grandmother for leaving her with servants, she had travelled home too infrequently. She had avoided too much contact with the old woman for fear of the accusation she might read in her eyes. Easier far to breeze in for a night or two at the most, talk loudly and fast to her grandmother, examine Bella's scrupulous housekeeping accounts, have a word or two with the doctor and rush back home. Heather was not yet mature enough to entirely disregard the critical opinion of others, but what she thought of herself deep down mattered still more. Bella was a constant unremitting accusation.

As was Malcolm, but for different reasons. Her feelings for him were ambivalent, on the edge of repugnance and distrust. Yet she had never found him dishonest or openly insolent. She could not fault him, his manners or his stunning good looks, but she did not like him. Nor could she ignore him. The child who had manipulated her grandmother, the boy who had spied on her, the adolescent who had lain on her darkened bed, had turned into a man who both repelled and attracted her, and, who sometimes, unbidden, crept into her sexual fantasies. To know that he was attracted to her filled her with a sort of disgusted lust; fear too, for he wore the black aura of those haunted rooms. Fear and sexual excitement ran on the same emotional channels through her flesh. She could recognise now that her fears of the old Hall were not altogether disagreeable, the sweats and the tremblings not entirely unpleasant. Malcy was, in some ways, symbolic of the old Hall.

Thus her guilt towards him was complicated for while she was prepared to use him in her fantasies yet she abused him in her thoughts. Though she would be glad never to have to see him again in the flesh, yet she knew she would not readily part with him in her dreams.

In the train north, Miles had asked, 'What do you want to do about those two? Bring them to Nightingales if you like. God knows we could do with a couple of reliable servants.'

'I suppose so,' she said aloud, but inwardly she cringed. She would prefer to turn them into memories rather than continuing responsibilities.

Looking at them now across the grave she knew that decency dictated that she offer them a home. They might, she hoped, refuse.

Bella

The graveyard was a right mess, Bella thought, as the funeral party dispersed. Straggling September grasses withered against the tombstones. Thistles seeded unrestrained. She stopped to look at the Goulds' stone and saw that it was almost obliterated by bishop's weed.

She thought of the dead below, row after row, layer upon layer, Ladymuir through the centuries, ready to rise again. Her mouth opened as the image grew in her mind. The village today was only the top of the tree. Beneath her feet were the roots of the community, 'the dead centre of town', as Mr Gould had called it, mothers and dads, grandpas and bairns, wasted under weeds.

It was all wrong, so it was. As she watched the seeding willow-herb blow across the cemetery like soft snow, an idea settled in her mind. Maybe there was a job going here. She would start with the fairmer's grave and work her way outwards, pull out every worm of weed, dig up every clod of couch grass, cut and trim the verges. Her fingers curved in anticipation of the feel of soil. Maybe if 'Parks and Cemeteries' approved, she could grow roses, row upon row between the layers, and daffodils, but maybe no. Daffies were a pest in summer with their straggling leaves. She could concentrate on daffs in areas and circles alternating with clumps of crocuses and snowdrops. Folk would come in and breathe the fragrance of the flowers fed on the substance of their ancestors. She no longer saw plants as a form of life equal to, yet different from, folk and beasts, but as an advanced species, closer to the angels,

104

the manifestation of souls, the final and eternal triumph over death. Flowers should flourish in this place.

Malcy's fingers poked her between her shoulders. 'Shut your mouth, Crawface, or you'll catch flies.'

He prodded her towards the gate where Miss Snooty and the Major were shaking hands with mourners.

'Yessir, nossir, three bags full sir.' He could speak without moving his lips. 'One day it'll be me pulling the strings.'

'Aye, that'll be right,' she said dryly.

'And you'll jump, like the rest.'

Bella was used to his talk. 'You'll miss her,' she said unexpectedly.

'Who? Lady Muck? Sure I'll miss her like a pain in the ass. What a daft thing to say.' He was irritated. Regret was a sign of weakness. She should know by this time he was hard.

'She was good to you,' Bella persisted.

'Nah,' he sneered. 'I was good to her.' He laughed. '*Javohl.* Better than you'll ever know.'

Lady Mowbray's solicitor detached himself from the group by the cemetery gates. They both knew him for he had been a regular visitor to the Hall.

'Miss Gould, Mr Malcolm Gould? His voice was educated Edinburgh. 'I would be grateful if you would accompany the family to the Royal Hotel. You are both beneficiaries under the late Lady Mowbray's will.'

So what's new, Malcy thought behind a deferential nod. Bella's mouth dropped open again. When the solicitor turned away he dug her again in the ribs.

'Come along, you two,' Heather called out in her high clear voice. 'You'd better drive with us.'

They sat facing the Percy-Drakes in the back of the hired Daimler.

Miss Heather talked all the time about the service, the mourners, the occasion, throwing out comments and questions without waiting for answers. Her over-prominent brown eyes were circled with exhaustion. He head poked anxiously from

105

the long thin stalk of her neck. Her fingers were weighted with rings. The firemen had found Lady Mowbray's jewel case among the remains but looters had come out from as far as Glasgow and taken most of what the fire had spared. Thousands of pounds worth of stuff stolen, so it was said. As the red flowers of flame had sprung into the kitchen, Bella had run outside for help, but Malcy had been called a hero, battling through suffocating smoke to get to the old lady. All he managed to save was his bible. The Percy-Drakes had been impressed by that.

The Major finally managed to get in a word. 'Have you two given any thought to your future? Bella,' he asked, 'what are you going to do when Malcolm does his National Service?'

She had been about to tell him her plan to tidy up the cemetery but Miss Heather was too quick

'I think we ought to see what grandmother has done for her first, darling.'

He winked at her, closing one eye solemnly in a dead-pan face making her giggle.

She liked the Major. Now that he was sitting facing her she could see him properly without craning her neck. She had been right enough. He was the spitting image of the Duke of Edinburgh with his short sandy hair, his joky blue eyes that could freeze over like ice, his long strong nose. Taller maybe, and older. She marvelled at the length of his feet.

Privately she had always thought that Miss Heather resembled the Queen. Not in looks. The Queen was a dainty wee lady with blue eyes, but their voices were alike, high and clear and confident. Since Nanny's death she had kept up the old woman's scrap-book of the Royal Family but it had gone up in smoke like everything else. Of the two couples, royal and commoner, she admired the Percy-Drakes most. They had the height and they were hers. Bella knew she had given them their chance but she saw no merit in the act. It pleased her more to gratify Miss Heather than to lie in Ginger's bed with a ring on her finger.

The Percy-Drakes had engaged a private room at the hotel. Bella and Malcy were called in immediately. They both sat on the edge of dining room chairs, Malcy, calculatingly, leaning slightly forward, ready to spring into service; Bella so that her feet could touch the ground. She loosened the swagger coat, loaned and shortened by Mrs Bain at the Lodge where she and Malcy had been staying since the fire. Her knees had horny pads after years of scrubbing floors and kneeling to weed. When she was nervous she picked at them. Malcy eyed her eloquently, but she did not notice.

'Well Bella, Malcolm, if I may be informal,' said the solicitor eyeing them over half-moon spectacles from the other side of the table. 'You are to be congratulated, I believe. Before she became ill, Lady Mowbray added a codicil to her will to this effect. I quote: - *If Bella Gould is still in my employment at the time of my decease, I bequeath to her life rent of the property at 176 Glasgow Road, otherwise known as the Lodge, in the hopes that she will become, as was always her wish, head gardener at the Hall as soon as is practicable after my decease. Should the said Bella Gould be unable for any reason to undertake the post of gardener, life rent of the Lodge or the equivalent in kind shall continue to be hers until her decease when the property shall revert to my heirs. To Malcolm Gould, I bequeath the sum of five hundred pounds payable to him at my decease, or when he reaches eighteen years of age, in the hope that he will use it to further his education.* And now,' continued the solicitor, 'may I congratulate you both?' He stood up, leaned across the table and shook each of them by the hand.

Malcy's first reaction was anger. The old cow owed me at least five times that amount and could have well afforded it, but all he said was, 'Thank you, sir,' managing to blend into his voice gratitude, surprise and deference.

Mentally he was doing sums. With what he had disposed of before the fire, he would now have close on two thousand pounds stashed away in the Post Office. The bequest offered another advantage in that he could now splash out from time to

107

time with no questions asked. 'Thank you, Miss Heather,' he added, touching up his voice with fervour.

She ignored him, being more interested in Bella's reaction. She could not wait for it. 'There Bella, isn't that marvellous? A home of your own.' She was ashamed of her relief.

'Leave a little room for furniture among the aspidistras and potted plants,' the Major joked.

Bella's response was muted. 'What about the Bains?'

'I anticipate no problems there. They will of course be given the customary three months notice,' the solicitor replied.

Bella thought about the Bains. Davy had been a corporation gardener in Glasgow and invalided out of the army with a wound in his gut that gave him continual discomfort. Mrs B. was a martyr to bronchitis, a lonely wife who missed the street gossip and fug of the city. On the mornings she helped out at the Hall she tended to trail after Bella with a tin of Mansion polish in her hand and a Woodbine in her mouth.

Lady Mowbray had not found them satisfactory. She had engaged them on the Major's recommendation - he had been Bain's commanding officer - and because they were the only applicants willing to accept a house with an outside convenience. Together they had turned the Lodge into a little palace and installed a lavatory which Lady Mowbray had been obliged to pay for. Mrs B had a talent for crochet work and every cushion cover, tablecloth and bedspread was a tribute to her industry.

'I'd not like to see them put out,' Bella said anxiously.

Heather smoothed her voice with reason.

'They'll have to go, Bella. You'd better know now for it will be common knowledge soon; we're selling the land. The Town Council have already approached us for the site and we have no thoughts of rebuilding.'

'Sadly, can't afford it,' said the Major lifting his eyebrows and spreading his hands.

'So you see the Bains will have to find another job.'

On the wrong side of fifty with his guts mangled. That would be likely, Bella thought but she said nothing.

'Miss Gould,' the solicitor said with a hint of impatience. 'If you don't want to occupy the Lodge yourself, you are at liberty to let it to whomsoever you please and collect a rent.'

From a man who was jobless in a tied house on a meagre pension? That would be the day.

Heather understood Bella's stubborn silence. With a feeling of inevitability she knew what she would have to do, but not before she had made a final appeal.

'Bella, Grandmother wanted you to have the Lodge. The Council can't touch it, and there's Malcy to consider. You want to make a home for him, don't you?'

'Malcy's going for the RAF,' she answered stubbornly.

'Well then, what will you do? Where will you go?'

Bella recognised that note of hysteria in Miss Heather's voice. The last time she heard it had been when her ladyship took the stroke. ('What will I do with her? Who will look after her?') Before she could tell Miss Heather that the Bains had already offered her accommodation in the Lodge, and that she had a job in mind with Parks and Cemeteries, the Major had risen, unfolding his great height, not joking now.

'Bella's quite right,' he said firmly. 'Can't put a chappie like Bain out in the street. Never do, what! Bella must come to us. You'd like that, Bella? Miss Heather - we both - need you at Nightingales.'

Heather did not look up. 'I still don't think it's right. Grandmother wanted Bella to have the Lodge.'

'And so she shall, darling, all in due course,' he told her. She could sense his growing impatience.

'We could certainly use you, Bella,' she said, reluctantly. She forced herself to look up and saw doubt in Bella's expression and blamed it on her own ungraciousness. She was drenched in shame. 'It would be super if you'd come, Bella,' she continued reverting to childish language to convey an enthusiasm she did not feel.

'Don't mind me,' said Malcolm as falsely as he meant to sound.

The Major turned to him. 'You'll be welcome for your leaves of course, even if you are joining the wrong outfit,' he joked. 'Always find you the odd job to fill your spare time.'

'Thank you, sir,' he replied, larding his voice with gratitude, for shit.

Bella had seen the mound of Miss Heather's womb. She did not doubt that she was needed. She put the seed-blown cemetery out of her mind.

She nodded. 'I'll come, then.'

Malcolm

Malcy saw to it that the Bains knew. His timing was calculated and accurate. Immediately after the session with the solicitor, Bella had gone to gather brambles in the lane. She had promised to make a boiling of bramble jelly for Mrs B and the fruit in the hedgerows was ripe.

'Heard about your new landlord, then?' he told Mr Bain. 'You'll never believe it. Pinched myself black and blue all over when I heard,' he began in mock-American.

'Go on,' said Mr Bain, lowering the *Evening Times*.

'You gotta guess.'

'Mrs P-D, I should hope,' said Mrs Bain who was setting the table for tea.

'Miss Snooty? Not her. Nor Major Swankpants neither. Go on, guess.' He grinned, knowing he had got them worried.

'Not the Council,' said Mrs B. There had been rumours of a new council estate on the Hall site. 'What would they want with the Lodge?'

'Access,' said Malcy triumphantly. He had told Bella the same. 'It'll be demolished to make way for a road and you won't get a cent. The property still belongs to the estate.'

Oddly he was not angry about Bella getting the Lodge. Anything that Crawface got was his for the taking. Nor did he

110

specially want the Bains evicted, though it amused him to taunt them. He looked forward to his new address. A/C Malcolm Gould, the Lodge, Ladymuir, was poor stuff compared with Flight Lieutenant Malcolm Mowbray of Nightingales, by Farnham, Hants. *Javohl.* A good address might be important one of these days.

'The Council would have to give us a new house if they put us out of the Lodge, wouldn't they?' Mrs B said doubtfully.

Malcy laughed. 'Who said anything about the Council putting you out?'

'You did,' said Mrs B flustered. 'You said - '

'Not guilty,' Malcy interrupted laughing. 'I said you gotta guess.'

'Pay no heed, mother. He's having us on,' said Bain, rustling the paper.

The back door opened and Bella came in with a pail full of fruit as black and shiny as her eyes.

'Here she is, folks,' cried Malcy. 'Say howdy to the lucky lady, the one and only Bella Crawface Gould, property queen of Ladymuir Lodge.'

Bain caught on. 'You're joking.'

Malcy grinned. 'Tell them, Bella. Who is the new landlord - beg pardon - landlady of the Lodge?'

'Me,' said Bella calmly, pulling a leaf out of the fruit and burning it.

The atmosphere was volatile.

'When do you want us out, then? Mrs Bain asked, aggrieved. Woodbine smoke curled up as the hot ash fell from her fingers.

'What's he been telling you?' Bella asked.

'Nothing,' said Davy Bain, 'and that's a fact.'

Bella explained.

Watching their expressions change, Malcy thought, and not for the first time, she only does it to get praise. She's a phoney, is our wee Crawface. The only way to make herself big and important is to put on the angel act. Bored now, he left the Lodge, and, without making a conscious decision, took the path

111

over the fields to the old Eyetie prison camp. Over the years he had often come here to mooch among the disused Nissen huts. Once he had found a button off a uniform. He had stared at it and without touching it edged it with his shoe into a crack in the concrete floor. Another time he had smashed all the remaining windows in one block. He had enjoyed that.

His memories of Mario and Niccolo were a wound. Sometimes it leaked and hurt.

Full of pain, he saw at once that the place had changed. Since his last visit, the huts had been re-roofed with tarpaulin, the windows replaced with rows of nesting boxes. The camp had been turned into a poultry farm. That made him angry.

He fanned his anger to burn up the pain. Rage coursed through his vessels, swirled in his head, assumed a huge distorted shape that dimly he recognised as the farmer, black-faced, whip-fisted, vile of tongue, his ogre and his god. Anger transformed him both into his father and also into his father's scourge.

What filthy bastard had polluted this place with fowl?

He strode across the grass to the first hut and flung wide the door. The deep litter was filthy with shit, swarming with feathers, harsh with caw and cackle. He lunged and caught one bird by its scrawny neck. 'Bloody bastard birds!' They'll pay. They'll fucking be made to pay.

He gabbed another and a third, until, his anger broken, he began to sob. Leaving the door wide open he strode back to the grove where he had hidden the night the bomb fell on the farm; five oaks in a cluster, their leaves a dark and heavy shield. He sat down on a stone, his body still shaking with dry tearless sobs. Gradually as he grew calm again, cool-headed, in control, he picked the feathers carefully off his clothes.

112

Part Three

Nightingales

Malcolm

At 7 am the DC flung open the door of Flight E Squadron, RAF, Brignorth.

'Up! Up! Up! You stinking lot. Wankers awake.'

It was, Malcy supposed, to be a joke but none of the sleep-gagged erks were laughing as they rolled out of bed and staggered to ablutions.

The DC was a bastard with a bully's sense of humour and pudgy hands that left finger marks on everything he touched. Ox-shouldered, barrel-chested, Taffy had the means of getting what he wanted not by force of character nor out of respect, but by the surer methods of cruelty and fear. The hassle began with bed inspection and ended as often as not with horseplay after dark.

That morning he picked on Hunter, the biggest recruit in the hut, a fresh-faced grammar school swank from Cheltenham who, rumour related, had refused a commission to see how the other half lived. It was a moot question, which of the two men the erks disliked most.

Taffy pushed his hand deep down into the 'biscuit' while the younger man stood to attention, confident, unsuspecting.

A cunning smile curved round Taffy's face. 'This 'ere bed''s wet. We don't want no stinking piss-quicks on this flight.'

The scarlet-cheeked aircraftsman started to protest at the lie.

'Shut your mouth. Stand to attention and call me 'sir'.'

Someone sniggered nervously.

A week passed before he got round to Malcy;. The erks had settled for the night. Most had dropped off, too tired for secret tears, battered physically by square-bashing, and, mentally by tests, parade hour, and fall-out ODs for an hour of ''ware women and VD'.

113

At 11 15 pm, Taffy flung open the door of the hut and switched on all the lights. He marched down the length of the hut pulling off blankets, yanking pillows from under sleeping heads, shouting insults and laughing maniacally at his own crude jokes. He was full of rum.

Malcy was not asleep. He lay on his back and held his blankets to his chin, his eyes wide open in contempt. The big man saw him and straightway crossed to his bed. Malcy held the blanket firmly.

Taffy's eye grew crafty. 'What you got to hide, pretty boy?' he sneered as he yanked off the blankets.

Malcy lay quiet in his regulation striped pyjamas. He never took his eye off the NCO. The big man laid his hand across his private parts.

'Like that, pretty boy? Like it, Nance?' His pudgy hand trembled and Malcy knew he'd got him. He smiled.

Next morning he filed a complaint direct to the sergeant.

'Sure you want to go through with this?' The sergeant asked with more than a hint of menace in his voice. The loss of his junior NCO would inevitably mean the loss of the passing-out cup. Malcy refused to change his mind and Taffy was duly removed.

Though he was not fool enough to admit it, Malcy enjoyed square-bashing, driving his body to the word of command, striving for physical perfection. He grew almost an inch in those first eight weeks and his shoulders squared and broadened.

He relished the neatness demanded of person and possessions and he excelled in all he was required to do from orderly duties to aptitude tests. He looked good in burnished boots, his battledress blue uniform with buttons that twinkled like stars.

He was regarded as a hero by his mates and though the nickname 'Nance' stuck, he was as close to happiness as he had ever been in his life. When his posting came through, the Flight Lieutenant commended him and told him that after a further six weeks training he would be going to the Reception Centre at

Padgate, back to where he had started but no longer as a ballsed-up recruit but as a fully-fledged Aircraftsman Class 1, working in the case paper room.

It was a cinch. Benches were laid out like a village hall where the erks queued, desks for himself and his mates as close to the high-chimneyed, zebo-blacked stove as they could get.

Everything went down on those forms from body scars to borstal sentences.

It was Bister who gave him the idea.

Malcy had one grudge against the RAF. His pay-book. On eighteen shillings a week, his savings would hardly grow. His target, modest enough, he thought, to be attainable, was £10,000 before he reached the age of twenty-one. His bible with three savings books locked within was safe at Nightingales. At Padgate, he had opened a new Post Office account into which he put a paltry ten shillings a week. He badly needed that idea.

Bister was a minister's son. He spoke posh and should have been an officer only he stammered and was as empty as a NAAFI wad between the ears. He was also self-conscious, home-sick and scared.

Malcy led him through the questions, patiently waiting for each stuttered answer. Incredibly Rupert Edward Collingwood Bister had had a conviction which he was reluctant to divulge. Out it came at last.

'U-u-u-urinating against a l-l-l-lamp-post.'

Malcy was genuinely shocked. 5469252 Bister saw his expression and blushed to the roots of his close-cropped hair.

'L-l-l-look. D-d-d-do you have to write it d-d-d-own?'

That was what gave Malcy the idea. 'You want to put me in the glass-house, then?'

'Of c-c-c-course not. I j-j-j-just thought…'

Malcy grinned. 'How does 'knocking a policeman's helmet off during the course of his duty' look? Or how about 'popping a lamp-post with an airgun'?'

Bister smiled. 'The p-p-p-policeman.'

'Okay.' Malcy cut him short. 'Put five quid under the papers in front of you and push them over. Careful now. We don't want to share our little secret.'

Bister's smile shrank but he obliged.

There were others, not a lot, but enough to make the risk worthwhile.

Malcy made a friend, a handsome dark-eyed lad with an unpronounceable name known to his mates as Romeo. His Italian father owned an ice-cream business in Bradford and his Irish mother prayed thrice daily that God would call him to the priesthood. She admitted to dreams of him in a black soutane and a gold halo. He spoke broad Yorkshire which sounded a little odd with his Latin appearance.

Malcy took to him not just because he was half-Italian but because he was neat, scrupulously clean with long-fingered artistic hands scented with Imperial Leather soap

His one thought grooved into his mind was sex, his sole topic of conversation the art of getting laid. According to Romeo, birds keeled over at a glance from his sexy eyes and lay down panting for it. He'd had them behind doors, up alleyways, on couches, but mainly against the back wall of his father's café in the dark.

'Sex,' he told Malcy as they patrolled the camp on fire-watching duty one fine summer night. 'Sex is God's greatest gift to the human race.'

'Maybe,' said Malcy who had had his own ideas on the subject.

'What do you mean 'maybe'? There was this bird, Bianca, boobs like balloons. Took one look at yours truly doing t'paper round grabbed me by the short and curlies and before you could say fook...'

Malcy understood Romeo was playing a game, fleshing out his fantasies. Two could play at that.

'I got a woman too,' he said as they wandered into the cook-house searching for a left-over sausage or the heel of a loaf.

116

'She lives in a mucking great mansion house with regiments of servants. She's six foot tall with a shape like the figure eight. Leaves her bedroom door open …'

'You done it to her?' Romeo asked, cutting himself a wedge of cheese.

Malcy did not answer as the images reeled on. Watching, listening, wanting was no longer enough.

Romeo's eyes were hot. 'Fat chance of doing it for real with bromide in the NAAFI tea. The padre says all the birds round here have the pox.'

'I'm not paying for it,' Malcy said firmly.

Charlie's Café in Padgate was Mecca to the erks, who, when they could afford it, stuffed themselves with egg and chips and pots of un-doctored tea. Malcy considered the prices extortionate but preferable to paying bus fares into the city. On their third visit they clicked. Two local birds sat down at the next table, and, giggling, sought out through batting eye-lashes, the available talent. One was called Brenda. She had red hair and orange lipstick.

Romeo winked at Malcy, and, pulling down his tunic, stood up. 'Those seats taken?' he asked, flashing a sexy smile.

The redhead giggled; the other who was blond with a rash of little spots around her chin looked straight at Romeo and shook her head.

'Mind if we join you?' he asked.

'Suit yourself,' said the blonde dropping her eyes then raising them almost immediately. She spoke directly to Romeo showing plainly that he was hers.

Malcy looked at the redhead. She had indeterminate green eyes and reeked of Parma violets.

It was easy after that. Romeo and Malcy showed off, spurred on by the giggling girls. After tea and doughnuts they walked them home, the blonde ahead with Romeo, Brenda behind with Malcy. She did most of the talking. Outside the café she paused to repaint her lips. They glistened in the street lamp as she stretched and pouted them provocatively.

She slipped her bare arm through his. It was thin and brittle and freckled against his battledress blue sleeve. Her nails were painted scarlet. One of them was chipped and edged with grime. They reached a lane with high walls on either side. Romeo and the blonde moved into the shadows.

'Well,' said Brenda giggling,' this is it.'

'You live here?' Malcy asked. The smell of lilac hung over the wall. He knew she didn't.

'Our dad'd kill me if he knew I was with an RAF boy,' she said running her tongue over her orange lips.

In the dim light he saw Romeo and the blonde in a deep clinch. Her hair fell like honey over his embracing arm. As he put his own arms round Brenda's thin body he caught a sniff of her sweat. She smelled of blood and the shit house. Her hands with the dirty nail clasped the back of his neck. Her lipstick stuck to his mouth and moved greasily on his.

He tore away his head, closing his nose to her stink. Out of the corner of his eye he saw Romeo humped over the blond. His hands were kneading her buttocks.

Revulsion, the antithesis of desire, tore him apart. He would have liked to do it to the girl but her dirty flesh shrivelled him. He moved his hands to her upper arms and squeezing them too roughly he thrust her off him.

'Lay off,' she yelled. 'You're hurting me!'

Hurting her helped. He moved one hand to clutch at her breast.

Romeo pulled him off. 'Hey, man, what the 'eck are you oop to?'

The blonde was helping Brenda who was weeping with fright and pain. 'I'll get my dad on to you,' she sobbed, but he knew she wouldn't. 'You hurt me, you pig.'

'Come on, Nance, tell her you're sorry. You didn't mean it,' Romeo urged.

'Will I, fuck! She asked for it. Sat up and begged for it, the dirty cow,' he said scrubbing her lipstick off his mouth and throwing away the handkerchief. He wanted to retch.

Romeo was out of his depths.

'I'll take yous 'ome,' he said to placate the two girls.

'No fear! You leave us alone, rotten beasts,' said the blonde drawing Brenda away. 'I never want to see you again.'

'What did you do to her?' Romeo asked as they walked back to the camp.

'She tried to steal my wallet, didn't she,' Malcy lied.

Romeo believed him. 'Just goes to show. The padre was right. A bad lot, t'birds round here. Might have given us a dose.'

Malcy was silent. He had wanted to hurt the bird the way he had hurt those chickens. He had felt her fear and tasted power. It seemed to him that power was not just the ability to take what you wanted in life, but also the wisdom to know what you wanted and the nerve to take it. He had learned a salutary lesson tonight. He knew he would never make such a crass mistake again. He lay in his bunk awake for a long time, a little in awe of himself.

He spent his first leave at Nightingales. He was impressed. Miss Snooty had done well for herself marrying into this.

The mansion had been designed by Robert Hooke in the second half of the 17th century for St Henry Drake, financier and friend of Charles II who had made a fortune in trade with the Carolinas. Hooke, a distinguished scientist and no mean architect, had applied his considerable talents to the design of Nightingales. Although not large as country houses go, it was exquisitely formal with a central hall and a salon on the ground floor opening out into four symmetrical apartments, each with closets and offices, and a stair to the basement quarters. The first floor contained, in the west wing, the crimson and gold state bedroom of Charles II with its great canopied bed set within a railed recess. This was the chief cause of interest to visitors who spent summer week-ends strolling in the gardens and gazing at the Carolinian memorabilia for which Nightingales was renowned.

The family lived in the south wing sealed off from the rest of the house, with Bella and Mrs Orpen, the ancient cook, in the basement which included a comfortable, modernised kitchen. The rest of the staff and the estate workers either lived in the village and came in by day or in tied cottages in the grounds. Malcy was given a room in the attics, a Victorian addition from the days when there were enough servants to man a factory. It was not unlike his room in the Hall, small, spartanly furnished with rose-sprigged wallpaper, faded and pocked with age.

Unassumingly, he asked if he might decorate it and in two days had turned the shabby north-facing room into an eyrie of brilliant white that included the chest of drawers the rickety single wardrobe, the wooden chair and the iron bedstead. He ripped up the cracked linoleum and stained and varnished the wooden floor. Humbly he invited the Major's approval and received it. Only the bible with its shabby binding looked incongruous in the pristine room. The Major lifted it curiously.

'Where d'you get this?' he asked curiously.

'Lady Mowbray gave it to me on my tenth, birthday, sir.'

'Survived the fire, eh?'

'I saw to that, sir.'

Swankpants did not attempt to open the lock. 'Good chap,' he said approvingly, and put it down.

'Any other paint job you require to be done, I'd be happy to oblige, sir.

Malcy stood not quite at attention but squared up. The RAF had taught him how to speak to officers.

The Major laughed. 'You could be sorry you said that. Always painting to be done. This place is like the Forth Bridge.'

'I mean it, sir.'

And so he did. Adolf Hitler had been a painter too. *Javolh.*

While Malcy drew his brush carefully along the window-sill of his attic and looked out over the grounds where ancient trees cast rich if creaking shadows over mossy lawns, where water lilies starred the ornamental lake and roses graced the formal gardens, he knew what he wanted.

Three sentences from *Mein Kampf* made particular sense to him: - *The idea of struggle is as old as life itself, for life is only preserved because other things perish through struggle. In this struggle the stronger, the more able win, while the less able, the weak, lose...It is not by the principles of humanity that man lives or is able to preserve himself above the animal world, but solely by means of the most brutal struggle.*

In such a struggle there were no rules. Craftiness, the ability to lie and cheat and steal, to charm and flatter were signs of strength to be used fearlessly in pursuit of the goal. Power was upheld by the twin pillars of wealth and knowledge. Malcy was not interested in the power that changed politics, swayed mass audiences, led nations into war. Power for him was the ability to get what he wanted, subtly and secretly. He wanted Nightingales.

The breadth of his ambition was stunning even to himself, but he did not doubt his ultimate success.

Painting throughout the house with the same meticulous passion for neatness that was indigenous to his nature gave him an intimate knowledge of all that Nightingales contained. Unlimited access gave him undreamed-of opportunities to add to his store of wealth, but he took nothing. It would have been like robbing himself.

At night he borrowed from the well-stocked library, accounts of the old house through the centuries, mouldering ledgers, diaries, game books, letters. He learned with the dedication of a research student and he forgot nothing. Sometimes with studied casualness he dropped clues to his newly acquired knowledge. The Major approved. 'Knows more about the old place than I do, what!'

Thus his leaves passed busily. When he was demobbed, Swankpants offered him a permanent post. 'What do you say to 'general factotum', eh? Bit of handiwork about the place, bit of guiding on Bank Holidays, bit of butlering when the occasion arises? Trouble is you've made yourself bloody indispensable.'

Which was exactly what he had intended.

Miss Snooty gave birth to a bouncing boy. There had been complications during his birth with the cord, but it was not until William Miles Gareth Mowbray Percy-Drake was six months old that a paediatrician from Great Ormonde Street diagnosed mild brain damage caused by the prevention of oxygen to the lungs. Nothing that necessitated residential care but a probable inability to reach a normal standard of academic achievement.

The news came as no great surprise to his shattered parents or to the establishment at Nightingales. From the start he had been a difficult baby, slow, unresponsive, prone to long crying fits that drove his nannies, four in eighteen months, to despair.

Until his demob, Malcy saw little of him. He lived in his pram under a cat net in the rose garden or in the nursery wing on the second floor. No one told Malcy he was slow. It was too painful a subject for gossip. He saw him for the first time properly, strapped into a high chair in the nursery, lethargically refusing food which Miss Snooty - they were between nannies - was trying to push into his mouth. He knew instantly that the child was damaged. He was not so much surprised by this as by his own reaction.

Miss Snooty's head drooped on her graceful neck. Her beautiful brown hair lay drab on her shoulders. She was close to tears, unable to cope after a sleepless night in the usual hiatus between nursemaids.

Malcy repeated the telephone message he had come to give. The child, hearing his voice, smiled unexpectedly and held out a fat fist. He had two perfect front teeth, round unblemished cheeks and clean tear-washed eyes. Malcy was knifed to the heart, a feeling full of pain and yearning and regret.

'You look like you could do with a bit of a lay-down, Miss Heather,' he said reverting to deferential Scots. 'I'll mind the bairn.'

'Oh, would you, Malcy? Can you spare the time?'

He had been going to turn out the silver in the pantry, match it, clean it and study the hall-marks. Time enough for that.

Alone with the child, he tried to rationalise his reaction. This way, he thought, I get through to her. If I make him mine, I'm on the road to Nightingales. Even to his ears the sentiment sounded false. 'You and me together, pal, against the fucking world,' he whispered to the child. That was nearer the mark.

From then on, without reference to the Tarot, without having to pinch his chubby arms or feed him the chocolate buttons he loved, Malcy made Will his slave. He grinned and ate or stopped screaming in the middle of a temper tantrum at sight or word of reproof provided it came from Malcy.

To Crawface, who also occasionally took care of the child with considerably less success, he complained that the wee bugger ate up all his spare time. With Miss Snooty, he was modest, deprecating and reassuring. 'He's no trouble to me, Miss Heather.' Occasionally to himself he was honest and wondered at the pleasure he derived from Will's company. He could not account for it. It made him uneasy. To Malcy, whose curiosity regarding motivation in others he also applied to himself, these feelings of tenderness were dangerous, a sign of weakness. He must be getting soft.

Thinking about Billy-boy, as he called him, made him as uneasy as a blind man without his stick, but when he was with the child he felt curiously calm. Gradually he convinced himself that his ability to control Will was natural, considering his strength of character, but that did not explain the little boy's effect on him.

He dreamed frequently about the Eyeties, warm sunlit visions of the past that left him nostalgic by day.

At weekends he took his turn as guide. The cars began to arrive shortly after 10 am on Easter Saturday when the great gates were opened for the season. Families from the city, foreigners, coach-parties, historic tours and passing motorists, with an hour to spare, poured in on sunny days.

In the summer of '57, Miss Snooty opened a shop with postcards, tea towels and watercolours by a local artist, which sold well. Part of the coach house was turned into a café which Cook and Bella kept supplied with cream scones and melting moments. Villagers were recruited to sell tickets, fruit or plants from the garden and to wash-up and wait at table or sit unobtrusively in the open rooms just in case someone decided to stub out a cigarette on the gold leaf.

The Major with Malcy's assistance decided to design a children's play-ground with swings and a paddling pool, partly with Will in mind. The Major was seriously considering giving up the bank in the city and opening Nightingales six days in the week throughout the summer, to increase profits and reduce the continually rising overheads.

As a guide, Malcy was unrivalled. He knew the name and often the character behind every portrait, the period (and the price) of every antique. He made the tours interesting and informative. He looked the part in a dark blue blazer, open-necked shirt and narrow trousers. His hair, no longer cropped and slicked with Brylcreme shone cleanly, a thick, wavy gold. His skin had tanned to a healthy clover honey. By the frequent use of one small pronoun, he allowed the visitors to assume he was family. He never corrected the error. He also let it be known with much charm and deprecation that 'we' had fallen on hard times, forced to part with treasures that had been the family for centuries and were largely dependent on the good-will of tourists like themselves. He accepted the resulting tips pressed into his hand with dignity. He kept a large proportion and made over the rest to the communal box devised to be shared among all the assistants. He opened a new saving account under the name of Malcolm Drake.

There were opportunities to made bigger profits. One hot Saturday in August, an American tourist left his wallet stuffed with tenners in the pocket of his jacket slung over a garden bench. Malcy picked it up, made a quick assessment of the amount which was not less than two hundred pounds, and took it straight to the Yank who was cooling off in the tea-room.

'Excuse me, sir, I believe this would be safer with you,' he said in smooth upper class English.

The Yank clasped his hand to his empty trouser pocket and exclaimed, 'My Gawd!'

He then presented Malcy with a pat on the shoulder, a cigar and one of the notes as 'a small donation to the upkeep of your lovely home'.

Malcy smiled and shook his head. 'That's not necessary, sir.'

The Yank spotted the Major and called out to him.

'I'd sure like to congratulate you on this boy of yours. He's a credit to the family.'

It was a fraught moment but Swankpants never twigged that the American was referring to a son of the house.

'Glad to hear it,' the Major replied as if he had expected no less.

At the time Malcy congratulated himself that he had not succumbed to fouling his own nest. He did not doubt that he could have got away with the theft, but such loud acclamations of his honesty by the garrulous Yank in the presence of the family, villagers and visitors might in the long run be worth more than a couple of hundred quid. For Malcy lived dangerously. He knew it and was not dumb enough to take stupid risks.

Once in every ten days or so, Malcy had a whole day off. The Major encouraged him to get right away from the place, enjoy himself, go up to London. Swankpants gave him the key to a side door in case he wanted to be late.

His answer to friendly questions as to what he did with his day off contained enough of the truth to be plausible. Looked at antique shops in the Old Kent Road. Spent a couple of hours at the V and A. Saw a flick. Ate salad and chips at a Lyon's Corner House. Sometimes he told the Major he had gone to a pub for a pint.

'Best not to mention that to Bella, sir.'

The Major closed one eye in an owlish wink. It was their private joke that Crawface could come the sergeant-major.

Inwardly Malcy hooted. Nevertheless, he did not believe in lying unless it was necessary.

The last Tuesday of June was a particularly satisfying day. He caught the 8 20 to Victoria, went straight to left luggage and exchanged a ticket for a leather suitcase stamped with the gold initials MWPD which Swankpants had loaned him after one of his leaves from RAF Padgate. He locked himself in a cubicle at the Gents, and, ten minutes later, emerged transformed. He wore a dark grey well-cut lounge suit, cream shirt and quiet tie. His pearl grey felt hat sat on a non-descript brown wig which matched a small neat moustache. He carried a brief case with a telescopic black umbrella strapped behind the handle. His slim black shoes looked expensive. The whole rig-out had cost a bomb but it achieved its purpose. He looked anonymous and respectable.

After depositing the case which now contained his everyday clothes, he bussed out to Wimbledon. He preferred to travel by bus when possible That way he could suss out likely streets.

Wimbledon was awash with fans surging towards the All England Lawn Tennis Club. It was a sunny breezy day. If he had reckoned correctly most of the houses in the nearby groves and gardens would be empty.

He ate a sandwich and drank a cup of tea in a crowded milk bar, schooling himself to patience but already the adrenalin had begun to flow. A pulse ticked in his temple. He was alert, fit, excited, nervous, the way a great star felt before the cameras rolled,   or so he imagined. A tout offered him a ticket for the centre court.

'Stuff it, mate,' he said coarsely. The wide-boy looked as if he had entered a bank but found a brothel. Careful, Malcy cautioned himself. That twister would know him again. This was a dangerous time. He was as high as the planet Mars.

Melrose, Braemar, Crinan Avenues were leafy, flowery, opulent, swinging from sunshine to shadow under a fitful sun. He could tell at a glance if a house was empty and he was seldom mistaken.

There it was; 10 Balmoral Avenue. The windows were closed, the outer front door shut. The garden burgeoned with rose bushes, shrubs and standards. Pergolas and trellises rioted with ramblers. Crawface would be in her element.

He walked up to the front door and rang the bell once and then firmly again. The ring had a hollow reassuring echo, but he had his question ready. 'Does Lady Mowbray live here?' Always the same words, the same name. It was a foolish risk and time and again he made up his mind to say Jones or Smith but when it came to the point he could not do it. That name was both key and talisman.

No one answered.

Unhurriedly he walked round to the back of the house, his eyes alert for watchers, for neighbouring windows that overlooked. A blackbird sang piercingly from an overblown laburnum next door, but he saw no one.

He rapped on the back door with his knuckles. Not a sound from within, not even a dog. The door had a mortice - unlocked - and a Yale which yielded immediately to his quick neat manoeuvres. He let himself in and locked the door behind him. Once, in Hampstead, he had been inside when the owner returned. He had just found time to let himself out of the front door while she fumbled in her bag for the back door key.

He wore gloves. He was scrupulously tidy and he left no clues. Money was what he was after but occasionally he took jewellery too.

A leather purse in the drawer of an unlocked bureau contained £70. A further £50 were stuffed into the pocket of a velvet evening jacket in the dressing-room wardrobe. He took two good diamond rings and a Mexican gold bracelet that weighed comfortably heavy from an unlocked jewel case. A further five pounds with some loose change was stuffed into a money-box labelled 'Milk' on the kitchen dresser. That he left.

Half an hour later he let himself out by the back door and took the tube back to town. He flogged the rings for £150 a piece, a fraction of their worth, and the bracelet for £55. It was still his policy to take what was offered without fuss. He then travelled back by underground to Ealing and deposited £475 into his account.

After changing back into his home clothes, he returned the suitcase to left luggage, took in a Frankenstein movie at the nearest cinema, ate a plate of pasta and a slice of Black Forest gateau at a cheap restaurant. He felt as it he had won a five set match on the centre court.

On the journey home he added up his expenses for the day. Fares, cinema and food amounted to £3.4/2s plus an extra five bob for a celluloid duck that quacked and wobbled when wound up, bought for Billy-boy at the station stall. £3.9/2d – almost two weeks wages. Time he was asking for a rise.

Up in his attic room when the household was asleep he unlocked the bible. Seven savings book lay in the rectangular hollow. He shuffled through them like a pack of cards, arranging them in chronological order. Time to count the loot. He knew to a penny how much each book contained, including a rough estimate of the interest. Today's addition brought the total to £8837.10/4d.

He slept like a corpse that night.

Sleep was not always Malcy's friend. After days of bridling his tongue, reining his thoughts, working in harmony with the staff and his employers, the nights were long. Sometimes Bella received the back-lash of built-up tension. He knew where to find her alone usually in the basement laundry ironing the household linen. His voice coarsened as he paced the blue tiled floor between the old wash-tubs and the mangles on one side and the temperamental Bendix on the other.

'What way did you have to take on this bloody work? Why did you ever come to this fucking place? You had the Lodge. You had the chance to get shot of slavery, but you let it slip, you daft midget. It makes me sick to the stomach to see you crawling to the toffs.'

She did not raise her head from the Major's shirt she was ironing. All he could see were the wings of her jet hair and the bridge of her wide nose. He lashed out savagely.

'I hate this fucking hole. I hate the slick rich bastards who think they own the world. One day they'll get what's coming to them and it'll be me that doles it out.'

Bella folded the Major's shirt and laid it aside.

'Listen to me, you stupid bitch. One day I'll be master here and you'll crawl like the rest.'

'Sticks and stones, Malcy,' she said mildly as she damped a pair of Will's shorts.

'And eff you too.'

Already he felt easier. Her dumbness and passivity were essential to him for the Lodge was the last place he would want to be and the Drakes were as necessary to him as meat. The day she heeded him, he would have to hold his tongue.

Yet he was well aware that Crawface was no fool and while the abuse spilled out of him, images too swift for recognition flashed through his memory. Sometimes in the night he would waken from dreams of a noisome pit walled with shit and a child's voice that wailed through the vaults of his mind. On these nights he was scared to sleep again so he wandered through Nightingales alone.

One warm midsummer sleepless night he took the keys to the King Charles wing. Moonlight thrust through the high mullioned windows embroidering shadows with silver threads. Beguiled by the grandeur of the room, he crossed the balustrade that separated the bed space from the rest of the chamber and lay down on the brocade counterpane. Squared light fell on his face. Across his thighs, the heavy shadow of post and curtain cast a darker hue. Above, the canopy soared to a peak carved

129

with the royal arms picked out in gold. He did not imagine himself as king, least of all Charles II for whom he had no particular admiration, but rather as possessor, manipulator, the Magician.

Beyond the bed recess, a great tapestry depicted scenes from the Creation, the strange plants and beasts of Eden, Adam and Eve, the serpent and the tree diamonded with moonlight. His mind expanded to new limits of knowledge as if he himself had eaten of the forbidden fruit. *Genesis* took on a new meaning.

Adam and Eve failed not because they had disobeyed God but because, cowards that they were, they had betrayed the serpent. If they had stuck with the snake, they and their descendants might still have been in Eden. The idea enthralled him. Cringing obedience to God was the coward's way. Man's true abilities had been dulled by the dope of guilt. Morality was - in the words of the master - *a badge of stupid and sheepish docility.*

The truth was that when Eve took the apple, the serpent had won. Why had he not seen that sooner? The supremacy of God was the biggest con since the resurrection. Judaism, Christianity, Islam were all a load of lies. Before God made the garden, the serpent existed, all wise, all knowing, laughing his head off up his metaphorical sleeve.

Logically, then, it followed that the serpent was the true God, evil and good were just words, hell nowhere to be feared. Nothing. Another con. Take what you like in life, mate, it's all you've bloody got. *Javohl.*

He now no longer saw himself as Hitler's spiritual offspring. Only a man with the capacity of rage and hatred such as Gould possessed could have sired such a son as him. But the child had long ago out-wised the father. What the farmer had known and done instinctively, his son recognised as an acknowledgement of the serpent's supremacy.

Just as there were degrees of goodness ranging from saintliness down to do-gooding, so there were degrees of evil which encompassed war-mongerers, murderers and rapists

130

down to the heedless vandal in the street. Just as some chose to follow the failed God, others were called by the serpent. He, Malcolm, was of that elect. High priest of the serpent; the Magician. It was a concept that drew from him sentiments of awe. He rose from his bed, and in a gesture alien to his nature, prostrated himself on the panelled floor before the coiled and embroidered image of the snake.

Sometimes on his night wanderings he passed the nursery door. Billy-boy slept in the night nursery in a bed which had short white painted iron safety rails. He liked to shake them, a trick which drove the nurse in the adjoining room maniacal.

Hearing the creek, Malcy opened the door, and, in the moonlight that lit the room, saw Will squatting in a fuddle of blankets, rocking to and fro. Saliva ran out of a loose corner of his mouth as it widened in a smile of recognition. He held out a cold red fist.

'Hi, wee fella,' he said quietly. The last thing he wanted was to waken the starchy nurse.

Will made sounds of delight. His speech was as slow as the paediatrician had predicted, but it was coming. Malcy interrupted the jumbled chatter. 'Sure you're a cute wee bastard, so you are. Say, "You're my pal, Malcy".'

He child obliged with a mouthful of spit and vowels.

The stench of urine from the soaked nappy inside the waterproof pants soured the room.

'Ye dirty wee bugger, just look at you!'

Gingerly he lifted the child out of the bed to change him. His little body was cold and his rose running. Malcy unbuttoned the sleeping suit and sloughed off the soiled towelling. It was not beyond his ability to change the nappy, but the child's bottom was sore, scarred in places with urine burns, so he filled the hand-basin with warm water, washed and powdered him and buttoned him into a clean pyjama suit and took him up to the attic.

'Don't you pee my bed, or I'll skelp you,' he said mildly as he drew Will down into his narrow bed and held the chilled little body against his own.

'You're mine, so you are. You stick with your Uncle Malcy and he'll stick by you.'

The child laughed and pulled at Malcy's mouth with cold red fingers. After a while they both fell asleep. Malcy's built-in awareness of time awoke him to return the child to the nursery before seven. He cried at being left alone. Malcy thumped hard on the nurse's door with the flat of his hand as he returned to the attic to dress.

On other nights he went to Miss Snooty's room. He never saw anything for the key, whether turned or not, remained in the inside lock. He seldom heard anything either through the thickness of the walls. Perhaps there was nothing to hear. The Major slept in the adjacent dressing-room, but Malcy always stopped to listen.

Once, though, with his ear to the keyhole he heard her weep.

The sound lifted the hairs on his nape. Will crying was an every-day event, but this was Will's mother. Malcy could not remember ever having heard an adult cry. He could not conceive of himself in tears, or Crawface, still less Miss Snooty.

He was swamped in a mixture of emotions. Indignation; what had she to cry about, the stuck-up, toffee-nosed cow. What a nerve, the rich privileged bitch. Curiosity; why would she bubble like a brat? The boss was good to her, wasn't he? Gave her it all. Excitement charged every nerve in his body. Without thinking, he put his hand on the flower-painted round knob and opened the door.

The room was large and smelled faintly of her scent. The windows were open and let in a little starlight. She heard him at once.

'Miles? Is that you?' She had stopped crying but her voice was thick   He stood with his back to the door. A sense of uncertainty kept him still. This was a big mistake. It could cost him his job and he was not yet ready to lose it.

She leaned across to the bedside cabinet and switched on the lamp. Her dark hair was mussed up and her brown eyes swollen in the pinkish glow.

'What is it, Malcolm?' she asked, assuming her mistress-to-servant voice. 'Is something wrong?'

'You were crying,' he said deferentially.

'That's ridiculous,' she told him in her most superior manner but he heard the tremor in her voice as if there were more tears to be shed. That was all the encouragement he needed.

'What have you got to cry about?' he asked her more boldly. 'The Major give you a clip across the ear?' It was half meant to be a joke, but she didn't laugh.

Two moths attracted by the light flitted across the room, casting huge shadows on the ceiling, and bumbled into the lamp.

'Go back to your room,' she said coldly. 'You are being impertinent.'

'I beg your pardon, Miss Heather,' he said ingratiatingly and turned as if to leave, then waited. He knew exactly what she would do next. As always when she felt she might have been unjust, she called him back.

'Malcy?' He did not turn. Her voice contained that hesitancy he so despised. 'Thank you...' she groped for the right words '...for being concerned.'

He hated the fact that she could not sustain her anger. It implied not only that she was weak but also that he was too vulnerable to take it. One day he would give her something to be grateful for, the stupid cow.

Heather

After Malcy left her room, Heather lay awake for a long time. Because it was simpler than probing the reason for her tears, she allowed herself a measure of indignation. He had not changed. She remembered how he had crept around the Hall at night

133

disturbing shadows, waking old ghosts. He reminded her of an incident in her childhood when she had found a pretty tin on the river bank with a smiling child holding a bunch of bluebells on the lid. Opening it, she had found a heaving swarm of maggots, dropped, no doubt, by some angler. She had been revolted out of all proportion to the find. All Malcy had done was to ask her why she wept.

She often wept in her sleep waking to find her eyes wet and her throat sore. She had not realised that she could be heard. Even if she had chosen to answer Malcy's question, she could not have given him a reason. She could never remember her dreams.

Like fish in a glass bowl, her thoughts swam around uneasily examining all aspects of her life, searching for answers she could accept.

There was Miles, pre-occupied by his work and the affairs of the estate, overdoing it, depressed, uncommunicative, ageing before her eyes. Surely her subconscious mind was not so foolish as to try to attract his attention by tears. Both of them were embarrassed by displays of emotion. Aware of his exhaustion, she had once suggested he give up the bank but he had snapped her head off. If he gave up work he could not support the household. If he were to part with Nightingales he would be betraying his ancestors and his descendants. His son.

Will was the abscess at the root of his father's *raison d'etre*. For over three hundred years there had been Drakes at Nightingales.

Will's brain damage was a fact she had accepted as far as it was possible, or so she believed. Had he been born at home, it might have been a still birth. If, at the time, in the throes of post-natal depression, she had been given the choice of losing him or keeping him damaged, she would have chosen to lose him. That was the nightmare beyond the balm of tears. Her guilt manifested itself in the way she reared him; long spells when she left him entirely to hired hands followed by bursts of over-protective attention.

134

She still flinched inwardly when she remembered how - secretly - she had criticised the doctors who had brought him back to life. Even then she had known, deep down, that her reasons was rotten, rooted in personal pride. The careless child who had 'lost' her parents had now given birth to an imbecile. What would the world think? She still felt compelled to explain to strangers how it had happened so that no one would think she or Miles were in any way responsible.

Yet the shame went deeper. She found she could not love her child. No wonder she wept.

Malcy's devotion to him was a surprise; not that he made a particular parade of his affection, but because her own guilt made her sensitive. She was aware of how every member of the household regarded him. Miles treated his son as if he were an untrainable gun-dog, kindly, but with impatience. Nannies came and went without forming strong ties of affection. Bella cared for him cheerfully as she treated everyone else, but Malcy appeared to love him for himself. It was clear that Will doted on Malcy. This she saw as further evidence of his imbecility. He loved without discrimination. It was important for him to have someone to love, she knew that, that his plump outstretched arms needed to be grasped and held, yet to love Malcy and be loved by Malcy was perhaps another cause for concern.

Now, as her heart beat faster after his intrusive nocturnal visit, she wondered if it might not be better for Will in the long run if he were to lose Malcy's affection now rather than later when he had grown to be too dependent upon him. Not for the first time she wondered if Malcy should go.

After all what would Will lose that others could not make up to him? In time he would have brothers and sisters to protect and love him. He was not yet four years old. Plenty of time. Nightingales would still have an heir. So the doctor said. So she told herself.

Though with her mind she believed that another child was possible, her body, her instincts and intuitions told her otherwise. Her flesh and blood were afraid of bearing Miles another child. They were first cousins, and, in spite of the doctor's diagnosis, there was no actual proof that Will's brain damage had occurred after his birth. Her mind could not compel her body to conceive.

'I am not fit to have another child.'

The words dropped cold as stones into her head. She may even have said them aloud. Twisting hotly between the sheets she thought of Miles next door in the high mahogany bed he had slept in as a child and had had brought down to the dressing-room at the time of his first marriage, preferring its hardness to the suffocating heat of a double bed. He was by nature a reticent man, fastidious in his habits. Nor was sex of any particular importance in his life. On Friday nights he knocked on their communicating door, two small taps, and waited for her to answer. If she did not, he assumed she had a reason or was asleep.

After it was over, they smoked a cigarette and talked about the arrangements for the coming weekend. Occasionally during the week he came to her room but he always returned to his own bed well before dawn.

Sometimes she wondered if he had made love differently with Lena, his first wife, and came to the conclusion that he had not. A man's sexual habits were probably as ingrained as his finger-prints. A woman's too. Or did women act out the role required? Would she be the same unresponsive lump with another lover? On the whole she believed she was incapable of passion, just as she was incapable of love.

And this was the deepest shame of all; to be aware of Miles' kindness, his problems, his needs, just as she was aware of Will's vulnerability and yet not to be able to respond honestly with her heart. Love and guilt could not co-exist and she was enmeshed in guilt, not just towards her husband and her son but to every member of her family and household from her lost parents and neglected grandmother to Bella and Malcolm for whom she had made herself responsible.

Though they sometimes seemed like the albatross around her neck, the burden she longed to shed, she knew she would never let them go. Why not, she asked herself as she lay sleepless with aching eyes. Why not send Bella and Malcy back to Ladymuir, put Will in a home, look for a lover who would pet and kiss her, give her more babies? She had not that sort of courage. She was too afraid of losing the image of herself, the charming Mrs Percy-Drake, the picture on the tin, because she knew only too well what lay within.

Restlessly she turned on to her back. The memory of Malcolm standing at the door, immobile beyond the bumbling summer moths, moved behind her lids so that she saw him more clearly with her eyes closed. The old sensation of fear and revulsion returned, and, with it, something less easy to define. Suddenly all other thoughts and anxieties cleared from her head. Shamefully there was only Malcy, his gleaming hair as bright as a painted halo, watching her.

'By the bye,' Miles said at breakfast, unfolding the Times, 'Old Harry rang up yesterday. Suggests we go to Lords this Saturday.'

Harry Fever was an old school friend who shared Miles' passion for cricket. Once a year they had a day at Lords.

'Malcolm and the others can cope with the mob on Saturday. He's capable of running the show on his own. I've had a word. I must say we struck lucky with that chap.'

He was always saying that, so how could she tell him she wanted Malcy to go? Nor was she at all sure that she did.

Thursday was Malcy's day off. Without him, the house seemed lighter as if the old place had relaxed its watchfulness, settled back on its foundations in the sun. In the afternoon Nanny developed one of her heads so Heather took Will out to the rose garden, set him on the grass with a bowl of water to splash while she snipped off dead rose heads. At half-past four Bella brought out the tea.

'Stay,' said Heather impulsively, taking off her gardening gloves. 'Talk to me.'

They brought out deck chairs and Bella fetched another cup.

'Do you remembered those picnics in Scotland? I'd drag you away from the farm and we'd walk for miles. I made you act out all my fantasies. You were the princess and I was the Red Cross Knight.'

'Aye, and wee Malcy was always the monster with a runny nose.'

Bella took a cloth from the pocket of her overall and wiped the butter off Will's chin. Watching her, Heather said speculatively, 'They're rather alike.'

'Who?'

'Malcy and Will. I never noticed it before.'

She looked at her son, his large shallow eyes, his curving drooling smile, his fat tanned thighs and curly yellow hair. What a foolish remark. Malcy had been thin, tense, disagreeable, his hair as straight and white as lint. Will was affectionate and garrulous, if incomprehensible. Malcy had been surly and uncommunicative. Yet the resemblance was there. She sensed it without understanding it. Both had been to an extent, deprived, the one of affection the other of wits. Both, she realised with shame had been unwanted as infants, if for dissimilar reasons.

'Maybe,' said Bella after a while, 'that's why they're such pals.'

Heather unwound the mangled bread from Will's fist while Bella peeled the paper off a chocolate biscuit already melting in the sun.

'God, Bella, you can't give him that!' she exclaimed, half laughing. 'What would Nanny say?'

He smeared it everywhere. Only his teeth stayed white.

Heather laughed guiltily until there were tears in her eyes while Bella giggled and wiped him clean.

'Bella' she said impulsively when they had stopped laughing, 'are you happy here? Is Malcy?'

138

It was a question she had never asked not because it had not occurred to her, but because she could not predict the answer. She assumed they were content because the alternative was unthinkable. Friends reiterated tiresomely that both were devoted to her, grateful, 'jolly well off', and she had accepted their judgement without daring to question it. She assumed that their reliance on her for bed and board implied that they both must, at least, be content. She saw them as sucker fish or ivy on the wall with no life apart from the host.

As soon as she had asked the question she wished it unspoken. The words hung suspended in the air, looming larger by the second. At first she thought Bella had not heard. Her work-worn, starfish fingers kneaded the grass, smoothing, caressing the spongy, mossy turf. Suddenly she bent down to sniff it.

'I like the smell of grass,' she said not looking up. 'I'm awfu' fond of a nice green.'

The question itched like a scab. Heather could not leave it alone.

'Bella,' she persisted, 'didn't you hear me?'

'Aye.'

Just as the answer was about to come, Heather lost her nerve. 'What is the situation at the Lodge?' she asked quickly. 'Are the Bains still there?'

Bella looked up in genuine surprise. 'Where was the need for them to flit?'

'No need at all, so long as you are happy here, not missing Ladymuir.' The question had turned into a statement no longer expecting a reply.

Will stuck the last of the biscuit into his mouth. Bella rinsed out the buttery napkin and began to wash his face and hands with firm strokes just as she had washed Malcy all those years ago.

For the first time since that morning in the kitchen at the Hall when she had stared down with curiosity at the diminutive farm child, Heather looked critically at Bella. She saw that her red cheeks which always gave the appearance of good health were

139

netted with broken veins. The laughter wrinkles round her huge black eyes gave a semblance of cheerfulness that was false. Her short black hair which used to be as glossy as boot polish was lustreless even in the sun. She looks old, thought Heather, and she's not yet thirty.

Boldly she said, 'Bella is something wrong?'

Bella sighed. 'It's ma teeth. They're giving me gip. I've been bothered a while.'

'Why didn't you say so?' Heather cried, strident with relief. 'I'll make an appointment for you at the dentist tomorrow.'

'I'm no' keen on dentists.'

'How can you be so silly? Of course you must go to the dentist.'

'I kent you'd say that.' She laughed and with a characteristic gesture covered her mouth with her hand, but not before Heather had seen the painful evidence of decay.

It occurred to her that Bella had no more answered her question than she had wanted to know the truth.

Next morning Malcy came to the breakfast room where she was busy with her correspondence and the accounts. As always, he was immaculate in black sweater, narrow trousers and a grey dust jacket that he habitually wore.

'May I speak to you privately, Miss Heather?' he asked in his flat accent-less voice.

'Of course. Come in, Malcy,' she gushed to cover her instinctive reluctance to hear what he had to say. 'Did you have a pleasant day out yesterday?'

'Yes, thank you, Miss Heather,' he answered coolly and then there was silence.

She forgot that it was him who had asked to speak to her and thrashed about in her mind for some remark, but he had his sentence prepared, the silence also. At exactly the right moment, he began, 'I wish to apologise for my intrusion on Tuesday night.'

140

The last thing she had expected or wanted was an apology. Nevertheless she decided to accept it at its face value.

'Very well, Malcy. We'll say no more about it.'

She turned back to her desk but he did not go. He came closer and stood at her back. Her nape turned cold and she had an urge to shiver.

'I bought you a present,' he said softly.

There was a parcel in his hand. Remembering the brown wooden bangle and what it had ultimately cost, she did not want to touch it.

'You shouldn't waste your money on me.'

He put it down on the desk, a small square cardboard box with a jeweller's name stamped in gold letters on the lid.

'You used to like my presents.' He sounded aggrieved.

Before she could speak he turned and left the room. She thought of leaving the box unopened, returning the gift unseen, ignoring it, but if his apology had been genuine and she had no cause to think otherwise, she had no wish to hurt his feelings. Also, she had to admit to a certain curiosity.

The box contained a brooch that could also be worn as a pendant. A silver snake coiled round a dark cairngorm that looked like a sombre eye. An ornament of no great value, she suspected, but what an extraordinary choice.

She did not like it. In a strange way it reminded her of the old Hall. The serpent that had in her imagination coiled around the dank old rooms, the eye, the ever-watchful presence. It was as much as she could do to touch it. She wrapped it up in the tissue paper and slipped the box into a drawer in her desk. Out of sight, it remained obsessively in the forefront of her mind. Did he really expect her to wear it?

She thought of showing it to Miles. 'Malcy has given me this extraordinary present,' she would say with a deprecating laugh. 'What am I supposed to do about it?' She had no idea what he would say, but Heather knew she would not tell Miles about the gift. Nothing that Malcy did was spontaneous or straightforward. Her acceptance would herald a change in their

141

relationship, a subtle shift of role that was both frightening and infective, a drawing together of fact and fantasy. Ripples of alarm crawled across her skin. Of course she would return it.

She pulled out a sheet of writing paper and in her large flowing hand that yearly grew more like her grandmother's, began to scrawl:

Dear Malcolm,

I was touched by your gift. Thank you for the thought. It is, however, quite unnecessary and it would be unfair of me to accept it. Save it for the girl you eventually marry. She will appreciate it, I'm sure.

There is no need for any further apologies. The incident is forgotten.

Yours sincerely, Heather Percy-Drake.

She re-read it and crossed out the last two pompous sentences. Then she re-wrote it, folded the sheet of paper and sealed it in an envelope. She took the box and the letter and went in search of him before second thoughts or cowardice could change her mind.

In the kitchen, Bella told her he was painting in the stables, so, on impulse she decided to put the box back in his room. She seldom went up to the attics and could clearly remember her last visit. She had wanted a wedding present for a school friend who liked antique silver so she had taken the keys to go through the chests stored up there.

The musty cobwebby sky-lit room had been transformed with paint and polish. The boxes and chests had been arranged for easy access and the inventories re-written and taped under transparent paper to the lids. This had been some of Malcy's work during his leaves which had so impressed Miles. She had unlocked one of the steel-lined chests, found a Georgian salver in good condition, and, before coming downstairs, hesitated outside Malcy's door.

Her grandmother had always made regular inspections of the servants' rooms but it had seemed an impertinence to Heather. Since Mrs Orpen's retirement, only the nursemaid, Bella and Malcolm lived in and she trusted them to report any structural fault or breakage without having to intrude upon their privacy. That was her excuse. The truth was that bedrooms were like windows that revealed too much. The arrangement of the furniture, the choice of possessions, the smell of flesh and bedding were too personal, too revelatory of their owners for comfort. Even Miles' room with the framed photographs of school and county cricket teams, his regiment, the sepia tinted sporting prints on the wall, the ancient marble washstand arranged with his old fashioned shaving gear, made her uneasy.

So she hesitated outside Malcy's door, but not just out of sensitivity. She was also curious, and, despising herself for what seemed like an urge to spy, had deliberately passed on. Now that the opportunity had come again, she still hesitated, remembering the fisherman's tin.

But there were no maggots in the corners, no squalid twist of sheets, not even a dirty sock. The room was as white and antiseptic as a hospital ward, the window open to the July sun. The narrow bed sagged from age but was covered with a counterpane laundered so often that it was threadbare, the varnished wood floor dustless. A brush, hairless, and a comb with no dandruff between the teeth lay neatly on the chest of drawers. Apart from an old bible and the angle-poise lamp she and Miles had given him for Christmas, there was nothing on the bedside pedestal.

She pulled open one of the drawers and saw his underwear, y-fronts and aertex vests, folded in tidy piles. The wardrobe that matched the white painted chest contained one dark blue blazer with gold buttons, two pairs of trousers carefully hung to preserve the creases, a tweed sports jacket, two pairs of leather shoes, brown and black, honed to the same degree of shine as Miles' and a pair of blanco-ed tennis shoes.

Curious now, she began to search for some clue to his nature but could find nothing. Glimpsing a square tartan-patterned biscuit box on top of the wardrobe, she reached for it and set it down on the chest. Inside it contained a notepad and envelopes, a pen, some pencils and a packet of coloured rubber bands, two boxes of cuff links - more Christmas gifts - an unused tube of acne cream, a pair of nail scissors and a pack of Tarot cards. She did not like the Tarot. It belonged to the dark side of life, a doorway into a world she feared, the arch into the old Hall. It aroused in her that familiar sense of excited dread. It was also a clue, the only clue to Malcy's nature. The brooch with the serpent and the eye began to make sense.

Without thinking she lifted the cards and sifted through the pack. A small photograph fell out and spiralled to the floor. She picked it up and saw that it had been cut out of sheaf of old poly-photos of herself, not a good likeness, but recognisable.

The old familiar frisson of fear lifted the hair on her nape. The feeling grew until her whole body convulsed in a shudder. The thought of Malcy with the photograph menaced her mind. She glanced over her shoulder afraid he might be watching. The picture lay protected in the cup of her hands. She did not want to leave it yet if she were to remove it, Malcy would know that she had been prying. After she had put her letter and the box in a prominent place on top of the chest of drawers, she slipped the photo back between the cards and returned the tin.

Malcolm

He knew as soon as he opened the door that she had been in his room. Her scent, like azaleas in the spring sun, lingered.

At first he thought the letter on the chest of drawers must be to thank him. Perhaps the box contained a reciprocal gift. As he read the sheet, he was aware of each mounting stage of anger. First the shock and then the surge as each part of his body and mind filled up with the lava of rage. It hurt.

He had bought the brooch on the day that his savings topped ten grand, stopped and stared at it in the antique shop window in the Old Kent Road for fully five minutes before he committed himself. It seemed to symbolise their relationship the way he wanted it to be, with the silver serpent as himself dominant in her life. The brownish stone matched exactly her prominent brown eyes. He dreamed of it pinned to her breast, often took it out to admire, even showed it to Bella though he had not told her who it was for. He visualised her reaction when he gave it to her, surprised to find that he had such good taste combined with pleasure and gratitude. He remembered that plain brown wooden bangle pushed half-way up her sun-burnt arm that she had worn for a whole long summer holiday.

He crushed her letter in his fist and tore at it savagely. Then he took the tartan tin from his wardrobe, and, putting the pieces in the lid, set them on fire. Watching the flames lick round the sprawling letters brought a measure of relief. He shook the ash from the window, took the lid to the lavatory along the passage and washed away the stain. About to replace it, he sensed rather than saw that the contents of the box had been touched. Proof was that the photograph he kept between the Devil and the Magician was now wedged between the Sun and the Moon.

Immediately his feelings changed. Anger gave way to wariness. He crossed the room and picked up the bible, but the lock was intact. Relief gave way to contempt. Toffee-nosed Miss Snooty had snooped like any common tart. She'd found nothing except her own photograph. Partly he minded. Her finding it made him vulnerable. She would think he cared. Yet at the same time, he was gratified. That she should be curious showed that she was not indifferent. The more he thought about it, the less he minded. Her act lowered her, made her seem more attainable. It cemented their relationship in a new way for there was not a drawer, not a file or a paper in her possession that had not been scrutinised by him.

Try as he might he could find no convincing reason why she had returned his gift. Closing his fist over the brooch, he felt

145

the sharp pin of the catch prick his palm and suddenly he was swamped with a new feeling - humiliation. No doubt she did not consider the brooch good enough for her. He was not good enough...

It had cost him five guineas. She would have to pay.

Bella

Bella had a bicycle. With the seat lowered, she could just reach the pedals. Sometimes she stood up on them to give herself extra power. It had a steel tray in front for carrying mail-bags which was useful for shopping. When Jess Taylor, the post woman, retired with arthritis to be replaced by a cocky lad in a red van, the post office, having no further use for the bike, allowed her to keep it. She gave it to Bella in exchange for a couple of hour's work in her garden once or twice a week.

'Have you not enough work to do in that great barracks of a house?' Jess asked waspishly. She was touchy about charity.

'It's my own time. I can suit myself.'

'You're crazy,' Grace had said. 'Fancy digging a garden on your day off!'

Grace was Jess Taylor's twenty-year old niece whose parents had been bombed dead in the war. She was an assistant in the village shop. Meanwhile she was saving up to go to London where she had come from as an evacuee in the first place. She was waiting to get her weight down to ten stone before she left. She reckoned that her hair which was long and black and thick as a briar bush accounted for at least two pounds and thought about cutting it off.

Jess Taylor's garden was Bella's haven since Mr Betchworth, head gardener at Nightingales, had chased her off his herbaceous beds. 'I'll have no bleedin' woman interfering in my borders,' he had shouted at her, so she had left them alone.

There was always the Common.

Years ago it had been the villagers' grazing ground with grass and a pond and some tall oak trees. With the sheep and cattle

146

gone, it had gradually grown into a wilderness of birch and willow, furze and marsh, full of darting insects, croaking frogs, yes, and nightingales.

The Common filled Bella with awe. Sometimes on her way back from Jess Taylor's cottage, she would take the path across the wilderness, prop her bike against a tree and leave the rutted lane. The voices of the plants were like bats' twitter almost out of range, insistent, beautiful. One spring she stood close to a great clump of dandelions and when she stared into the strong yellow blooms she had felt the heat and beat of the plant as powerful as the sun. She had bent over a bush of pink clover and grown dizzy from the singing fragrance. She had lain in a patch of heather and heard its urgent appeal to the laden bees.

She found rare plants too; orchids sweet as vanilla, herb robert and ragged robin, slender golden flags and trefoils like rest harrow and white melilot. Gradually she began to understand wild plants, to admire them for their independence, their energy and their purity. She watched them thirst for rain and thrust for space, sun-strong, freely-bred, not needing human care. Once she had picked a bunch of meadow sweet for Jess Taylor's window-sill.

'What do you want to go picking weeds for?' she had complained. 'They'll be dead by morning.'

They were.

They knew their place. That had been one of Big Lizzie's favourite maxims. *A place for everything and everything in its place.* She remembered the patch of mare's tail under her window at the Hall that she had failed to tame. In the Common even the great marsh thistle had beauty, the nettle curved its head with grace, dock and hemlock grew to noble heights, yet when their seeds dared to germinate in Jess Taylor's garden, she, Bella, uprooted them, called them weeds and piled them on the compost to nourish the sweet peas.

She thought, as she hoe-ed and raked, that the same care had gone into the creation of the pesky ground elder and the fragrant rose; they were nourished by the same sun, rooted in the same

147

soil, yet one was acceptable, the other unwelcome. It was the same the world over. There were rabbits and there were wrens. With human beings the variations were just as wide. There were high and there were low, black and white, rich and poor, good and bad.

She did not question the situation, did not think to criticise or change it. She continued to weed Jess Taylor's garden, to nurture, feed and stake the chosen blooms, but in the Common she held her breath.

The summer night was cool and quiet. A wakeful wood pigeon coo-roo-ed from an apple tree while she thinned lettuces and hoe-ed between the flowering pea shoots. She looked at her watch and sighed. She could have stayed happily in the garden all through the July night with the moths and the bats and breathing plants. At the back door of the cottage she scraped the soil off her boots, removed them and set them on a sheet of newspaper and put on her shoes. The cat, on its way out, wound between her legs. It arched its back as she ran her hand over its silky fur.

'Keep that dratted pigeon off my caulies, puss.' She opened the kitchen door and called out, 'I'll be off, then.'

Jess was sitting in the dusk. 'Nobody's stopping you,' she snapped. Misery crouched on her back like a dowager's hump.

Bella changed her mind. She filled the kettle from the sink and lit the gas ring. 'I'll just make us a cup of tea,' she called out.

'Who said you could? Digging my garden doesn't give you the right to my kitchen. You're mighty interfering, Bella Gould,' Jess grumbled but the fight had gone out of her.

'Did you hear from Grace?' Bella asked, deliberately touching the root of the old woman's misery. Usually she left the subject of Grace's abrupt departure alone.

Jess Taylor sighed. 'It's been three months. Maybe it's that ape of a postman losing my mail...maybe pigs can fly. Well, good riddance to bad rubbish. She was trash, like 'er dad.'

148

Bella sugared the tea. 'Did you tell the polis yet?'

'Might have saved my breath. The whole village knew she wanted the city lights, so she went, and there's nothing the police or the Queen of England can do about it. She's old enough to please herself.'

'She'll be back one of these days.'

'As far as I'm concerned she's gone for good. I'm thinking of putting her stuff in the bin.' She indicated a pile of clothing in the corner of the room. Bella recognised Grace's red Sunday coat. It made her look like a plump scarlet poppy.

'Wait a wee while. She could be back tomorrow.'

Miss Taylor indicated a shallow cardboard box on the table. 'Did you ever see such rubbish?'

It was full of cheap beads, fair-ground rings, half-used lipsticks, grips and pins and half-full bottles of nail varnish. The brooch looked incongruous among the trash. A silver serpent curled about a big marble. Bella stared at it in the dusk. Jess picked it up.

'Dear knows where she got this. I never saw it before. Maybe one of the customers at the shop gave it her. She often got tips and presents. She was liked, the stupid minx. Here, you take it. I want you to have it.'

Bella shook her head backing away from the unwanted gift.

'Go on,' Jess insisted. 'Keep it for her. Maybe if I give it away she'll come back out of sheer perversity.' Her eyes were very bright under her cropped thatch of grizzled hair.

The ornament was cold and heavy in Bella's hand.

Half way across the Common she got off her bike and stepped out into the moon-silvered wilderness. She stopped at the edge of a brackish pool overgrown with rushes. She took the brooch from her pocket and thrust it down into the black oily water, deep into the concealing mud.

Heather

Heather kept her gynaecological reports in a paper file in the second drawer of her bureau in the breakfast room. The latest, dated July 22 1960, stated as previously that they was no physical reason why she should not conceive again, advised her to relax, cultivate other interests, be patient, and confirmed the date of a further appointment. There was also an account attached which had not yet been paid.

The first indication that Malcy knew about the file came in early August. She and Bella were washing the Rockingham dinner service on display in the dining room. It got surprisingly dirty. Malcy had carried the pieces into the butler's pantry as carefully as they deserved. Bella washed and Heather dried and laid them out for Malcy to replace when he had polished the great gleaming refectory table and cleaned the silver.

The dining-room was, in Heather's opinion, one of the most beautiful rooms in the house. Blue, gold and silver with Somerscales seascapes in gilded fames under a glittering Georgian chandelier were all reflected in a huge Chippendale looking-glass which dominated one wall. She enjoyed the soothing ritual of washing the elegant china and of Bella's undemanding companionship. She did not have to make decisions or conversation. She did not have to think while her hands were busy.

When Bella had finished washing the plates and had gone back to the kitchen, Malcy came into the pantry. Nothing had been said about the returned brooch or her visit to his room, so it came as a shock when he said in a soft insinuating voice, 'So you're wanting another bairn?'

For a moment she mistrusted the evidence of her own ears. Colour flooded her face.

'Quacks,' he continued, 'what do they know? They'll tell you anything for a fat fee.'

It had been a large account. She guessed he had been through her bureau.

'It's none of your business,' she said icily. She could see the rise and fall of her own heartbeat through the cashmere of her sweater.

'No - Madam,' he answered insolently.

His rudeness silenced her for a moment as she remembered how she had gone through his possessions.

'I'd like this distasteful conversation to end,' she said dismissively, turning her back on him to take out a new tea towel from the pantry cupboard.

He paid no attention. 'I can tell if you'll have another bairn,' he continued as if she had not spoken, 'with the Tarot cards.'

'Now you are being ridiculous,' she told him, picking up one of the dessert plates and running the cloth round the gold rim.

She could see that she had angered him. Her hands began to tremble. As she reached out shakily to put down the plate, it slipped from her fingers and shattered on the floor. For a moment they both stared down at the broken pieces in silence

Malcy was the first to move. 'What a pity, Miss Heather,' he said with what sounded like real regret as he squatted down to pick up the bits. 'I'll see if I can mend it.' Then he looked up at her, his expression intent.

'The Tarot is never ridiculous.'

She was still trembling long after he had taken the pieces away.

It seemed that everyone knew that Malcy used the Tarot cards.

Some days later, Angela Macbride, a middle-aged villager of dubious Highland extraction who sold tickets and guide-books, weighted down with bracelets and medallions, was talking about 'second sight' while they checked the diary.

'Your Malcolm has the gift,' she enthused. 'Surely you, being Scottish, must know that? He is positively inspiring with the Tarot.'

'Second sight has nothing to do with the Tarot cards,' she answered snubbingly. Miss Macbride's claim to Highland knowledge was as phoney as a cockney guru.

151

'Fortune telling, astrology, clairvoyance, second sight, they're all shoots off the same root, my dear,' she answered tinkling her charm bracelet huffily.

Heather had an image of thick dark roots thrusting like blind serpents through black soil. She shivered. 'I don't believe in tampering with the supernatural.'

'Why not?' Miss Macbride arched thin brows. 'The occult is so enriching, I always think. There are more things in heaven and earth, et cetera, et cetera.'

'Hell for instance?' The words came straight from Heather's subconscious.

Miss Macbride looked at her with surprise. 'I beg your pardon. I didn't realise you were a Catholic.'

'I'm not,' said Heather immediately apologetic.' I just don't like Tarot cards.'

The conversation ended there, but it continued to jabber on in her head. What was so wrong with the Tarot? It seemed to her that to rely on the chance lay-out of a pack of cards was to deny not only her own ability to make decisions that could alter the course of her life, but also the influence of a good God.

If she believed that, she must be a Christian after all.

The thought rather pleased her. It had been some time since she had given religion any serious thought. The village church was in Miles' patronage, the vicar an uncompromising Anglo-Catholic. She and Miles had attended services and taken a share in parish functions until Will's birth. She had immediately blamed the Almighty for his damaged brain. What sort of God could let this happen to an innocent child? It also occurred to that if she had been a better wife, mother, church-goer, Christian, God might not have punished her in this way. Even as the bitter thoughts arose, she rejected them as unfair. If there was good and evil in the world, then Will's affliction came from the evil side. God, so the vicar said, was able to mitigate the evil. A damaged child was permitted in order to draw out love. She supposed with her mind there might be some truth in that supposition but she could not comprehend it with her heart.

152

All her life she had been aware not just of the existence of evil but also that for her it held a kind of attraction not unlike the cobra's eye. She remembered Mr Urquhart's sermons in Ladymuir describing the dark pits of sulphurous fire. Terrifying yes, but at the same time she had been attracted to those hot images of hell. Evil was frightening indeed, but also intriguing and mysterious. She saw goodness, on the other hand, as clear and bright, the sun on ice. Between the pitch of evil and the frost of goodness she hovered in a grey area. 'I want goodness and God,' she insisted to herself, but even as she spoke the words, she was looking backwards at the shadows.

That Sunday she and Miles went to church. They sat in the family pew and sang *All things bright and beautiful* at the Family Eucharist. She felt safe in the sunny church surrounded by forces of light, a little smug.

One of the stained glass windows depicted a shepherd in a purple cloak leaning over a cliff to hook up a stranded lamb. Identifying with that sheep she wondered how long she had existed without the crook.

Nine hours later she was seated at the kitchen table while Malcy spread out the cards of the Major Arcana.

She had gone to the kitchen after dinner to make up the dogs' meal. Honey and Fudge, two very elderly Sealyhams who had belonged to Cousin Eva, were now her responsibility. Miles could not abide them, nor could Malcy who disliked their bad breath and uncertain tempers. Nanny was afraid of their yellowing fangs and would not let them near the nursery so they spent most of their lives in the basement out of the way, exercised by herself or more often by Bella. Heather kept them in Eva's memory for she had been devoted to the surly creatures.

Malcy was alone when she came in. He rose politely to his feet.

'Where's Bella?' she asked. At the same time her eye caught the spread of the Tarot cards on the kitchen table.

153

'Out with the dogs. I fed them,' he added as she went to the cupboard for their bowls.

'That was nice of you,' she said truthfully for she knew he disliked the chore.

Caught up in the crook, complaisant from church, she thought she was safe. What harm could there possibly be?

'All right, Malcy,' she said good-humouredly. 'Let's get it over with. What am I supposed to do?' She sat down at the kitchen table and indicated the cards.

He looked at her swiftly and she caught the gleam of triumph in his eyes. The Esse hummed comfortably and outside the crows in the creaking elms cawed drowsily as he picked up the twenty-two cards spread out over the table and fitted them numerically into his hand. His movements were deft, swift, neat. She noticed his nails, short and very clean; his fingers, though slender, were strong, artistic even, but not quite straight. The middle and forefingers of both hands splayed outwards from the centre joint. Strange hands.

When he had gathered them all together he gave her the pack and told her to shuffle well. She could sense his excitement. She thought, he really believes all this rubbish, and, as she took the cards, wanted to say, 'This is ridiculous.'

'Think about what you want,' he urged her. 'Wipe every other thought out of your mind. Concentrate on what is really important to you.'

Here was a different Malcolm from the quiet, sly, efficient servant, the youth who could be both deferential and unspeakably insolent. She tried to think about another child, to imagine herself pregnant again, but all she could see were his hands, those lean and crooked fingers.

I want him.

The three words dropped into her mind unbidden, unwanted. Horrified, she denied them hotly in her head but she could not thrust the sound of them entirely out of her mind. In silence, she handed him the shuffled cards.

154

'The Tarot contains two powers,' he said, taking the pack from her. 'They can interpret and they can influence. Be sure you know what you want.'

'Are you trying to frighten me, Malcy?' she said with a laugh, but the sound was forced for the symptoms of fear were already affecting her, weakening her muscles, chilling her nape. She shivered.

It was as if she had not spoken. Beginning with the first card from the top of the pack, he placed it face up in front of him.

'This card represents the influences that surround you now.'

She sensed his intense interest and thought, he is doing this for himself. It was not enough for him to see her daily face to face, to intrude into her bedroom at night. He had to dig deeper; his curiosity was obsessive. She wanted to put up barriers.

'It's a dual sign,' he explained touching the upturned card with the tip of his forefinger. 'See how the figure points with his wand to the sky and with his right hand to the earth. He has the power to give you what you want. You are in the hands of the Magician.'

She gazed down at the card, saw the youthfulness of the image, his fair hair, the knowing smile.

'He's a bit like you,' she said facetiously.

He looked up swiftly and she saw that he was gratified. He believed it! But then Malcy had no sense of humour. On the other hand, for the moment at least, it could be said that she was under his influence. Suddenly she did not want to go on with this foolish game, but he had already turned over the next card to cover the first.

'The Emperor,' he said. 'He represents the immediate obstacles to your heart's desire.' He spoke of how reason and intelligence, rank and worldly power stood in the way of the emotions and passions of the heart. This was obviously Miles. Uneasily, she was aware that if the cards had picked up on that spontaneous, unwanted arrow-swift thought; then it was Miles who stood in the way. She kept her eyes lowered for she had no wish to give Malcolm the chance to read her thoughts.

155

'And now for your objective.' He laid a third card to the left of the other two   She looked at the Lovers in silence and embarrassment.

'This card is all about love. The struggle between the spirit and the flesh….' He was quoting straight from the textbook, she realised, but she was not really listening. How right she had been to distrust the Tarot. They were evil, mischievous, uncanny. They had conjured up that ugly wish as she had held them in her hands and now they were interpreting the thoughts that they themselves had implanted. She was ashamed to be playing such a game. She wanted to stop, but not enough.

'Now to go back to the past, to discover the major influences that have made you what you are, brought you to the present.'

He laid a fourth card to the right of the others. 'The Burning Tower.'

She was mesmerised. This could surely be the Hall.

'The Tower,' he was saying, 'is the House of God. Struck by lightning it becomes the devil's abode. It has to do with danger, evil influences, insecurity and fear.'

'It's upside down,' she noticed.

'Yes,' he said, looking up at her briefly, intensely. 'That means the oppression is still there. You are caught, trapped, imprisoned by your fears.' He paused for a moment. 'Does that make sense to you?' he asked slyly.

Not by a blink of the eye did she betray just how well she understood, how uneasy she felt. 'I think this is quite ridiculous,' she told him. She could hear the tremor in her voice.

Before she could stop him, he turned over a fifth card quickly and placed it below the central pair. 'Temperance,' he explained. 'This one relates to your recent past, to what's happening to you now. Look,' he urged her, ' you can see the angel pouring out the essence of life into an urn. The waterfall represents the flowing of the past into the future. Temperance usually means harmony and happiness, but see, it's upside down again.' He looked up at her knowingly. 'That way it stands for sterility and unfulfilled desire.'

'I want you to stop,' she said, but he paid her no attention. She tried to rise but it was as if her body had taken root.

She might never have spoken. 'The sixth card tells the future'

With a huge effort she pushed back her chair. 'I'm not interested,' she said, and, at the same time, he laid down the Devil. He looked up at her inviting her to comment or question.

She stood still for a moment staring at the card.

'Bondage,' he said, 'violence, enslavement, death.' He grinned at her widely. 'That's what it says in the book.'

The skin of her nape chilled, lifting the hairs. She could not move. All the old unnamed fears that had haunted her in the Hall returned. Then the door burst open and the dogs bustled in, followed by Bella, who looked at the spread of cards on the table and clicked her tongue disapprovingly.

'Tck, tck. Is that you bothering Miss Heather with all your nonsense?' she rebuked him. 'I thought I told you to get that table cleared.'

'We're not finished,' he told her sulkily.

The spell was broken.

'I assure you we have, said Heather firmly. With an effort she made herself touch the cards, sweeping them together into a pack and handing them back to Malcy in symbolic denial of all he had said.

'You're wrong,' she said to Bella. 'There is nothing ridiculous about the Tarot.' Then she turned to Malcy. 'If you want my advice, you'll get rid of them. It's a sick game and it could be dangerous.'

After bidding them both good-night, she moved to the door. Malcy was there before her to open it deferentially. As she passed him, he whispered out of Bella's hearing, 'You shouldn't have touched them. That was a big mistake.'

Upstairs alone - Miles had not yet returned from London - she poured herself a brandy and sat in the window until the azure dusk grew dark.

Miles

Miles sat alone in the first-class rail compartment. A long business dinner with an American client had tried his temper and drained his energy. The anxieties of his work wrapped him round like a mantle, uncomfortably tight, as he stared unseeingly at the *Times* crossword on his knee.

Halfway home, he looked out on the darkening landscape, sentinel trees, motionless cattle in painted fields, and it seemed that his life was accelerating. He was rushing, lemming-like, through time towards disaster. Filled with a crushing sense of claustrophobia, he stood up and pulled down the window.

The sky-line was as familiar to him as the plane of his palm. He had made this journey countless times returning to Nightingales from school, from the war, from his work, to his mother, to Lena, to Heather, always with a sense of anticipation. Not tonight. The thought of Nightingales was depressing.

As usual the boy had waited up for him, ready to give an account of the happenings of the day.

'Not tonight, Malcolm,' he said wearily. 'You can lock up and go to bed.'

He was aware that he had given the boy the brush-off rather often of late, but he found it increasingly hard to face his youth and enthusiasm, his ideas for expansion, his general air of complacency.

'Very good, sir. I'll say good-night, then.'

Although he spoke civilly, Miles suspected he was disappointed. He understood it. Malcolm was that *rara avis*, a loyal servant whose existence depended upon house and family. He deserved more support from his master.

'Good night, Malcolm. We'll have a good chat tomorrow.'

Alone, he poured himself a whisky and soda, had a brief look through his mail and felt the tension drain from his limbs. Half an hour later he put out the lights and crossed the hall.

A trick of the darkness or a symptom of his exhaustion, he did not know which, filled the house with ghosts. He knew them all. Their faces caught in paint were as familiar to him as those of the living who inhabited his home. He saw his failure reflected in their eyes, read disappointment in their unsmiling mouths and understood. Loyalty to dead Drakes was as demanding as his responsibility for the living. Like the inner rings of some ancient tree they were as much part of the whole as the outer branches.

Heather was sitting up in bed, reading, waiting for him, when he called in to say good-night.

'Had a good day?' he asked, not wanting more than a perfunctory answer, his hand still on the door handle.

She laid aside her book. He noticed that the anxious line between her brows had deepened of late. 'I need to talk to you, Miles. It's important.'

He was irritated. Could she not see that it had been a long day and that he was dead beat. 'Won't the morning do?'

She was equally annoyed. It was always the same when she had a problem. He procrastinated. 'No,' she said firmly. 'Why do you always run away from me? It's insulting.'

Both of them knew she was talking about something else.

'Steady on,' he said shortly, but he closed the door.

She forced herself to be rational. 'I'm sorry, Miles. I know you're tired, but if I don't speak now, I never will.'

Reluctantly he moved across the room.

'I want Malcolm to go,' she said in a low defiant voice, aware that he might be listening outside the door, and, at the same time, prepared for an argument with Miles.

He was annoyed. On top of a heavy day such a demand seemed to be grossly unreasonable. To conceal his irritation he lit a cigarette and blew out a lungful of smoke.

She waved it away. 'Please Miles, not in here.'

'Sorry,' he said automatically. 'Why on earth do you want to get rid of Malcolm?'

She did not look at him and she spoke too fast. ' He came to my room the other night - and, quite frankly, I found him - 'she groped in her mind for the right word ' - impudent.'

159

'Impudent? How?'

She was foundering. 'Oh, you know, familiar.'

He did not entirely believe her. Malcolm was far too intelligent to risk dismissal on such a charge, but he was not, for the moment, prepared to argue.

'So you want me to give him notice?'

She was immediately hesitant, guilty, no longer so sure of herself.

'What do you think?'

He was silent for a moment. Then he said, 'It's probably for the best. I didn't intend to bring this up just yet but I'm afraid the time may have come to let Nightingales go. The south wing is full of dry rot. The window frames will have to be replaced sooner rather than later and the roof needs extensive repairs. Last year the heating bill alone topped £3000 I've written to sound out the National Trust but there's no certainty they would be interested. Stately homes are two a penny these days. We may have to put it on the market.'

She was aghast. 'But you love this place.'

'Then there's the future to consider,' he continued as if she had not spoken. 'I would not want to burden you and the poor child. It might have been different if Lena and I had had a son. He would have been old enough to consult. As it is…'

'Oh, Miles, are you sure?'

Shamefully she realised her first thought was not for him. All her life she had lived in Nightingales or the Hall. The one had gone irretrievably. To lose the other seemed unthinkable. 'How can you bear even to consider it?'

'To tell you the truth, very easily.' Now that he had told her, spoken his thoughts aloud, the relief was enormous.

'But where would we go? What would we do?'

'The tenants in the Dower House are leaving. We could live there very comfortably, I should think.'

She thought with distaste of the ivy-clad Victorian villa on the outskirts of the village built for a long-dead mother-in-law. 'If Malcolm were to stay, would that make a difference?'

160

He rose from the bedroom chair to get rid of his cigarette and crossed to the window. 'Malcolm has nothing to do with this.'

He looked old and tired. Touched with pity, she got out of bed and crossed the room to join him. Outside against the moonlit sky they could both see the up-stretched arms of the fifty-two poplars that bordered the far shore of the lake. There should have been fifty-four but two had died and their replacements had not survived.

'If we had had another child,' she asked in a low voice, 'would it have made a difference?'

Of course it would have made a difference. Both knew that it was not entirely the dry rot, nor the expense of maintaining Nightingales. It was the lack of an heir that had brought him to this decision. Each felt the pain that hurt the other.

Later as she lay sleepless she fancied she heard the creak of the floorboards outside her room. Let him listen, she thought. There's nothing he can do.

Malcolm

'Malcolm has nothing to do with us, ' was the way he heard it and that was all he heard. It was enough. The plan, devised when the Major had first started to drop hints about the future, was, from that moment, operational.

He glanced at his watch. Well past midnight. *Achtung.*

Back in his room, he changed into dark green coveralls, pocketed a pair of fine rubber gloves, covered his gleaming hair with one of Billy-boy's woollen caps. Cat-sure, he stole downstairs to the cloakroom where the boss kept the garage keys and took the torch always kept beside the fuses boxes. Down in the basement he entered one of the utility rooms to pick up the appropriate tool. Next door, the dogs grumbled. One of them yapped. He poked his head round the door and told it to shut up. Reassured, both of them settled back to sleep.

Outside the night was warm. Bats, caught in the tail of his eye, darted across the star-lit sky. Somewhere not far off a nightingale was singing. He kept to the shadows.

The garages were new, converted from part of the old stable block beyond the tea-room. He unlocked the side door and switched on the torch. The Merc was parked between Miss Snooty's Renault and the estate Landrover, a gleaming white monster of a car that he greatly admired. He breathed in the not unpleasing fumes of petrol and after a moment slipped down on his back and inched below the chassis.

He had taken the car to be serviced at the local garage on two occasions and had questioned the mechanic carefully. He knew exactly what to do. He shone his torch till he had found the nut securing the track rod. Deftly he removed it and let it fall.

'Malcolm has nothing to do with us.' The words re-echoed through his head. He could only guess at their connotation, but whatever the context, the phrase excluded him. No one did that to him. *Nein, Herr Major.* This is *kaput.*

Still, it was a pity about the car.

Heather

Next morning Heather slept late. Miles left without waking her to catch the 7 50 up to town. She never saw him alive again.

The road to the station was clear, unfenced, with beeches and chestnuts that arched greenly overhead. Miles was a fast driver, but accurate. Driving was one of his accomplishments. There had been no rain, no reason to skid and yet he had driven straight into the trunk of a two-hundred year old beech. He had been killed outright.

Accidental death due to the failure of the steering system, the official report stated. The nut was duly found on the garage floor and the mechanic censured for the car had only recently been serviced.

Dark days followed while the harvest flourished and the sun shone. Heather had never before been without older support,

Nanny and her grandmother, her headmistress, Eva and finally Miles. Without him she felt lost, broken, adrift.

Malcy and Bella went about their work with quiet efficiency. Staff and villagers played their part, solicitous, protective. The house was closed to the public. Letters poured in from friends and acquaintances. She took valium and mogadon.

On the evening after the funeral, Malcy came to the breakfast room, his face pale, his features suitably sombre. She was crouched on the window seat staring out at the glassy lake, weighted down with regret, remembering only Miles' virtues, her own shortcomings. It seemed to her that she had given him nothing, neither tenderness nor companionship, not even an heir. Always she had regarded her marriage subjectively, never looked at herself as seen through his eyes, always been jealous for her own rights and comforts, ignoring his. She was consumed with guilt.

Looking up, she saw that Malcy was in the room. 'Bella made you some chocolate, Miss Heather, and there 's a wee drop of something stronger in it to make you sleep.' He placed the tray on a table in front of her. 'Better drink it,' he added with the correct blend of familiarity and respect, 'or I'll get stick.'

She thanked him but he did not go.

'Bella and me,' he continued in the same quiet voice, 'we want you to know how sorry we are about the Major. He was a fine man as I've good cause to know, but you don't need the likes of me to tell you that. Maybe it's not my place to say, but we just want you to know that we'll look after you and Master Will, just the same way we looked after your Granny at the Hall.

Unexpected tears, not the first she had shed, welled up in her eyes. She wanted to thank him but she could not speak.

He gave no indication that he had noticed.

'I'll make Nightingales a place the Major would be proud of,' he said intently. 'I'll watch out for you and the wee fellow. I swear it on the bible.'

As suddenly as they had started, her tears dried up and her shoulders twitched with the familiar frisson of dread. Now was the time to tell him that she was contemplating a change in her life and that he must go. She looked up, knowing it was important to assert her authority. For a moment their eyes met; and she was amazed to read in his expression a naked, blazing need. A kaleidoscope of memories tumbled through her mind. She remembered the snotty-nosed, unwanted child in the push-chair, the waif from the orphanage; his rejected gift to her. For the first time it occurred to her that Nightingales, herself and her son, were Malcy's only family, his only home, Bella's also. The two servants were her responsibility, the only family they had known since the fire at the farm, and so she hesitated.

All she could say was, 'Thank you, Malcolm. I appreciate your's and Bella's loyalty.'

After he had gone she sat on in the twilight, the chocolate untouched. Perversely, it occurred to her that if he had overheard her last conversation with Miles - and she did not honestly believe he had - he could not have chosen a better time or way to plead his case. But that was unjust, paranoid. The truth was that she had never really liked Malcolm and for that reason she needed to be scrupulously fair to him. It was also true that Nightingales, for as long as she chose to keep it, needed both Malcolm and Bella. So did Will. Deprived so cruelly of a father, he was nowhere near ready to be separated from his chosen friend.

She recognised the familiar taste of brandy in the cooling chocolate but it was not enough. She poured herself a cognac and guiltily - Miles had despised the mixture - added a dash of ginger ale.

Bella

Jess Taylor, crazed and embittered by Grace's continued silence, moved to a charitable almshouse for the elderly, so there were no more bike rides across the Common to dig the

164

rich dark soil in her garden or try out new varieties of sweet pea. Just as well. Since the Major's death the work at Nightingales seemed endless and she had only one pair of hands.

Outwardly Bella went about the extra chores as usual, laughing as she had always done, still behind her hand in spite of her new teeth, feeding the workmen who had come to remove the dry rot - an obscure Carolinian charity had come up with a generous grant - taking her full share in preparing Nightingales which had been closed after the Major's death for a gala opening in April 1962. Miss Heather had agreed to Malcy's suggestion that she open the house every day of the week from Easter to Hallowe'en and to use the newly renovated south wing to house exhibitions. Malcy believed he could turn Nightingales into a financial success. He put away the Tarot and spent the evenings juggling with charts, projections and figures.

Inwardly Bella withered. Nor could she account for her dry heart. In contrast, as the visitors poured in, Malcy seemed to swell with contentment and confidence. She did not resent his new self-esteem though sometimes when he boasted that 'our' investments were picking up or that 'we' had been in touch with the Duke of Bedford for advice on this that or the other, she felt obliged to check him.

'Who's this 'we' you're on about?'

'Jealous?' He looked down at her with a grin. He was too cocky by half.

She said no more, yet her anxiety remained. Nanny had used the proprietorial 'we'. With her, the small pronoun denoted loyalty and affection, yet on Malcy's tongue it sounded impudent. Her thoughts swung uneasily around to her employer. Miss Heather allowed him too much responsibility. She should keep him in his place. Yet how could she blame her? Miss Heather needed someone reliable and Malcy was certainly obliging. She, Bella, had no right to criticise Miss Heather after all she'd been through, and no good reason to grudge Malcy his chance. So she frequently told herself, but anxiety lay queasily like moving water at the bottom of her mind.

That first season was a success. Too busy to think, Bella worked her way through the summer months but afterwards when the gates were shut for winter, her depression returned. At night when she knew that Betchworth was snug in the pub throwing darts, she took to wandering through the grounds drinking in the odour of dank leaves, wood smoke and late roses.

One night, leaving the dogs to snuffle in the shrubbery, she was overwhelmed with a longing she could not explain. Instinctively she went to the walled garden where chrysanthemums and Michaelmas daisies glimmered under a misty moon. The gate was locked. Like a prisoner, she grasped and shook the iron stanchions. Suddenly she was weeping for no good reason that she could understand, Turning to cross the dew-soaked law, she leaned down to touch the cold grass, but it was not enough. She sank down on her knees and spread her fingers and kneaded the mossy cushioned lawn, but it was still not enough. Stretching her body flat, she laid her mouth on the grass and touched the thin green blades with her tongue. Pressed hard against the ground, she was engulfed in the damp and chilly comfort of the earth. She had no thoughts, only a longing to sink underground, to become rooted and grafted in soil, to hear the great heart beat of the turning planet.

The dogs found her, snuffling and licking her face, they nosed and pawed her till she rose.

Malcy was in the kitchen working on a stained silver salver. 'What have you been up to? Digging for coal?' He was in an amiable mood.

'I think I'll go back to the Lodge,' she said unexpectedly. Until she spoke, the idea had not occurred to her. Now it seemed the obvious solution to her life. Mrs Bain had written to say her man was ailing and they were thinking of going back to the city.

'No, ye'll no',' he said quietly in heavily accented Scots. Then he picked up a toothbrush and began to work at the blackened grooves around the rim of the tray.

'And who's to stop me?' she retorted, brushing the dirt off her coat with a hard firm hand.

'Oh, you'll be stopped all right, no fear of that,' he said still in the same quiet tone, still not looking at her.

She saw herself at the locked garden gate with her hands on the stanchions. 'Why would you want to stop me?'

'Why would you want to go?' he retorted hard on the heel of the question.

He looked up at her and she saw right down to the source of vision, the child in the noisome privy, arms outstretched. She hesitated and his expression altered.

'You'll never leave me, Crawface,' he mocked. 'You and me, we're stuck with each other. For better for worse, for richer for poorer, till death us do part.' He laughed and turned back to his tray.

She made a final attempt. 'I just wish I had a bit of ground.'

He glanced at her with the indulgence and contempt of a man who has won too easily.

'Is that what this is all about? You should have said.'

Betchworth

On December 26, Samuel Betchworth was dressing the empty dahlia beds with bone meal, two and a half ounces to the square yard. Through a drift of pipe smoke he visualised the summer. A riot of colour, as the catalogues boasted, pools, lakes, oceans of Blithe Spirit, Amethyst, Chinese Lantern and starry yellow Klanstad Kerkrade, but he could not sustain the image for the rage in his head.

Thin to the point of hollowness, with penetrating grey eyes over-hung by shaggy, tobacco-stained brows, he was a surly, uncommunicative man who believed in dominating women, youth and nature in that order. He was confident he had succeeded. His wife had been a slut so he had put her out. His sons were layabouts so he washed his hands of them. The grounds at Nightingales flourished obediently.

In fact Betchworth was a failed dictator. His wife had run off with a greengrocer from Basingstoke, his sons preferred city life, and, in the garden, dahlias had taken over. Every year another herbaceous bed was uprooted to make way for a new variety culled from the latest catalogue.

He had no friends. The labourers employed to mow the lawns, dig and sweep and prune seldom stayed longer than a season. Miss Heather tolerated his surliness for the sake of his skills, Bella kept out of his way, but recently Malcolm had cultivated his acquaintance. Cautiously Betchworth responded. He admired the lad's drive, his dedication to the house which matched his own to the grounds, yet he reserved his judgement. Friendship implied weakness.

How right he had been! Gould was nothing but jumped-up Scottish trash with both eyes to the main chance. Once again, the conversation which had taken place in one of the greenhouses two days previously, ran through his mind.

'Ever thought of market gardening here, Mr Betchworth?' the lad had asked impudently. 'Soft fruit and veg, bedding plants for sale to the visitors? Greenhouses stocked with house-plants, a garden shop, that sort of thing?'

'No,' he'd answered. Just the one word snapped to shut the lad up.

'Trouble is,' the lad had continued not taking the hint, 'trouble is we're short of the readies up at the house. The grounds are a waste pf space as far as they go. We could be coining it in with fruit and veg and plants on sale.'

'Turn my gardens into a bleeding greengrocery? You're off your rocker, mate.' He'd given Gould the rough edge of his tongue. Gone on for a while.

'If you won't, Mr Betchworth, there's others that will.'

The impudence! The sheer bloody cheek of the bastard.

'You threatening me?' The blood had pounded in his head. 'The boss'll have something to say about that.'

'The boss 'll do exactly what I say, 'he'd answered, cool as a cucumber, with a grin all over his pansy face.

That tore it. He'd grabbed a stake from a coleus, and lashing out, caught him on the shoulder. 'Get out of my sight. You'll not touch a spadeful of bleedin' sod in my garden. I'll swing for you first.'

He'd had the last word and the pleasure of seeing Gould hop it, but the conversation nagged in his mind. He realised that he cared about his garden. Such unexpected tenderness bewildered him, lowered him in his own esteem, made him vulnerable. An image of his wife with her hand on the door and pity in her eye whipped through his memory.

Then he saw the rabbit. It sat on its haunches and stared at him. How the blazes had the bugger got in? Someone must have left the gate open. Wouldn't put it past Gould to leave it open out of spite. But this anger was simulated. His hatred of rabbits was more than balanced by his enjoyment of their destruction. As he hurried back to the shed where he kept the rifle loaded for just such an occasion, his heart lightened and the re-iterated conversation in his head faded. He picked up the gun and bided his time.

The explosion raised all the rooks for miles round.

He was not killed outright, but he was as good as dead, blinded with his right arm amputated at the shoulder.

The barrel of his gun had been obstructed. The coroner was of the opinion that Mr Betchworth had shown a sad negligence in the cleaning of his firearm.

Bella

On January 12, Bella was washing up the dinner dishes when Malcy told her the garden was hers.

She laughed in disbelief. 'You're joking. What will Mr Betchworth say when he gets back?'

'Him? He won't be coming back.'

She reached for the special cloth to dry the silver. 'You're daft. How could I do a job like that?'

'You said you wanted a piece of ground. You've got it, hen, like it or no'.'

'Miss Heather'll never agree. You've got to be qualified for a job like that.'

He frowned. 'It's yours, if you do what you're told.'

She laughed again. 'Right. Let's hear it. I kent there'd be a catch somewhere.'

'You've to make it pay.'

He explained. She had visions of sweet peas brightening city window-sills, sugared strawberries in basement bed-sitters. She could feel her heart thump.

'What about the kitchen?'

'Mrs Bushy in the village wants the job. I've already twisted her arm.'

'I'll need to see what Miss Heather thinks.'

'You're on a three months trial. Is that all the thanks I get?'

She looked at him doubtfully, distrusting his motives. 'Why me? There's loads better qualified would jump at the job.'

'You're cheap,' he said crudely.

That convinced her. Mr Moneybags, she called him, for he never spent a penny if he could help it, except on the bairn. He also knew she would have taken the job for nothing more than her keep. Joy swelled up in her till it seemed she was as tall as a mountain, as high as a star, not just at the prospect of the garden, but also because Malcy had fixed it for her.

Heather

Within two and a half years Nightingales was financially secure. Miles' insurance and the sale of a Gainsborough had covered the death duties. The dry rot had been removed. By judicious cuts the household accounts had almost halved. She could have done none of it without Malcolm. His capacity for work was astonishing. His tact and efficiency with the extra staff recruited from the village made him respected if not exactly popular. She was told repeatedly that she was lucky to have him. Almost she believed it.

For Will's seventh birthday, Heather arranged a party, a few local children, villagers and friends. Mrs Bushy, the daily cook, baked a cake shaped like a train and there were games in the drawing-room.

Will spent most of the time clinging to Malcy's arm shrieking with laughter as they bounced though Musical Bumps and the Grand Old Duke of York played with great verve by Angela Macbride on the grand piano to the tinkling accompaniment of her charm bracelet.

Bella, who had changed from her habitual cut-down cords and stout leather boots, into a blue wool dress, looked vivid and happy. To Heather's surprise she seemed undaunted by the gardens. Malcy had more or less blackmailed her into that strange decision to move her out of the kitchen.

'She has no experience of gardening whatsoever. What training has she ever had?' she had argued when he had told her what he wanted.

'The best,' he had told her, adding slyly, 'you'll remember Mr Fraser at the Hall? He and Bella were thick as thieves.'

She did not want to be reminded of that misfortunate whose corrupting influence had probably affected both the farm children.

'I suppose we could let her try,' she had agreed doubtfully.

'You'll lose her if you don't,' he had warned.

So Bella got the job, and though there was little outward change except in her apparel, Heather was aware of her deep contentment. Watching her now with her cheeks scarlet from the fire inside and the frost without, Heather automatically wished that Miles was there, but the thought had become a reflex. With a prick of guilt, she realised that she no longer missed or needed him.

When the guests had gone and Nanny had taken Will to his bath, she helped Malcy tidy the room.

'I'm glad Will has had such a happy day,' she said plumping cushions and picking up pieces of balloon. 'It'll be his last birthday at home for some time.'

She did not notice that Malcy had become still until she turned to him. 'As always, I'm grateful to you…' The words died on her lips.

He was standing with his back to the guarded fire, himself ablaze with anger. His eyes raged. She had not seen that look on his face since she had scorned the Tarot.

'What did you say?' he asked insolently. 'What do you mean "Will's last birthday at home"?'

'Oh that.' She laughed nervously. 'Nothing sinister. Only that this time next year he'll be at school. His father made all the arrangements before he - . It's a special school in Scotland. A marvellous place.'

'No,' he said shaking his head, his voice reverting to Scots. 'Never. The wee fellow stays here.'

She supposed she should not be angry with him for caring about her son. 'I don't think you understand,' she said patiently. 'If Will were normal he would be going to his prep school next year as a matter of course. Because he's the way he is, we ought not to deprive him of a full education.'

'It's you who dis nae understand. How can ye think of it? To send your own bairn away to the jail.'

'It's not like that,' she protested.

'Jist how would you know? How can you tell?'

'Because I've been away to school. I loved it.'

'And so have I. I hated every minute.'

'That was different.'

She thought, I'm pleading with him. I don't have to make excuses and give explanations. She still believed she had to justify herself.

'How do you know the wee man will be content shut up with a bunch of loonies?'

172

She winced at the ugly words. 'They're not - . It's a risk I have to take.'

'You have to take,' he sneered. 'It's his risk. You just want shut of him.'

Stung to anger, she cried, 'Do you think it's easy for me to part with my only child?'

Guilt fanned her anger. She was not at all sure that her motives were entirely pure. Reason told her that Will needed to be educated up to his potential, taught and guided by experts. He was fast becoming wild and unmanageable at home, a danger to himself, controllable only by Malcy. Conscience told her that reason took second place to expediency.

Her anger quietened his. 'There's other schools, ' he urged. 'He could go there by day.'

'I want him to have the best available so that he can learn to survive when I've gone.' She said firmly. This was always the ultimate argument.

'I'll watch out for him.'

'I know that and I'm grateful for all you do but I have to look further ahead. This is what his father wanted.'

'His father's dead,' he said callously. 'You leave Billy-boy to me. I'll see him right.' He moved inches closer. His voice changed. 'I told you, I'd watch out for the both of you. I'll not let you down.'

She sighed and shook her head. 'I'm not going to argue with you, Malcolm.' She got up and would have left the room had he not reached out and caught her by the wrist. His hand was burning hot.

'Why not?' he asked her urgently. 'You could do worse. I'm as good a man as ever the Major was. I can manage the house. The bairn needs a dad. I'd give you anything you wanted. Don't think I can't.'

Taken completely by surprise, she opened her mouth. He drew near enough to put both hands on her upper arms. She could feel their heat and bony strength through the silk of her blouse. Close, she saw that his skin was flushed, unblemished, his eyes unguarded, pleading, his breath like Will's tinged with onion from the salad sandwiches.

When she hesitated, his expression changed from need to triumph. 'I've seen the way you look at me. I've read it in the cards. We could get wed. I'd be good to you.'

Afterwards she was not sure if it was his presumption or her shock that prompted her extreme reaction. In one quick movement she freed herself, raised her right hand and brought it stingingly across his face.

'How dare you! How dare you take advantage of your position here? I can only put it down to the fact that you are upset about Will.'

He stared at her in unfeigned surprise, then, as the colour raced into his cheek, his expression hardened. She knew had gone too far. She was afraid. Instinctively she knew better than to show it. Before he could speak, she moved to the window and turned her back on him.

'I want us both to forget that this conversation ever happened,' she said icily, managing somehow to control the tremor in her voice, though inwardly she was shaking. 'I'm prepared to do that if you are.'

He ignored her words. 'You'll be sorry,' he threatened. 'One of these day you'll change your tune.'

'That's enough,' she commanded, amazed at her outward calmness. 'Now go if you please. I have other things to do.'

He took his time, but he went. She waited for the door to shatter shut but he left it open, on an insolent gape. When she was sure he had gone she went straight for the drinks' cupboard in her private sitting room and poured herself a generous measure of Courvoisier. Her teeth chattered against the rim of the glass.

As always she could not hold on to her anger. Perhaps it was her fault; by her increasing reliance on him, she had unwittingly encouraged him. If that were true, then she had been cruel. Any other man who had proposed marriage to her would at least have received a courteous refusal, a word of thanks. Guilt engulfed her.

She was still agonising over the scene when Mrs Bushy rang up from the kitchen extension to tell her that Malcy had gone out. 'In a right mood, he was,' she complained. 'Just took the Renault and left without a word. Something's upset him. Do you want me to serve you dinner before I go?'

Now her guilt was coloured by a new anxiety. What if he did not come back? It would take months to find, let alone train, a suitable replacement. Few had Malcy's knowledge, his dedication and his drive. If he left, Bella might go too and what would happen to the garden with spring approaching? And there was Will. He would break his heart if Malcy were no longer here.

She realised that Malcy had made himself indispensable and not only to Nightingales.

She kept the brandy bottle at her side.

At twenty minutes past two the next morning Bella heard him return. He passed her basement bedroom door on stealthy feet. In the kitchen he made himself a pot of tea and two ham sandwiches.

On his way to the attic he paused outside Heather's door, but she heard nothing. Brandy had induced a deep, forgetful sleep.

Harry

Harry Fever eased his sixteen stone out of the pampered 1930 Rolls and paid the garrulous retired army sergeant who kept the car park at Nightingales. Instead of taking the direct route to the house, he decided to follow a path through the bluebell carpeted beech grove that led to what the painted sign-post described as *Pleasure Gardens*.

He had not visited Nightingales since just before Lena's death in that black-edged spring of '43. At Miles' funeral he had promised himself to keep in touch with the widow which had resulted in two perfunctory cards a year at Christmas, and,

175

enclosing a cheque, at the boy's birthday. Three years later, obliged to call on a client within ten miles of Nightingales, he decided he ought to visit Heather.

As the trees thinned and woodland gave way to great bushes of overblown rhododendrons - Lena had once told him she had counted three hundred in the grounds - his hands sweated and his asthmatic breathing quickened. The memory of Lena at the front door, her body already corpselike, his violet eyes huge and pitiful in her thin face, with the old house pulled round her like a shroud, was as painful as it was precious. No other woman had remotely approached her shrine within his heart. For her sake he had intended never to visit Nightingales again.

Yet he had liked Miles just as he had once loved Lena long before he had introduced her to his friend, and, for the sake of that comradeship, he had come back.

As he emerged from the shrubbery and saw the great house, cared-for and complacent under white bowling clouds, the parterre garden lavish with roses, the great sweep of nourished lawns sheltered by magnificent trees including Lena's beloved Japanese cedar, the curved line of the lake gaudy with children in colourful paddle boats, he realised that this was not the Nightingales he remembered.

Although there was a strong streak of sentimentality in Harry's personality, he was also a businessman, a stockbroker of considerable reputation in the city. He expected efficiency and good manners from his own employees, and, as he walked through the grounds peopled with families enjoying the plentiful amenities from croquet to clock-golf, ice-cream and home-made teas, he stopped to talk to the discreet officials. He was impressed.

He was also relieved. Until that moment he had not grasped how little he had wanted to become involved with Nightingales again. The past, although permanently enshrined, was over. He led a comfortable bachelor existence, frequently dining with friends of both sexes, golf at weekends and September holidays on a Scottish grouse moor with a client. Now, it seemed, he could return to London with his memories intact, his obligations to Miles met. With a lighter step he entered the house to look for Heather, congratulate her on her enterprise, and see the poor boy, his somewhat neglected godson.

Angela Macbride was on duty in the hall. Attracted not so much by his air of prosperous abundance, though she liked big men, but more by the rich quality of his cigar-smoker's voice, she was reluctant to let him go. Without too much effort she sold him a comb of honey 'produced by one of our villagers'; a guide brochure; 'one of our assistants is a local historian' and a herb pillow; 'my own humble effort. You'll find you sleep like a top'.

'I congratulate you all,' he told her sincerely.

'Thank you,' she said beaming at him. 'Yes, I think we're on the right path. We were all so afraid that when the Major was killed - such a tragedy - that Nightingales would be closed for good.' She looked beyond him and her smile widened, ' Ah, here is one of our team now. I do advise you to take the guided tour. Malcolm is excellent.'

He turned to see a pale, slight young man on his way out. On hearing his name he turned expectantly. 'Malcolm,' Miss Macbride gushed, 'I'm sure this gentleman would appreciate a tour.'

'Certainly,' he said in a quiet educated voice. 'Do you know the house at all, sir?'

'A long time ago,' he answered. He had not intended to go through the rooms he had once known well but he was curious to find out more about this good-looking, self-assured young man. As he followed him along the set route roped and signposted for one-way traffic he concentrated on his guide rather than his words.

He could not place him. There were so many contradictions. At first glance he looked no more than eighteen years - it was doubtful if he needed to shave more than once a week - yet he had the shrewd expression and self-confidence of a mature man. He appearance was casual, yet calculatedly so. His navy blazer

177

and fawn slacks were too well-pressed, his shoes too highly polished. The deferential way he ushered Harry through doors seemed at variance with the arrogance he showed in handling items of interest and value. Although his accent was flawless, his manners were too careful for good breeding. Harry suspected he was no gentleman.

The house was in excellent condition as far as Harry could tell. The breezy sunlight set the chandeliers twinkling. There were flowers in every room, gracefully but not artificially arranged. He commented on them.

The young man's smile was suddenly possessive. 'Mrs Percy-Drake arranges them herself.'

Watching him reach to unlock one of the glass-fronted bookcases in the library, Harry realised that he had seen him before. At Miles' funeral he had taken one of the cords. Harry had assumed he had been a relative of Heather's. He wondered now if he were a cousin or younger brother.

'You might be interested in this, sir,' Malcolm said handing him a Moroccan leather-bound notebook which contained faded but recognisable water-colours of the house and grounds dated 1807. 'Humphrey Repton's improvements on Capability Brown's original lay-out. You can see that the ballustraded garden was his idea. He brought colour back to the gardens in the belief that landscaping should act as a back-drop to plants and flowers rather that be an end in itself. We have always kept very much to that tradition here at Nightingales - inside and out.'

Harry turned over the pages. The young man was beginning to annoy him. What did he know of Nightingales and its traditions. Lena would have known how to keep the fellow in his place.

'This must be an exceedingly valuable document,' he said a little stiffly, handing it back.

The young man took it with a smile that was not quite ingratiating. 'We don't show it to everyone, sir.'

Harry was aware that he had charm, but, on this occasion, he was not moved by it. He looked at his watch.

'I hope you'll sign the visitor's book before you go.' Malcolm indicated the table in the vestibule and offered a pen.

'You one of the family?' he asked casually as he sprawled his signature across the page.

He neither denied or acknowledged the question. 'I'm Malcolm,' he replied, a little surprised as if Harry should have known.

Harry did know. This must be Miles' 'Scottish retainer' as he had humorously called him. It had not occurred to Harry that he would look so young. Yet it made sense. Since his early years, Miles had always shown a certain naivety in his assessment of quality, judging character by outward appearances, impressed by good manners and good looks.

'Of course. Malcolm.' He said smoothly. 'Malcolm,' he repeated, 'I wonder if you would be so good as to let Mrs Percy-Drake know that I'd like to see her?'

'I regret, Mr Fever,' he replied after a quick glance down at the visitor's book, ' Mrs Percy-Drake is away for the day. I'll tell her you called.'

Instinctively Harry disbelieved him, and, uncharacteristically, for Harry was not a vindictive man, it seemed important to prove the servant wrong.

He started his search in the walled garden. A woman was weeding among a clump of dorondicums. 'Excuse me,' he interrupted her. 'I'm looking for Mrs Percy-Drake. I'm an old friend of the family.'

She rose. In spite of her shortness, he was aware of her strength, not so much in the breadth of her shoulder and power of her wrist, but internally, a force that shone forth from her huge deep-set black eyes. She regarded him without curiosity but with a benignity that betokened approval.

'If she's at home, she'll likely be in the herb garden. It's private.'

In a strong Scots accent she gave him directions.

'How is she?' Harry asked impulsively. There was something about this little woman that invited trust.

'Needin' friends,' was all she said. Then she smiled showing big, white, too even, china teeth.

The herb garden was a sun-trap enclosed within a thick high holly hedge, grassed over except for one wide border full of great clumps of lavender, rosemary and lemon balm. This, he was to discover, was his godson's domain on fine days when the grounds were full of visitors where Nanny pushed him in his swing or played with him in the revolving summerhouse on colder days.

Here he found Heather. She was mending an old tapestry, bent over the tiny faded stitches when Harry opened the wrought-iron gates. She recognised him immediately.

'Harry, how nice! What a wonderful surprise,' she called out, putting down her work.

He embraced her, feeling her thinness through the silk stuff of her dress.

'Your Malcolm said you were out,' he remarked later when they were both seated in the shade of the summerhouse. He felt rancorous towards the servant for misleading him.

'Oh, did he? Well we should have been. It's Will's day for the centre but when it turned out so fine - it's not as if they can do anything…Don't tell Malcy, though.' She laughed, but he sensed she was not entirely joking.

'It's hardly his business, is it?' he said dryly.

'Anything to do with Will is Malcolm's business,' she said soberly, 'and thank God for it.' They both turned to look at the child who was playing in a small sand-pit on the other side of the summerhouse under the watchful eye of his nursemaid. 'Nanny,' she called out, 'be an angel and bring us some tea, will you?'

When they were alone, Harry reached out to touch her hand. 'Well, my dear, how are you really?' he asked kindly.

Though he did not know it, it was his capacity for caring expressed in that deep, rich smoker's voice, that had once

180

attracted Lena. It had an immediate effect on Heather. She wanted, suddenly, to cry. 'Surviving, ' she answered.

He saw then that she was not the confident, efficient, chatelaine that Nightingales and his first glimpse of her had suggested. She seemed nervy, and, looking at her closely, he noticed that her looks had changed. The rich brown hair that had been such a feature of her beauty looked lifeless and her skin had coarsened.

'A bit of a burden all this, is it?' he asked indicating with a wave of his hand the house and grounds.

She did not answer directly. Instead she said, 'Did you know that Miles planned to sell up?'

He had not known but he was not surprised. Miles had wanted rid of the place when Lena died. It was his mother who had forced on him a strong sense of duty, his mother who had engineered his second marriage.

'Why do you stay, then?'

'It's a question I constantly ask myself.' She smiled with a pretty air of deprecation, shrugged and added, 'What else would I do?'

He was aware that she had charm. 'A great many things to judge from the way you run this place.'

She shook her head. 'Malcolm runs Nightingales.'

'Is that a good idea?' he asked carefully. It was too soon to criticise.

She laughed. 'It's an excellent idea as far as I'm concerned. He does it very well.'

'He struck me as a - 'he hesitated, searching for the right word ' - as a pushy sort of chap.'

'I can handle Malcolm,' she replied with a hint of defiance that made him wonder.

Nanny came back with tea on a painted tray which she set down on a wicker table.

'Tea-time, Will,' she called, holding out a red plastic cup. 'Come and get your juice.'

181

He looked up. His placid stare focused. He saw Nanny's smiling mouth, the red mug temptingly held out, his mother pouring tea. Between them sprawled a monster, fat with gigantic chins, who ate up boys like bread and butter. Fee-fi-fo-fum. He screamed.

When the nursemaid tried to take him in her arms, he ran away from her. His face reddened, his eyes screwed up in their sockets, saliva ran in glistening threads from his mouth as he ran in mindless circles round the sandpit.

'Fetch Malcolm,' she told the nursemaid, and, to Harry who had started to rise, embarrassed and disturbed by the tantrum, she murmured, 'there's nothing you can do, I'm afraid.'

By now Will had cast himself down on the grass, kicking and tearing at the turf, his body convulsed with sobs. He would not let her near him.

At last Malcolm appeared followed closely by the nursemaid. Without a word, he picked up the heavy child. Plump brown arms reached out and clung to his neck while his legs gripped round his waist. All the time Malcolm spoke softy, inaudibly into his ear and rocked him in his arms.

'I don't know what set him off,' Heather said almost apologetically.

'Can't you see the wee man's scared?' said Malcolm with a genuine tenderness that surprised Harry.

'He was perfectly all right a moment ago.' Heather's voice shook as she turned to Harry. 'He hasn't had a tantrum like this for weeks. I was beginning to hope he had outgrown them.'

'Wee Billy-boy's fine so long as he knows you,' said Malcolm smoothly, adding as he turned to look at Harry, 'he doesn't take kindly to strangers.' Although his eyes were bland, expressionless, Harry was aware of his hostility.

Still holding the child, though he was a considerable weight, he spoke to him in an entirely different voice. 'Hey, wee fellow, let's go and feed the ducks, if Mummy can spare us a sandwich.'

Nanny held up the plate. After a moment the boy reached out, took one and bunched it up in his fist. Then he gave a long shuddering sigh and laid his head down on Malcolm's neck.

When they had gone, Heather tried to smile. 'I think we need a drink.'

Impulsively Harry leaned towards her. 'Let me take you out to dinner.'

Bella

That same night in June, Bella picked up what she called her first-aid bag which contained twine, secateurs, a small fork and trowel, and, starting off in the kitchen gardens, began her rounds.

Evening was the best time of the day. After Tim, who mowed the lawns with his outrageously long hair caught back in a rubber band, and Copperwheat, who was happiest with tomatoes but adaptable, and the part-timers - students and pensioners from the village who worked in the greenhouses and nursery beds - had gone home for the day, the gardens belonged to Bella.

'Time you were sprayed,' she said to the raspberries, stooping to feel the hard white nubs of setting fruit. 'Lift your head, hen' to a great pale blue shaft of delphinium as she adjusted the stake. 'There, now, you can breathe,' to a cluster of pink sidalcea as she forked out a dock weed. 'My, you're early this year,' to the sinister dark cowls of Monks Hood.

She picked up toffee papers, snipped off dead heads, noted a trace of black fly in the broad beans and silver leaf in the orchard. First thing tomorrow the jobs she noted tonight would be allocated to her workforce.

She was aware that the garden staff did not altogether trust her, but she was not bothered. Mr Betchworth had kept graphs and lists and diaries dating back over fifteen years containing weather notes, dates for planting and cropping and endless comments on his dahlias, written in an upright legible hand.

Bella kept it all in her head. She was an instinctive gardener knowing by the taste of the wind when frost was likely, by the feel of the soil when to sow.

'What's the good of it on paper? It's here I need it,' she answered outright criticism, tapping the side of her head, 'and here,' holding out her earth-etched hands.

When it came to cropping, however, Malcy insisted that she keep daily records of every lettuce and punnet picked.

'You grow them,' he told her. 'I'll sell them, but mind, there's to be a profit,' he added unnecessarily. Bella needed no telling.

At first she had been daunted by the responsibility. No longer. A big garden was essentially the same as a small garden and she had all day and plenty of extra hands to tend it. Sure there were many things she did not know; how to cure leaf spot on the water lilies and when to mulch Jerusalem artichokes, but she had a tongue in her head and she could usually find someone who knew. She filed away the answers in her head, nor had she forgotten any of the things Fraser had taught her at the Hall. She could summon him to her side and hear him say, 'Pepper the peas before you sow them, hen, if you don't want the mice to eat them,' or 'catch-crop your lettuces and spring onions between the celery trenches before you earth up. Never waste good ground.'

The final treat in a day full of pleasure was to visit her favourite flowers. On the ground that Betchworth had planned for dahlias, Bella planted sweet peas, four hedges of them trenched and composted, sown under glass, planted out and tended in her free time. Loving them so much, it seemed wrong to spend time on them in working hours, so she saved them up for the evenings.

The sky turned golden and the rooks grew drowsy as she snipped off shoots and tendrils and tied the main stems to the stakes. After a day of sun there were already buds on the rows. Miss Heather would have a picking soon.

184

Sometimes on those mellow evenings she remembered a past spent scrubbing stone flags and scraping out dead ash from the old range. The relief when she realised these tasks were no longer hers was always a wonder.

After a quick look round the rose beds in the parterre she crossed the lawn towards the lake. A small breeze shivered the poplars, fingered the water and stirred the paddle boats tied up to the miniature pier. Ducks roosting on the island, breasted the water towards her hopefully, their offspring in tow.

'I'm as hungry as you are, pets,' she told them, scattering crumbs from the heel of a stale loaf she had pocketed earlier.

A skitter of coots skimmed the far end of the water where the lilies grew. She bent down to examine a leaf. That mould was still there. Copperwheat would need to go over the whole lot in the morning.

A nightingale 'tucked' and 'kerred' in alarm as she crossed the strip of woodland that led to the drive. She peered down at the gravel but it was now too dark under the trees to see if that new weed-killer was working. A pool of silence in the rustling night made her look up. Malcy was standing under a flowering lime. She sensed his mood. Like the other night creatures within his orbit, she grew still. They regarded each other in the glimmering dusk.

Then he said, 'She's still out. A rich fat bastard crooks his finger and like a bitch on heat she follows.'

His voice was harsh but not loud. The silence around them deepened. In her contentment, Bella had grown careless. Her mind, like night-scented stock, was now wide open. She saw clearly what she had not allowed herself to recognise, understood what she had not wanted to know. There, in the man before her, stood the bairn no one had wanted. Her pity was too big for words. At the same time, she knew she had to speak.

'Miss Heather's no' for you, Malcy.'

He was not as angry as she had expected.

185

'Aye, she is. She comes with Nightingales and the wee fellow. No other bastard's going to get her.'

She tried again. Remembering why he had got her the gardens, she believed she had some influence over him.

'Miss Heather's entitled to choose her own friends, who she goes out with and who she entertains.'

'Not if she knows what's good for her,' he said softly.

She clicked her tongue. 'Och, Malcy, I've no patience with you. Miss Heather's pleased with you, I don't doubt, for the way you work, but that doesn't give you the right to run her life.'

'You'd better believe it.'

She saw the white gleam of his teeth in the dark.

Harry

Harry was not sure why he had come back. Each of the four times he had taken Heather out to dine he had asked himself the same question. He was concerned for her of course, not just on account of the child but also for the responsibilities she had inherited. He wondered about her future. She had turned out to be a little too clinging, nervy, and, in his opinion, she drank too much. All his instincts warned him against further involvement with her, and yet, against his better judgement, he had come back.

He did not allow himself to become easily attracted to women, fearing rejection or ridicule because of his size. He did not think of Heather as a sexual partner, nor did he want a wife. He enjoyed bachelorhood. The more he saw of marriage, the better he appreciated his own freedom and lack of responsibility. There had been times in the past when he had thought he would have liked a son, but no longer. When he saw the hippies and drop-outs sired by his contemporaries and now poor Miles' son, he was thankful he was childless.

He did not think it was altruism that continued to bring him back to Nightingales. He was too lazy for good works. It was not until she was seated beside him in the car that he understood. She was obviously so pleased to be there.

'Where to, to-night?' he asked perfunctorily, for he had already half decided to take her to an Italian restaurant recommended by a friend, but, instead of leaving the choice to him as she usually did, she turned to him impulsively. 'Do you know what I would really like?'

He glanced at her briefly. She was wearing dusky silk, the colour of clover. Her fists were clenched nervously over her thumbs in a characteristic gesture. Her mouth was slightly open showing the tips of her teeth.

'I'd like to see your home.'

'Of course. Easily done, but let's eat first, shall we?'

'The thing is,' she said after thanking him. 'I really need to talk to you, Harry. Seriously.'

He did not want her confidence but he knew there was no avoiding it.

'Will is due to go to a residential school soon. I'm going to have a battle royal with Malcolm when the time comes. You've seen how they are together? I want to do what's right for poor Will. The worry is driving me crazy. What do you think?'

Now was his chance to say what had been in his mind since his first visit to Nightingales, and, what he had hinted at whenever the opportunity arose, that of course she should get rid of Malcolm, that it was iniquitous to allow a servant so much influence, but he hesitated, aware of her need for support and not sure he wanted to become involved.

'If I do send Will to school,' she continued, 'Malcy will probably leave and Bella will go with him. I can't manage Nightingales without them.'

He saw the trip wire though it was well concealed. He could advise her to sell Nightingales. If Miles had been prepared to do so, why should she have qualms; or he could advise her to sack Malcolm if he made trouble. No one was indispensable. Either answer, however, involved himself in her future.

'Maybe Malcy's right,' she continued wretchedly, 'Maybe I should keep Will at home. On the other hand he is becoming difficult and would probably benefit from a bit of discipline and some sort of education. What do you think I should do?'

He resisted the temptation to tell her exactly what he thought. 'Let me sleep on it,' he said firmly.

'You promise to tell me what you think?'

'Of course.'

'Oh, Harry, you can't think what a relief it is to have someone to talk to. I feel so pressurised at home.'

'In the end it has to be your decision,' he said with a hint of impatience that she sensed at once.

'Sorry to be such a bore,' she said apologetically.' The trouble is I get so confused between what I ought to do and what I want to do, but of course you're right. It does have to be my decision.'

They ate in a small restaurant a street away from the tall three-storey house off Reuben Gardens that had been in the Fever family from the turn of the century. Since the death of his grandmother, Harry had altered it very little. He felt comfortable with the worn Indian carpets, the huge upholstered leather chairs and Tenniel prints in the living room. He was proud of his Whistler original and the good silver on the mahogany sideboard in the dining room and the library which contained a first edition of Trollope's Barchester novels, displayed in a late 19th century revolving bookcase he had picked up in a sale. A dull house possibly when compared with Nightingales but *Dulce Domum* to him none the less.

'I feel like Mole,' he said as he found his keys, 'about to let you into my "shabby dingy little domain". Don't be too disappointed.'

She looked up at the bay windows painted in black and white, the lilac and laburnum bushes in the garden. 'If you only knew how much I covet a house like this.'

As soon as he unlocked the outer door, he knew that there was something wrong; a subtle disturbance of the atmosphere, a

188

faint unpleasant odour, the sense of an alien presence. Uneasily he opened the vestibule door. Nothing to be seen in the hall, but the feeling of disquiet deepened. Seizing a stick from the umbrella stand, he told her to stand back as he opened the drawing room door. The stench was now overwhelming as he snapped on the light.

The leather chairs were slashed with deep knife cuts, one of them thrust so deep that the stuffing had spilled out. Papers from the bureau were torn and scattered, pictures smashed, the walls streaked with faeces.

'My God,' Heather whispered at his elbow. 'What's happened?'

The other rooms were, if possible, worse, the Whistler savagely knifed. Framed photographs of his family and friends, including one of Miles and Lena, strewed the carpet of his bedroom, the counterpane was soaked in urine, and, along the length of the Regency striped wallpaper above the bed, the obscene words traced out in shit, 'Fuck you, fat arse'.

The stench was feral as if wild beasts had rampaged through the house.

The police arrived within five minutes. She overheard a young constable murmur to his superior officer when he thought themselves out of earshot, 'Cor, someone had it in good and proper for the poor guy.'

Nothing, it seemed, had been stolen. There were no clues, except for a pair of filthy yellow rubber gloves, Boots brand, which did not belong to Harry. The forensic report suggested that the vandal or vandals had probably worn socks over their shoes as well as gloves for there were no prints of any description. Entry had not been forced as a downstairs cloakroom window had not been properly closed.

Harry was stunned. Such evidence of hatred appalled him. He sat down on a chair in the kitchen - the only room that had not been vandalised - and gasped asthmatically. Heather called his doctor who sent for an ambulance. She would have gone with him but he waved her away. Unreasonably, unkindly, with no possible justification, he connected the incident with her.

Afterwards, in his right mind, he believed that his rejection of her in his hour of need was an instinctive act of self-defence. All very well to play 'good old Harry' in the background, but when it came to the point he did not really want her in his life.

Heather

Heather felt the silence, like the November mist outside, settle in her soul. One by one, the old anxieties re-ran on well-worn tracks.

Harry.

She missed not so much his person but rather the idea of Harry. Though certainly not in love with him, she would have married him if he had asked her. Harry represented a doorway out of Nightingales which she had deliberately set out to go through. She still winced when she remembered how firmly it had been shut. Her messages, flowers and offers of help had been rejected. One short note of thanks, nothing more. She had not heard from him again.

Nightingales.

For the first time since the end of the season the house was quiet. Under Malcy's direction, squads of villagers had scoured, polished and shrouded the public rooms; mildew, woodworm, repair jobs noted and marked down for attention. In the grounds, the paddle-boats, swings and croquet hoops had been lifted and stored. Leaves had been swept up and burned. In the garden, while Tim and Copperwheat turned the soil, Bella concentrated on Christmas flowering plants in the greenhouses. By the end of October most of the villagers had gone and the silence, broken only by Malcy's shrill whistling while he painted the moulded ceiling in the library, or Will's occasional cry penetrated the quietness.

Will. Always her thoughts came back to Will.

190

She had been sorting music in a Sheraton canterbury, great yellowing books bound in black leather, containing the works of Chopin and Beethoven which had belong to Miles' grandmother who had been an accomplished pianist, when Nanny came in. She was dressed in a fringed afghan coat that smelled faintly of goat. It was her afternoon off.

Nanny's boyfriend was Tim who wore his mousy hair combed back and contained in a rubber band.

'I'm going out now. Will is in the playroom. Do you want to come or will I tell Malcy?'

Heather thought she had said, 'Tell Malcy,' but afterwards Nanny swore with tears that she had said, 'I'll come.'

William

Will squeezed the saturated paper between his hands and opened them. He had made a duck. He liked ducks. He wanted to feed the ducks. He looked up. No Nanny. No Malcy. No matter. He knew where the ducks lived. He was a big boy now.

He tried to open the playroom door. It was not locked. No one about. Into the kitchen. No one there. In the bread-bin there were two loaves, one with slices so he took a handful, squashed them up and stuffed them into his pocket.

The back door was very stiff. He needed to use both hands.

'I'm a big boy,' he said pleased with himself.

The sky was very close and white and nipped his fingers and his nose. His breath came out like smoke. He stood on the gravel blowing smoke till he was out of puff. He forgot about the ducks.

After a while he picked up a pebble and threw it on to the grass. It made dark streaks on the silver-wet lawn. He threw another and another till he made a bare patch on the drive. Then he remembered the ducks.

He ambled across the lawn down to the lake. Water sprayed up as he shuffled his feet. He shunted around in circles making patterns on the grass.

191

The lake was as flat as a grey plate. He stood at the end of the pier and looked down. A boy stared back at him.

He didn't feel too sure about the boy. He moved away for a moment but when he peered down again the boy was still there staring right back at him with unsmiling eyes. He dropped a piece of bread on the boy. The ducks swarmed round and the boy disappeared into the weeds. He was glad about that.

The ducks ate all the bread, and, after some beak dives and tail kicks, swam back towards their island. The boy came back.

'They're my ducks,' he told him firmly.

The boy seemed to be speaking to him but he couldn't hear him. The boy looked cross. He didn't like him staring.

'Go away,' he said but the boy still stared.

He took a step forwards and stamped on him.

The boy caught his foot and yanked him into the icy water and the weeds held him tight.

Malcolm

Malcy stood with his left hand curved round the oak cornucopia of fruit that adorned the newel post at the top of the first flight of stairs.

Without the protective drugget used in the tourist season, the royal blue carpet was threadbare in patches and sun-bleached. Fifty years old if it was a day. Red, he thought, rich as plums with a thick velvet pile... Bold, no doubt, against the crimson satin-finished paper, but a coat of cream paint on the moulded plaster panels that underlay the second flight of stairs would bring out the flesh tones of the cavorting goddesses in the huge gilt-framed pictures and lighten the predominance of his favourite colour, red. His hand tightened as he visualised long beams of sunlight from the staircase falling in pools at his feet.

He would suggest it. Permission would be granted eventually.

He was always right whether in the choice of paint, price of guide-books or employment of casual labour. Yet every time she repeated the same dreary ritual of doubt, hesitancy, procrastination, finally followed by a grudging agreement, not because she ever had better ideas, but because they came from him. Not his place to have ideas.

She'd asked the fat ass for advice on that carriage clock that he had already taken to the Museum of London which had an identical model. The fat ass had said try Sotheby's and she had beamed on him as if Confucius himself had spoken.

A new carpet, though. He might have a tough job selling her that idea. Cost a bomb. She had enough money, just. He kept the household accounts, marked down each day's takings set against expenses with scrupulous care. Worked late in the office every night counting each ticket receipt, every cup of tea and postcard sold. On Friday nights he presented the books to her. She'd stopped checking them, though, just signed them and thanked him - irritating habit that, always thanking him for what he was paid to do - not that she ever needed to check up on him. He was honest. Almost. Lately he had opened a new account in the name of William Drake. He aimed to cream off roughly a hundred quid each month for the wee fellow, just in case of any funny business. Week by week it mounted. Nothing noticeable, nothing that would hurt Nightingales or herself. For example that bill for paint. Came to £282. Easy to fake the receipt and write in an extra tenner or so. Undetectable now that he paid most of the bills by cash.

As for his own account, nothing to complain of there. The bible still held a sheaf of bank books, but lately, since his windfall, he'd branched out. Had a London stockbroker like the fat ass who asked no questions and did as he was told. Not so easy to estimate exactly how much he was worth but it was over fifty grand. He still smiled to remember that particular night. The Wheel of Fortune had come up between Death and the Magician and he'd walked away with five grand.

It had rained on the evening he'd paid a visit to the fat ass's residence, bucketed down so he'd taken shelter in Belsize Park. A tall secluded house it was, isolated from the road by

193

overgrown bushes. A broken window in the basement let him in to what he believed to be an empty house. It stank of cats. He'd climbed the stairs to the first floor landing when he heard the radio. *Any Questions* boomed from one of the bedrooms. 'If the team members were left a fortune what would they buy?' Ha.

The door was open, the stench outrageous. Then he got the fright of his life. An old woman was staring at him, propped up on a sea of pillows in a wide brass bed. She was well dead. No wonder the cats had gone.

He had remembered Nanny as he had picked up the handbag, cheap imitation leather, empty except for her pension book and a war-time Identity card. Out of habit, he searched the room.

There was money everywhere, behind the wardrobe, between the drawers, hidden within the folds of ancient darned underwear, behind the framed cross-stitch text on the wall, under the edge of the carpet, fivers and tenners neatly folded and sealed in brown manilla envelopes with the correct amount written on the outside.

He had not gone near the bed but the rest of the house had revealed surprising hoards. It was the greatest game of hide-and-seek he had ever played. His canvas bag which already held the filthy coveralls he had worn in Hampstead bulged as an hour later he let himself out by the back door, waited under the dripping bushes until the coast was clear and caught a bus to the station.

He hadn't found it all. Some days later the *Express* blazed a headline, '£5000 left to Hampstead Cats'. The doctor, summoned by the police, had found a will and further caches under the mattress and between the sheets.

He had put half his loot into Premium Bonds. With his luck he would be bound to win.

Slowly, surely his plans were maturing. Crawface was well stuck into her garden, Nightingales his, all but in name. Will was entirely his. There remained only Miss Snooty.

He did not altogether blame her for her rejection of him. He'd have despised her now if she'd fallen for what he'd been then - a comparative pauper. She'd soon see the light. With a hundred grand in his accounts he'd be worth a duke's daughter. She'd come running when she knew, pour his tea, warm his slippers, yes dear, no dear, three bags full, dear. A champagne wedding with the guest list like a page out of Debrett's and the fat ass to give her away. He'd order that claret carpet throughout the house, best Axminster. A wedding gift from Malcolm to Malcolm. He'd shut the gates of Nightingales for good, keep the trash out and live like a fucking lord.

Shoulders straight, fingers tipping the banisters, chin at an arrogant tilt, he descended the stairs and paused to look out of the landing window.

The silvery lawn was circled and slashed with dark streaks as if some animal had cut crazy capers on the grass. But the old dogs had long ago been put down.

Billy-boy.

Heather looked up from the music books. 'I thought he was with you.'

The playroom was empty.

He ran down the sloping lawn, his feet whipping through the wet grass. He saw him almost at once. The water was no more than three feet deep over a mat of weed.

He knelt down to reach for him. It took all of his strength for the child was water-logged. Dragging him out on to the pier, he pushed and pummelled his chest. Water leaked from his open mouth. He lifted his head and breathed into his mouth. The ribs moved a bit and for a moment he was fooled.

There was a weight on his own chest greater than any volume of water, a wetness in his own eye that blinded him and he breathed as if he were drowning. He thought he heard the baying of hounds but it was only the sound of his own sorrow as he crouched over the small body clasped in his arms.

195

That night after the doctor and the police had gone and Heather lay deep in drugged sleep, Malcy drove out into the dank November night. One side of his brain was alert, able to make decisions to take this road or that turning, knew how much petrol remained in the tank, exactly what he was going to do, aware of the risk, the need for caution.

The other part of him was in nightmare, constantly reliving that journey from the lake to the house through the wet grass with the dead child in his arms. That part of him was weeping, the insistent howl of misery. That part of him was confused so that at times he held the child, at times he was the child, unwanted, damaged, dead.

But the cleavage in his mind was not complete. The wire that linked the two halves was anger, a stunning deadly rage that could only be assuaged by revenge.

'She'll pay. She has to pay. I'll make her pay.' These were the words that chattered continually in his head.

At 2 35 am he slowed down behind a white Lotus Elan. A woman was at the wheel. For several miles, he followed her along a twisting country road under trees until she turned into a short narrow lane. Her headlights outlined a white harled bungalow. The house was in darkness.

He stopped the Renault at the side of the road, careful not to leave tyre marks on the grass verge, switched off his lights and drew on a pair of supple leather gloves that matched the smooth texture of his leather jacket. Then he got out of the car and walked down the tar-macadam lane.

The headlights of her car outlined the woman struggling to open the garage door. She had long white-blond hair and she wore a cream mock-fur coat over a black evening gown. He heard her swear.

'Need any help?' he asked on the edge of the light.

She whipped round.

'Where did you spring from?' She handed him the key. 'Bloody locks!'

While he wrestled with it, she stood at his elbow hugging her coat across her breast. 'I saw your car. Bleeding headlights blinded me. I suppose you followed me from the club.'

He opened the doors wide and handed her the key.

She saw his face.

'It's not on, mate, so you can just eff off.'

He caught her arm and spun her round forcing her back into the head-lit garage. The engine of her car was still running.

'Get off me,' she spat at him. 'I'm a singer not a tart.'

That almost made him smile. 'You're a woman, aren't you?'

'My husband's in the house. He'll kill you.'

'You have to pay,' he said softly.

She opened her mouth. He could hear the inrush of her breath. Before she could scream he closed it with his hand. The feel of her teeth under her soft lips, the tear of her skin excited him. He moved his fingers to her throat and forced her down on the garage floor.

She fought him all the way, going straight for his groin, but, like a ferret he held on till the end.

'Bloody murderer,' he repeated over and over again. 'You'll fucking pay.'

He spent what was left of the night in a hotel on the outskirts of Birmingham and slept round the clock.

Thirty-nine hours after the drowning, he was back at Nightingales. He took in the mail. Among the pile of letters there were already some black-edged envelopes.

Heather sat crouched over the breakfast room fire. She looked up, white and haggard, when he came in. 'Thank God you're back,' was all she said.

Bella

Bella tapped on the breakfast room door, and, after a pause, entered. Inside the chrysanthemums drew all her senses. Pots of Little Charm and tumbling Cascade, a crystal vase full of delicate Koreans, pink and gold and bronze that she had brought up earlier from the greenhouses, brightened the November gloom.

'Yes, Bella?'

Miss Heather sat in a corner of the sofa, her tea untouched, the *Times* unopened beside her. Her hair was pulled back and tied unbecomingly at her nape giving her face a bony unnatural harshness.

'I just wanted a wee word.'

But she could think of nothing to say. Five minutes earlier she had been breaking the ice on the lake to make water holes for the ducks. Warm to the bone in the frosty afternoon, contented as Adam in a winter Eden, she had watched the water well up gelatinously through the cracks. Then suddenly she had remembered that it was a year to the day since Will's death and all the hidden anxieties of the past year frozen in the pit of her mind flooded up into conscious thought.

Poor Miss Heather.

'Give her time,' said Miss Macbride. Depression was the doctor's diagnosis. Guilt, according to Malcy. Whatever the reason, she had not visited the garden in months, nor had Bella set eyes on her for at least a week.

Needled with pity, Bella had left the lake, crunched over the crisp iced lawn, entered the back door, pausing only to change into house shoes, climbed the basement stairs, crossed the hall, walked down the carpeted corridor and knocked on the breakfast room door.

'Miss Heather,' she began again, not knowing what words to use.

Heather frowned. For a moment Bella thought she was going to be sharp with her, but instead, her eyes slid away to the fire in he grate.

'If something's wrong, tell Malcolm.'

Bella wanted her to be angry. 'It's you,' she said bluntly, 'just look at the state of you. You're a sight, so you are,' but still Heather refused to be angry. She stared down at her idle hands and said nothing at all. 'What Lady Mowbray'd say if she were alive today, I shudder to think.'

Heather looked up then and Bella felt the full force of her misery like a blow to her belly. 'But she's not alive and my parents are not alive and my husband is not alive and my son is dead. What a silly hypothesis.'

Though she did not understand the word, Bella recognised her pain. She searched for something to say that would comfort and heal. As she looked down on the woman she served, she saw again the child who had been her friend. All she could think to say was, 'Would you like a game?'

Heather's lips curved but the smile did not touch her eyes. 'Oh Bella, is it true that we were once children? Sit down. We'll have a drink. What would you like?'

Deeply conditioned by the fairmer's thirst to distrust alcohol, Bella shook her head. 'No' for me.'

'Yes you shall,' said Heather rising. 'How can you refuse? Not today. To remember Will.'

She took a bottle of Remy Martin from the drinks cupboard and poured two generous measures. To Bella's she added half a bottle of ginger ale. To her own, a meagre splash of soda. Her hands shook as she picked up the glasses.

'It won't harm you,' Miss Heather said handing her a glass. 'Brandy's a clean drink. Medicinal, whatever Malcolm may say.'

Bella obligingly took a sip, held the stinging liquid in her mouth till she was forced to swallow.

'Is Malcy behaving himself?' she asked.

Miss Heather's drink was almost finished. She took another mouthful before she answered, nor did she look at Bella when she spoke.

'Do you remember I once saved his life? Yet I let my own son drown.'

A kaleidoscope of memories tumbled through Bella's memory, the river, the drowning toddler, the farm, the fire, the ferrets. The vision widened. All the people she had ever known

199

stood like she had once done with their hands on the iron stanchions of the locked garden gate. She yearned to let them in.

'Maybe it was for the best.'

That remark shocked Miss Heather. 'How can you say such a thing?'

Bella had no notion, only a deep and strong conviction. 'Death is a safe place.'

Miss Heather poured herself another drink. 'What makes you so sure?' she asked with anguish in her voice.

Bella shook her head. How was she to explain the inexplicable? 'Maybe we get the words mixed up. Maybe pain and grieving and fear is death and being dead is a chance to come alive.'

Heather laughed harshly. 'As far as I'm concerned, death is just a hole in the ground.'

'Yes,' said Bella earnestly. 'That's where it starts. Life.' She had a sudden image of tiny Shirley Poppy seeds.

The door opened and Malcy came in.

Still charged with knowledge, she saw how he had changed. His slenderness was no longer youthful but emaciated with the look of a man who never rested. His golden hair was thinner, darker. Although his outward manner inspired confidence, suggested self-control, Bella was aware of his inner restlessness. Lately he had taken to cracking his finger joints. He was like the blue touch paper of a fire-work primed to explode. Immediately he noticed the brandy bottle and the two glasses.

'It's not six,' he said shortly.

Miss Heather flinched. 'Today is an exception.'

'Least of all today. From today, the mistress of Nightingales ceases to be a lush.'

Bella froze. His presumption shocked her, but no more so than Miss Heather's compliance. She watched as he crossed to the drinks cupboard and began to take out all the bottles. 'Bella, get a bag,' he ordered.' I want shut of all this poison.'

200

She found her tongue. 'I'll do no such thing. Not without Miss Heather's say-so.'

Malcy looked across the room. 'Tell her,' he said quietly.

'It's for the best,' Miss Heather said in a low humiliated voice.

'Why?' Bella asked stubbornly. 'Just because he says so?'

'Malcy's right. I drink too much. I promised after a year - '

'Don't let him bully you.'

Miss Heather smiled thinly. 'I shan't let either of you bully me.' She got up, crossed the room and opened the door. 'Fight it out between yourselves,' she said on her way out.

Open-mouthed, Bella watched her go. The change in roles confused her. Surely it was Miss Heather who should have sent them both packing. She should have told them to get out.

She turned to Malcy. 'What have you done to her?'

He was not quite angry. 'Since you're so blind, I'll tell you. I run this house and make it pay. I've wiped her snot, mopped up her vomit, listened to her whines. I've worked like a bleeding slave. That's what I've done for her and she knows it. It's pay-back time.'

'What more do you want?' As soon as she'd asked, she wished the question unspoken, because she already knew the answer.

He grinned. 'You ken fine what I want. I want her in my bed. Oh,' he held up his hand to ward off her outrage, 'it'll be all legal and respectable. I'll even take on her name. Percy Hyphen Drake Hyphen Gould. Has a ring to it.'

Why should she be so disapproving? He was seven years Miss Heather's junior, common to her quality, poor to her wealthy. So what? Nowadays these hurdles were not insurmountable. Yet the idea appalled her.

'No Malcy. It's no' right. She's not for you.'

Suddenly he was angry. 'I'm not rich enough, posh enough, is that what you think? You daft midget. Little do you know.'

Why should she be afraid for Miss Heather? She had a tongue in her head and she could say no for herself. Yet, she trembled

201

for them both. She saw his strength as pitiful, his obsession as weakness, his work as a hide, his skills as blinds. Poor wee Malcy. He would always be the unwanted bairn. She remembered him at wee Will's death, frozen on the surface, boiling beneath. What had he done with all that anger? Where had he hidden his own grief?

'Oh Malcy, son, leave her alone,' she pleaded.

Some of her anguish must have touched his core for now he was no longer angry. Instead he shook his head. 'I can't. Don't you see? I can't.'

She tried once more; the familiar way. 'The day you ask Miss Heather to wed you, I walk out.'

His answer came swift as an echo. 'The day I wed Miss Snooty, you get the sack.'

Heather

The bedroom door loomed and faded. Heather closed her eyes and immediately the bed dissolved beneath her and she was spinning dizzily down through purple space past an infinity of stars.

The first night she had gone drunk to bed she'd been scared sick. No longer. 'I have acquired the taste,' she said carefully. 'Nanny always said I was adaptable.'

'You're stoned.'

She opened her eyes and the room lurched to a standstill.

'Hullo Malcy.' She smiled at him. He looked nice with the edges blurred. She almost fancied him when she was drunk. The drunker she got the better she liked him. Odd old world. 'Have you come to kiss me good-night?' she said provocatively.

'Where's the bottle?' he asked tersely.

'Find it!' She giggled, hugging it under the bedclothes.

'Oh, I'll find it, never you fear.'

She giggled again. 'What a bear you are. A grizzly, snapping bear. All tooth and claw and growl. I like you when you're a bear.'

With one sweeping gesture he pulled down the quilt. Her wool dress was hitched up to her thighs.

'Naughty, naughty, ' she teased, hugging the bottle to her breast.

As he reached down to take it, she caught him with both arms around the neck.

'Kiss me good-night, Malcy.' He twisted away as her lips brushed his cheek. 'You're so smooth and pretty. Like a little boy.'

He held up the bottle. 'Who gets you this stuff?'

She rounded her eyes and put her fingers to her lips. 'I wonder.'

He reached out and dragged her upright by the front of her dress. ' Who gets it for you?'

The room lurched and somersaulted around her.

'I feel sick,' she wailed. The fun was over. 'Malcy, I feel sick.'

He pulled her out of bed, half carried her through to the bathroom, pushed her down on her knees in front of the lavatory pan. 'Vomit,' he told her, holding her head.

'I'm sorry,' she gasped between the spasms. 'I'm sorry. Oh God, I'm so sorry.'

Back in her room she sat on the side of her bed feeling cold and ill. She had no thoughts, only dizziness in her head. Tears leaked weakly from her eyes. With practised fingers Malcy unzipped the back of her dress, lifted it over her head, unhooked her bra and slid the should-straps down her arms before covering her with her nightgown. 'You can manage the rest.'

She opened her eyes. Malcy's fingers had turned into fat pink worms. They were crawling out of the sleeves of his jacket.

'Go away,' she screamed, covering her face with her hands. 'Leave me alone.'

He gripped her arms and pulled them away from her face. 'Was it Bella got you the drink?'

The fat worms were in his mouth, crawling out of his eyes. She began to shake.

With an expression of disgust he let her go.

Harry

Harry Fever enjoyed his breakfast. Every morning he rose in good time to prepare and savour freshly ground coffee, iced grapefruit, bacon and eggs, toast and marmalade made especially for him by his daily woman who came in for two hours three times a week.

While he ate he read his letters. That particular morning there were two early Christmas cards, an invitation to dine over the festive season, a couple of circulars and a letter addressed in a simple, painstaking hand which he did not recognise. He opened it with interest believing it to have come from the youngest of his three godchildren to whom he had sent an early Christmas cheque.

When he saw the address inside, his appetite diminished.

Dear Sir, he read
Excuse me for troubling you but knowing you were once a friend of the Major and Mrs Percy-Drake I took the liberty of writing. Things are not good at Nightingales. Miss Heather never got over the death of Master William. If ever she needed a friend, it's now.

Leaving the matter in your hands, I remain your obedient servant, Bella Gould.

Remembering the short, rather odd gardener at Nightingales his first instinct was to reject the letter as cranky. If Heather had really needed him, she would have surely replied to any of his three unanswered letters in all of which he had inquired for her health and state of mind. His first letter had been to thank her for the flowers and note of good wishes she had sent to him in hospital. A few months later he had written again to re-assure her that he had fully recovered and that the Whistler had been remarkably well repaired. The third was sent with flowers after he had read the announcement of the boy's sad death in the *Times* and an apology for missing the funeral. He had been in bed with flu. Perhaps he should have persevered, but her continued silence had daunted him, not even a card at Christmas.

Strangely enough their short relationship had quickened emotions and needs that he had thought long dead. The pillage of his home had made him more vulnerable. When he met the middle-aged wife of a client on a fine spring day walking her dog on the Heath, a friendship had started that had grown almost by accident into a comfortable relationship with no strings, no responsibilities, no demands. Julia had a full and busy life apart from him. Anchored to this affair, he had nothing to fear from Heather. Yet he shrank from returning to Nightingales.

So it was with some reluctance he opened his diary and saw that his weekends were engaged until after the New Year. True he had one or two free week-day nights but he did not care to drive out of town on dark, possibly icy December roads. He was giving a luncheon party on Boxing Day. He could ask her to that. Put Julia in the picture. She was well able to cope with any possible histrionics. He would write a note from the office. Better still, he would get his secretary to telephone the invitation which he would then confirm by post.

That afternoon when he returned from lunch to the office his secretary confirmed that she had contacted Nightingales.

'Mrs Percy-Drake thanks you for the invitation but she won't be able to accept as she is entertaining herself that day.'

He was both put out and relieved. It had seemed such an excellent arrangement. At the same time he could not help thinking that there was probably not much the matter with her if she was able to entertain.

'How did she seem?' he asked. 'All right do you think?'

'Mrs Percy-Drake was not at home. A gentleman answered the telephone.'

Malcolm. Harry felt uneasy. Taking a sheet of paper from his desk drawer he wrote:

My dear Heather,
I'm so sorry you can't lunch with me on Boxing Day. Perhaps you will have a free day early in the New Year? Meanwhile have a Happy Christmas and all my good wishes for 1965.
Yours as ever, Harry Fever.

As with all his other letters, Heather did not receive it.

Malcolm

At seven o'clock on Christmas Eve, Malcy opened the small square jeweller's box. Three emeralds clawed into a gold band lay on its velvet cushion. In his mind's eye he saw it heavy on Heather's finger. Four hundred quid's worth and new. He would propose tonight and make the formal announcement at the annual estate party.

It was true that Heather was entertaining on Boxing Day, a tradition that the villagers and employees had come to expect. The buffet supper had been prepared as far in advance as was possible and much of it only needed to be defrosted. The gifts for the kids, chosen and wrapped by himself, for he would trust no one else with that particular task, were stowed in a gaudy plastic sack. He had already supervised the lifting of the drawing room carpet and winced as the hefty groundsmen knocked into one of the delicate Anthemion backed 18th century chairs which he was replacing with stackers from the café. Next year he swore he would keep the yobbos out. Allowing that the party was necessary to keep the villagers sweet and that he enjoyed his role as Santa, he decided he would hold next year's 'do' in the tearoom.

There would be other changes too. He was thinking of decorating and re-furnishing Swankpant's bedroom. For himself. He'd open the communicating door any time he bloody chose.

But now he had a decision to make. Inside the wardrobe zipped up in plastic covers hung two new items of clothing, a new lounge suit bespoke in Savile Row, dark grey with a narrow, barely perceptible pin-stripe and a black dinner jacket with brocade lapels and matching trousers. He had intended to dress up for the Boxing Day 'do'. Heather would most certainly be in a long dress and the Major had always make it a point of honour to put on a dinner jacket, but it occurred to Malcy that it might be more appropriate to put on the lounge suit this year, less toffee-nosed. Instead he would wear the dinner jacket tonight. Add a touch of old-fashioned class to his proposal before which he would join her for dinner at eight. No more below-stairs meals for him, he thought, as he stripped to the buff and began to wash himself. Pity Mrs Twenty Questions Bushy, the cook who came in every morning, would have gone home by that time. She'd enjoy the joke. 'I'm as good as the toffs and so are you, ' she frequently repeated like a chorus between verses of complaint. As for Bella she would have to lump it or pack her bags. Just as well she was out for the evening. Thick as thieves with Copperwheat and his family. He'd need to keep an eye on that.

He dressed with care. New underwear, silk socks, patent leather shoes - the real McCoy none of your cheap imitation muck - lawn shirt discreetly ruffled, bow-tie but not the vulgar made-up job. One last brush of the hair, a touch of the tingles with Yardley's aftershave and then he pocketed the ring. Looking into his spotted attic glass, he liked what he saw. 'Fine feathers make fine birds,' as Lady Muck used to say.

He was reminded of a film he'd seen a while back. Guy with a pansy name, handsome as Gabriel, ponced about in black and white living a life of larry, never ageing, until you saw his portrait in glorious technicolour. That came as a shock. George Sanders was in it, but he couldn't remember the name of the film.

He closed the attic door and hurried down the two top flights, then slowed down as he crossed the first floor landing to tread the new plum-coloured carpeting with deferential feet. Automatically, with a householder's eye, he checked the great Christmas Tree lights for safety, and that the doors and shuttered windows were locked, corners and surfaces for dust, the central heating radiators for warmth. He was very sure of himself. If his heart beat faster it was only in recognition of the occasion.

The sitting-room fire burned with old applewood logs; bowls of white and blue hyacinths scented the room; Christmas cards and holly decked the mantelpiece. Miss Snooty was at her desk. Her frail nape burdened by a thick coil of dark hair stirred his gut.

'Heather,' he said tentatively. It was the first time he had omitted to use her title and the name sounded naked, intimate. She did not appear to have heard.

After a moment she looked up from the stack of envelopes she was addressing and noticed him.

'Good gracious, Malcy,' she said in her grandmother's voice spiced with dry humour. 'What on earth are you doing tarted up like a waiter?'

Turning back to her desk, she did not see his look or hear him leave or notice he had gone until the draught from the open door chilled her.

Dorian Gray, he thought in the instant before a tide of anger swept over him. That was the name of the film, *The Picture of Dorian Gray*.

Heather

At 8 15 Heather finished signing Boots tokens, this year's gift to all who had helped at Nightingales during the year. She checked the number against her list and stacked the envelopes ready for distribution from the tree. In the past she had always chosen the presents personally, taking pleasure in finding

208

appropriate gifts, but this year she had left her shopping to the last minute, continually postponing what had loomed as a mountainous chore. In the end Malcy suggested tokens, bought them and left them for her to sign. No doubt he would have written them too, if need be.

She looked up at the clock surprised to see how late it was. What had happened to dinner? She actually felt hungry. The feeling of nausea which had never properly left her since that appalling night when she had hallucinated, had finally gone. Though she found it hard to admit even to herself the reason for that horrific occasion, she had not had a drink for almost two weeks. Not that she couldn't, for there was still a bottle of Martell hidden in her sponge bag, smuggled in by Tim when he brought up flowers from the greenhouse, in exchange for a generous tip. Ridiculous really, when there was a cellar full of drink in the house, only she seemed to have lost her key. She suspected Malcy had taken it off the ring in her bureau. Knowing how much he disapproved of alcohol, she could not bring herself to ask him.

She was pleased by her abstinence because it had been voluntary which showed she must still have some strength of character. More important it proved she was not an alcoholic. She could stop drinking when she chose which meant, conversely, that she could have a drink when she liked.

Meanwhile she was actually hungry. Picking up the house telephone she rang down to the kitchen. No reply. Perhaps Malcy was already waiting in the dining-room. She crossed the room and opened the door.

'Malcolm?'

The grandfather clock at the end of the passage ticked steadily through the silence. Crossing the hall, she pulled her cardigan closer. The tree glittered and blinked at her with a hundred eyes.

'Malcy?'

She was conscious of every door, every shadow, every black-mouthed passage and fear came bounding over her in chilling

209

strides. Just as she had done as a child, she ran up the wide shallow stairs to her room two steps at a time with the clutch and breath of innumerable demons at the back. She went straight to her sponge-bag, found the bottle and with a sigh of thanksgiving unscrewed the cap. She did not bother to find a glass. After one long swallow she felt better.

Malcy, she remembered, had been wearing, of all extraordinary things, a dinner jacket. He must have been going out. Why hadn't he told her? Another swallow. He may have mentioned it and she had forgotten. Why should he not go out? It was, after all, Christmas Eve. Party time.

Christmas Eve.

She remembered parties before the war. She had worn a white muslin dress embroidered all over with little rosebuds and a pink taffeta petticoat which rustled. The tree had glowed with real candles that flickered in their green metal clips. They had played and sung, *Here we go round the Mulberry Bush.*

Another swallow.

Christmas Eve. A night of frost and stars and angels. Nanny used to know a poem about angels. How did it go?

The little angels in heaven
Each wear a long white gown
And they lean over the ramparts
Waiting and looking down.
But they shall know keener pleasure,
And they shall know joy more rare
Keener, keener pleasure,
When you, my dear, come there.

'Will is an angel now,' she said aloud. Maudlin tears filled her eyes. Will was in heaven.

'No more drinkies,' she told herself screwing the bottle cap. 'I have to go to church.'

She knelt down to hide the near-empty bottle under her dressing table. It was difficult to stand up again. She kept

210

holding on to the wrong things like her hair brush and the lace runner, but finally she managed, and reached for a tweed cape in her wardrobe.

Nothing was easy any more. The cape swayed away from her and when she wrapped it round her shoulders the buttons would not fit in the holes.

'Hat and gloves,' she told herself. Nanny had always insisted on hat and gloves.

'Don't be ridiculous. Black and pink?'

Painstakingly she exchanged her gloves for a pair of sheepskin mitts.

She fell down the last five stairs and lay for a moment muzzily arguing with herself 'I can't be drunk. Not on three small sips,' but somewhere underneath the fuzz and buzz in her head, she knew that she was.

'Mustn't drive,' she said aloud, and added as the idea dawned on her, 'I can walk.'

Outside the stars twinkled and danced and there was a moon.

'My Will's up there,' she said aloud and then because it was Christmas Eve she began to sing, *I saw three ships come sailing in.* She had never before realised that it was such a tongue-twister.

She was early for the Midnight Mass but not the first. The vicar was rifling through the bible at the lectern and an altar boy was setting up the hymn board. He stared as she walked carefully up the aisle but when she smiled and waved he turned away.

Just in front of her there was a crib with Mary and Joseph, three shepherds, two cows with the plaster ears chipped and an angel. She stared at it for a long time unaware that, behind her, the church had filled. Her eyes closed. She was almost asleep.

The service started. Jerked awake by the boom of the organ, she watched the choir, red-cassocked and bright-eyed, led by a solemn crucifer walking up the length of the aisle while everyone sang *Hark the Herald Angel Sing.* One small boy had yellow hair and plump pink cheeks.

211

Suddenly she began to cry. Tears poured uncontrollably down her cheeks.

Angela Macbride slipped into her pew, handed her a hanky and whispered something in her ear.

When Heather nodded, Angela took her arm and supported her all the way down the aisle, her charm bracelet a tinkling accompaniment to *Oh Little Town of Bethlehem.*

She was not drunk now. She was aware of the averted faces, pitying eyes. One of the churchwardens insisted on driving her home. She would not let him in, nor the anxious Angela. 'I'm all right,' she assured them shame-facedly.

'Of course you are,' said Angela encouragingly.

'Compliments of the season, Mrs Drake,' said the churchwarden heartily.

When they had gone her tears returned. How could Malcolm and Bella have both left her alone on Christmas Eve?

Emma Coleman

At 1 20 that same night, Emma Coleman was walking the lonely road by Odstock, three miles south of Salisbury. Her head rang with carols and the greetings of the congregation outside St Mary's church and in happy anticipation of the day ahead.

Ted would have cocoa ready to heat up on the stove, the stockings filled ready to be hung and a Christmas kiss. They'd neither of them get much sleep. Last year the children had come in before five to snuggle down in the big bed and open their presents. Ted was on early shift at the farm.

The turkey weighed twelve pounds. At twenty minutes to the pound and twenty minutes extra, she would need to get it in the oven by nine. That recipe had said roast it breast down for the first hour. She'd need to sleep on that idea.

A car passed, a sleek dark foreign make. Ted would like a car. She wished she could give him one for Christmas. Stuff it in his stocking, but pig-men with three kids couldn't afford more than a bike. Still, the boss was generous with the Land

212

Rover in an emergency. Nice of the vicar to offer her a drive home after the midnight service, but she hadn't had the face to accept knowing he had a heavy day ahead and kids of his own with stockings to fill. He'd given her a big tin of biscuits to help out, getting a bit heavy to carry on her arm.

Just ahead of her, the car had stopped, pulled into a lay-by under the trees, lights off. A courting couple no doubt. She smiled. She and Ted had done their courting under trees. Never felt the cold.

Her court shoes clattered on the road and nipped her toes. She wished she'd worn her boots but they were too shabby for church.

A man climbed out of the car as she approached. Nice looking, well-dressed in a leather jacket and leather gloves. A bit of money there. His hair shone like a halo in the moonlight. The angel of the Lord in modern gear. Must tell Ted that joke. She'd accept a lift if offered.

She smiled as she approached him. 'You lost, then?'

He looked at her. Flat shiny eyes that caught the moonlight. Ted didn't like her walking alone at night. She had argued, 'Who'd look at me, fat and forty with three kids?' All the same she wished she hadn't spoken to the stranger. Those eyes made her uneasy. 'Merry Christmas,' she said awkwardly.

Then he smiled.

'Like a lift, hen?'

She recognised a Scottish accent when she heard it. The boss's wife was a Scot. She'd always liked the Scots, trusted them. Her misgivings vanished.

'Wouldn't mind, if it's no bother. Just a mile down the road. These shoes are killing me feet.'

Talking cheerfully, she followed him round to the near side of the car. He held the door open, quite the gentleman. ...

Malcolm

Mid-Christmas morning the telephone rang. Malcy answered from the kitchen extension.

'Happy Christmas, Malcolm.' It was Miss Macbride. 'Is Mrs P-D available?'

'She's still in her room, I believe. If you wait a minute, I'll find out.'

'No, don't waken her. I merely wondered how she was this morning?'

He was on his guard. Not knowing the true reason for her call, he waited to find out. The silence stretched.

'Dear Malcolm,' Angela gushed. 'I'm sure you know how much we all admire your loyalty. Personally, I think you're marvellous the way you protect her, but really there's no need. We all know about our Heather and we're all desperately sorry.'

Silly old cow. He picked up the telephone ballpoint and began to doodle on the pad, elaborate intertwining circles.

'We didn't waken you last night?'

'No, Miss Macbride. My room's in the attic. I was out like a light.' Important to make that point. She took it.

'I'm not surprised, all you do. Heather is at least fortunate in that respect…. Of course I knew the moment I saw her in church that there was something wrong. You can tell at a glance, can't you? When she got so upset, I felt it would be kinder to take her home. Luckily Mr Richie offered to drive her back. How she walked there in the first place in the state she was in, I'll never know.'

The ink circles grew darker. The pen point stabbed through the paper, but his voice was expressionless. 'Was Miss Heather drunk?'

Angela retreated flustered by the word. 'I wouldn't put it quite so strongly. She wasn't raving or - '

'She was drunk,' he interrupted firmly.

'Well, yes, I suppose she was,' she agreed reluctantly, adding, 'Malcolm, I think - we all think - she needs professional help.'

Interfering old bag. What did she know about it?

'Exactly my own sentiments, Miss Macbride,' he replied politely.

'I'm so glad you agree. It's such a relief to have talked to you about it. I know you'll do something positive...I take it the party is still on tomorrow?'

'Of course.' Why the hell would it not be?

'Of course,' she echoed. 'It's just such a pity it had to happen in church. The whole village was there.'

'Don't upset yourself on account of Miss Heather,' he said stifling an urge to yawn. He had not got in till seven. 'I'll tell her that you called. May I take this opportunity to offer you the compliments of the season, Miss Macbride?'

He put down the receiver before she could speak again.

When had she got the booze? He had searched the house and removed every bottle, even hidden the cooking sherry. The cellar keys were under the mattress of his bed.

Bella came into the kitchen with a bowl of peeled potatoes, as Twenty Questions had the day off. He turned on her savagely. 'Where were you last night?'

She looked up from the oven where she was arranging the potatoes round the roasting duck. 'You ken fine where I was. At Copperwheat's.'

'Well you should nae ha' been.'

'It's a free world,' she replied mildly.

He turned on his heel and strode upstairs. He had a headache and his eyes stung. There was a time when he could stay up all night and never turn a hair.

The room was a midden. A box of talc lay spilled on the floor, mixed up with her cosmetic jars and tubes. Her clothes, pulled out of the wardrobe, were strewn about the room. The brandy bottle stood blatantly empty on her bedside cabinet. Uncertain December light turned her skin grey. She frowned in her sleep. What a slob.

'Miss Heather,' he said, loading the syllables with disgust.

215

She opened her eyes and immediately closed them again. She held out her long thin arm. The palm of her hand turned upwards partly in supplication, partly to ward off his anger.

'Malcy, where were you last night?'

With a stab of triumph he knew he had her. If he were to say, 'We're getting wed in the morning,' she'd probably agree, but suddenly, without question, he realised that he didn't want her. This pathetic drunk would only clutter up his life, drag him down to her degraded level.

The knowledge rocked him on his feet and for a moment he was overwhelmed with a sense of loss, a shadow of how he had felt at Will's death. He had wanted her for so long that he was bereft without the need. The moment passed. Nightingales was what he wanted, unshared, unencumbered. There were other ways of getting it without marrying the boss.

Filled with a sense of freedom as if he'd escaped from a straitjacket he was the Magician again. Nightingales, without this woman who sickened him when she was drunk and humiliated him when she was sober, was all he wanted. He'd give her a year to destroy herself. All he had to do was return the cellar keys.

Smiling down at her almost with tenderness, he said, ' Happy Christmas, Miss Heather.'

Then he left to run her bath.

Bella

'Haddock and chips, love.' The waitress dumped the plate in front of Bella. She splurged a dollop of tomato sauce on the side and picked up her knife and fork.

'Okay, is it?' Curly asked anxiously as his great hands enfolded his own cutlery.

Bella looked up. 'Aye,' she answered with her mouth full. 'No' bad.'

She liked looking at Curly. He was handsome, so he was, with his black hair bubbling all over his head, and olive skin

216

that looked like suntan. His broad strong hands were strong and smooth, and, unlike hers which were permanently etched in grime, entirely clean.

Curly was a long-distance lorry-driver whom she'd met on Christmas Eve at the Copperwheats. He was a pal of Copperwheat's son-in-law who worked for the same company and he had lodgings in Basingstoke. He didn't have much to say for himself but he laughed a lot and jiggled the Copperwheat grandson up and down on his bony knee. Sometimes he caught her eye. Once he handed her a plate of mince-pies and one of them toppled on to the floor. They'd had a good laugh about that.

'You ever go to the panto?' he asked her, looking at his feet, while the others were discussing the annual family outing.

'No' me.' She'd never seen a pantomime in her life except on the telly.

'Would you go?' he asked, still not meeting her eye.

'I'll try anything once, me,' she had said with a laugh.

Three days later Arthur Copperwheat brought her a message.

'Curly said he'd call for you on Saturday. Dress up warm, he said. You two clicked, then?' he asked winking at her over the water-barrel outside one of the greenhouses.

She pretended not to hear, but her face grew warm.

She wore her good blue dress with the casual swagger coat bought from a catalogue on Malcy's insistence - he'd called her a right tink - and shortened. Her legs felt cold and naked in nylons. Her apple-round cheeks glowed from the frost under her short black hair.

'Where are you going, dolled up like a dog's dinner?' Malcy asked, coming into the kitchen with Miss Heather's tray.

'Out.'

But even if she'd wanted to keep him in the dark he'd soon have found out. Five minutes later the peace of Nightingales was shattered as a great black monster of a motor-bike roared up the drive spattering the gravel like bullets, and Curly in an

217

orange wind-cheater and helmet with 'Gertie' printed on it in large black letters above a winged skull, honked on his hooter.

'*Gott in himmel*,' Malcy muttered peering out of the kitchen window. 'Hell's Angels are on the loose.'

Bella could tell he was joking. Malcy was in a great mood these days.

Curly handed her a helmet like his own, and made her change into trousers and her duffle coat. 'Thought you'd like a spin on Gert.' He patted the handle-bars lovingly. 'Ain't she something?'

Bella covered her mouth with her hand and laughed nervously.

Surprisingly it was all right. She tucked her coat carefully under her bum, wrapped her arms round Curly's waist, screwed up her eyes under the visor and in no time at all they arrived.

'You're a sport,' he told her admiringly once they were safely seated in the theatre.

The pantomime was a real laugh. Aladdin reminded her of Miss Heather, all legs and brown hair; the way Miss Heather used to be. She stopped laughing. Those needles of anxiety had started to prickle. Miss Heather was getting worse. Malcy did his best. Told Tim off good and proper for getting her the stuff.

'What's up?' Curly whispered anxiously.

She shook her head and smiled obligingly. He bought her ice-cream in the interval and they went out into the foyer so he could have a fag.

'You enjoying it?' he asked.

'It's a laugh a minute.'

'You went quiet. I just wondered.'

'Ghosts,' she said. 'They've gone.'

After the interval, Widow Twanky got them all singing, 'I'm a silly-billy!' 'Oh no you're not!' half the audience roared while the other half shouted, 'Oh, yes you are!'

In the café eating fish and chips they were squashed side by side in a booth by the window.

218

'Those ghosts,' he said. ' I get them too. Sometimes at night when I'm on the road they all crowd in.'

'Aye,' she said, and again the needles inched out of their sheathes.

They were silent for a while finishing their meal. Later he said, 'I'm on the Glasgow run for the next three months.'

'I've got a wee house in Scotland,' she told him, pouring out more tea.

'That right?' He was intrigued. 'Come to think of it,' he added, spilling tea into the saucer in his excitement, 'I've got room for a little un in my cab. Why not come with me?' The idea was so novel that automatically she was about to refuse. 'Go on,' he urged. 'Don't tell me you can't get a couple of days off from that garden of yours in January 'cos I won't believe it.'

As she stared at her reflection in the café window superimposed upon a dark and unknown world, she was overwhelmed with a sense of inadequacy. England, Nightingales, the great demanding garden loomed and over-shadowed her like mountains. Miss Heather, Malcy, Tim, the Copperwheats and all the other staff oppressed her with their needs and expectations. She was filled with homesickness for Scotland, for Ladymuir and the Lodge, for the uncomplicated company of the now widowed Mrs B and above all for the wee garden that would be all overgrown by now.

'I'll need to think about it,' she told him.

High up in the Leyland cab, pounding up the road, Bella's stomach churned. She remembered the first time she had been car-sick. Lady Mowbray had taken her with Miss Heather to St Andrews. She had first glimpsed the sea between two rows of tall stone houses like a great blue topsy-turvy sky. She had ridden on a donkey on the sands.

On the way back she had been sick, which, together with petrol rationing, had put paid to car outings during the war. She was feeling a little sick now. The build-up of anticipation, the

219

strangeness of the day unguarded by routine, the need to savour every minute, had been too much.

'Penny for 'em?' Curly shouted over the noise of the engine.

She laughed and shook her head.

It had all been so easy. Copperwheat had told her to scarper. The garden would still be there when she got back. Malcy had said grudgingly, ' I suppose someone had better take a look at the Lodge. It's family property. Make a note of any repairs.'

Coming from Malcy this was unexpected encouragement. She had anticipated a hard time.

Miss Heather had said, 'Do what you like, Bella, only remember to come back.'

Though she had smiled, making it into a joke, Bella had seen with sorrow her shaking hands and clouded eyes.

The further north the lorry rumbled with Curly showing off a bit at the wheel, the more her stomach heaved. When she thought of Malcy, Miss Heather and Nightingales, the needles of anxiety turned into spears.

I don't want to go back. The words lit up her spirit with relief that they had been spoken, if only in her mind.

Curly was great company. He bought her tea at transport cafes and pointed out places of interest on the road.

'We're in Bonnie Scotland now,' he told her just north of Carlisle. 'Feel like doing the Highland Fling?'

On the A74 just as a drizzling January dusk descended, he drove into a lay-by and switched off the engine.

'Bella,' he said in the quiet of the cab. 'I need to tell you something. I've got a son.'

She looked at him and saw his bowed head, the startling white nape of his neck below the spring of hair, the curl and clutch of his hands on the wheel. He was just a great bairn himself.

'I got this girl into trouble, see? We were married but she was no good. Went off and left us before Darren was a year old. He's in care now and there's nothing I can do about it.'

For the first time, Bella saw Curly as a man with needs. The seemingly uncomplicated stranger who made her laugh, the one-

220

dimensional figure who had brought a bit of fun into her life had gone for good.

'That's too bad,' she said quietly.

'I just wanted you to know,' he told her engaging gear.

Five minutes later he was singing, ' She loves me, yeah, yeah, yeah!' a little off key. After a while she joined in.

From the outside, the Lodge was a miniature pile of Victorian architecture, a precocious infant originally attached to the Hall by an elegant tree-lined umbilical cord. In spite of the imposing masonry, it was small with two darkish rooms downstairs and an even smaller one in the square castellated tower. Inside, it was similar to its siblings in the High Street, for the miners' rows of Ladymuir had also been flag-floored, damp, with outside water-closets.

Just as Ladymuir stood on a Lanarkshire moor south of and almost midway between Glasgow and Edinburgh, so the Lodge had been built on the threshold of two worlds, a gateway that separated the farm and parklands of the Hall from the long narrow street and black bings that overhung the village.

Today it was an anachronism. Most of the beeches had gone to make way for council housing. The gravelled avenue, now tarred and widened, led to a collocation of rectangular flat-roofed blocks. A concrete and glass primary school stood on the site of the Hall and the farm had been turned into an industrial estate comprising a machine shop, a baby-clothes factory and a food-processing firm.

In the village, the miners' rows had been demolished to make way for private housing, a supermarket and a public convenience. The old Miners Institute was a restaurant-cum-inn. The coal bings had been bull-dosed and landscaped into a smart new golf-course. Instead of ending up another derelict mining village, Ladymuir had turned itself into a new town full of commuter families who preferred the rural scene, and retired couples from the cities. In the twelve years since the fire at the Hall, Ladymuir had become almost unrecognisable.

The Lodge, curtained with overgrown shrubs, set in its own walled garden, was an oddity, a hangover from a vanished world, taken for granted by the residents, occasionally noted by passing motorists who stopped at the filling station across the road. Curly drove past it, before Bella recognised the street and even then she was not sure. The image of the Lodge had loomed so large in her memory that she could not believe the reality to be so insignificant.

'It's that good to see you!'

Mrs B stood in the doorway, shrunken and bowed, a frail old woman with tobacco-stained hair and a tremor.

'Come away in, the both of yous.'

She would not hear of Curly leaving. 'Upstairs is all set. Bella can bide with me.'

When he had parked his lorry, they sat down to a high tea of cold gammon and tomatoes, fruit scones and fancy cakes all washed down with strong milky tea in cups painted with yellow roses.

'What rare china,' Bella said admiringly when she could get a word in. Mrs B talked with the compulsion of the old and lonely who have few visitors.

After they'd eaten, she sent Curly out to stretch his legs. 'I know men,' she said nudging him with a bony elbow. 'You'll not be satisfied till you've sampled the local brew.'

'You coming?' he asked Bella

'She is not,' said Mrs B, lighting a Woodbine. 'She's better things to do with her time, I should hope.' So Bella had no choice.

She leaned back against the familiar crocheted cushions, stretched her feet towards the fender and looked around her. The old black range had been replaced by a beige-coloured tiled hearth and there was an electric cooker in the scullery. The walls were papered with big, red, overblown poppies.

'You've made it awful' bonnie,' said Bella admiringly.

'I'm thinking of flitting,' said Mrs B. 'The place has changed. The council tenants dump their muck over the garden wall and their kids steal the apples and bang on the door. The village is full of fancy folk and fast cars. My sister's got a bungalow in Largs. She was widowed in October and she's forever at me to move in beside her.' She leaned forward and threw her fag-end into the fire. 'That should suit you grand.' Catching Bella's look of surprise, she continued, 'That's the reason you came, isn't it? To give me notice so that you and that lad can get wed? Well, I'm saving you the bother.'

'I'm not thinking of getting wed,' Bella told her firmly for the idea had not occurred to her. 'And I was nae thinking of putting you out.' That was certainly true, but the idea of never returning to Ladymuir had suddenly become tempting. She had a bit put by. She could get a job. She remembered the weedy cemetery. She'd take a wee walk up there in the morning.

'I've a letter written these past twa months, but to tell you the truth I canna abide the bother of it all. Flitting at my age is no joke,' she added with an accusing look at Bella.

'You're welcome to stay.'

'Oh no,' she cried with a triumphant toss of the head. 'I'm a limpet once my mind's made up. I'll leave you the furniture and my pots and pans. What else would I do with them? My sister's bungalow's like Buckingham Palace, so I suppose. Who's to help me get there, I'm sure I don't know.'

Two slow tears oozed from her eyes and lay on the inside rim of her glasses. 'It's no joke being old and alone. You marry that lad, Bella, and have a bairn of your own. They say children can be a sorrow and a cross but it's no life at all without them.'

'I'll help you flit, Mrs B, if that's what you want. Miss Heather'll no' object if I take a few more days off.'

Mrs B wiped her eyes. 'You're a good lass, Bella Gould. You'll get your reward in heaven.'

Bella made her a cup of tea and got her laughing at memories of the Hall and later in the lumpy double bed, the old woman sighed and curled up against her like a lonely child.

Bella was never sure if Mrs B precipitated Curly's proposal, dangling the Lodge in front of him like a carrot, or if he had spoken spontaneously out of his own need. In the end it made no difference.

She did not mind him putting Darren first, the prospect of a home in second place and herself someway behind. Love was not a sentiment she expected, no more, perhaps, than he did. He told her he had been brought up in an institution. 'A nice enough place, mind. One of the house-mothers - she was a titch like you - once made me a birthday cake with candles.' The supervisor had once or twice taken him fishing. 'Trouble was there were so many kids coming and going, so many changes that as soon as you made a pal, he was shifted and you never saw him again. My past's littered with brothers and sisters, mums and dads that lasted maybe as long as six months. I've got a book with my life story all written out by a social worker with photos in it. My mum was a real raver with blond hair and big blue eyes. Darren's her spitting image.'

'I was fostered too,' Bella told him shyly.

'I don't want Darren fostered and I don't want him brought up in care. I want to be his proper dad,' and then in the same breath, 'you'd make a smashing mum, Bella. Darren'd take to you. We could have more kids, be a real family - you know what I'm getting at?'

The idea was as unreal and remote as a South Sea island to an Inuit, technicoloured on the surface, yet snagged with unknown, undreamed-of dangers. Superficially, no doubt, she and Curly would get along fine together. The Lodge would house a tidy, ready-made family where they would live like Adam and Eve, innocent in the garden, yet all her instincts told her to reject the offer.

She sensed in Curly a simplicity that was false. He trailed behind him a life-time of loss. Lost parents, lost home, lost friends, a lost wife and a lost child who in his own small wake carried his own immeasurable pains. If she could take them into the garden of her heart she would surely do so, but she could not. Her spirit ached with a sense of her own inadequacy. There was no room for them in her heart. Every corner was taken up with Malcy and Miss Heather. Those familiar needles of anxiety jagged at the skin of her soul.

'I'm sorry, Curly, I like you fine, but I'm a gairdener, no' a mam nor a blushin' bride. See me in a wedding goonie marching up the aisle!'

Though she tried to make a joke of it, she could not laugh. Curly did not seem unduly upset. 'No hard feelings?' he asked her next day when he drove off leaving her behind at the Lodge to help Mrs B to flit.

'We're still pals,' she re-assured him.

'Sure you won't change your mind?'

She shook her head.

Malcolm

From the office where Malcy kept the files, ledgers and other documents relevant to the running of Nightingales, he could keep an eye on the drive. Though he tried to concentrate on the receipts he was preparing for the accountant, his eye kept wandering to the window. He would never admit, even to himself, that he missed Bella or needed her, yet when she had rung from a public telephone to say she would not be home till Saturday, he had blown his top.

'Don't bother to come back,' he had told her grimly. 'Who needs you anyway?' Then the pips had gone and he had hung up.

It looked as if she had taken him at his word.

Closing the ledger, he stood up and moved to the window. Outside it was dark and the wind murmured peacefully in the trees but he was not soothed. He was as jumpy as a cat in a shower. He'd been like that since Bella left.

It made no sense. With Bella out of the road, he'd taken the opportunity to make a few changes one of which was to move down to the Major's room. He'd taken his things there that

225

morning and shut the attic door behind him for good. He'd already restocked the cellar with brandy as supplies had been running low. He'd even fixed the light on the cellar stairs. He wanted no accidents - yet. The accounts showed a small but steady profit, and yet deep down inside he walked in a windy desert, lost and alone.

Glancing at his watch he saw it was after seven. Well stuff Bella. He'd be better off without her anyway.

Upstairs in the Major's room he fixed gold cufflinks into a new Pierre Cardin shirt and changed into his grey suit, carefully pressed earlier in the day. He drew on a pair of slim elastic-sided boots polished to mirror shine, and stood in front of the cheval looking-glass to consider his appearance, but the act of dressing up, usually so enjoyable, lacked credibility. Hamlet without an audience. Twice he drew back the curtain to look out on the sweep of gravel below, but all he saw was rain lancing the terrace lights.

Suddenly he remembered the child he had once been, fingers splintered by the five-barred gate as he willed the dumpy schoolgirl that Bella had been to come home. Not for companionship, not out of affection, but because she was as necessary to him as four walls and a pair of pants. Without her he felt cold and naked.

He could not account for this dependency. Angrily he lashed out at her under his breath. 'Try coming home at this hour and see what you'll get,' he muttered but inwardly he wailed. The evening so carefully planned, stretched out ahead of him as flat as a plate. He needed the peaks and valleys of her opinion, to see his triumph reflected in the water of her eyes. Only then could he savour it.

Mrs Bushy had gone home and as was usual at weekends, left a cold dinner; salmon mousse and a broad bean salad, Poire Helene (which he disliked) and a consommé that only needed to be heated. This he did, and when he had filled the tureen, he put it on the lift hatch and went upstairs.

The dining room - not the great refectory that was open to the public in the season - but the converted smoking room which was above the kitchen, had been set earlier for three. Old English silver glittered on the french-polished table. The centre-piece, a favourite of his which he had discovered in one of the chests in the attics, depicted a pair of lovers under a palm tree, electro-plated on German silver. Starched damask napkins rolled and folded into silver rings lay on the side-plates, a subtle indication that this new arrangement would now be permanent.

Without further hesitation he removed the third place.

Heather

Darkness in the corners of the room crept closer. Heather crouched by the fire and watched the dwindling white-ashed logs. Two library books by Lillian Beckwith brought in that afternoon by Angela Macbride ('Do read them dear, they are about our beloved Highlands.') lay unread on the hearthrug. She had tried a page or two and finding them not to her liking, blamed herself. She could settle to nothing, least of all the tapestry that she had begun a while ago in an effort to keep her hands occupied. All she could think about was the bottle in the wardrobe in her room.

When she had got up at noon, headachy and hung-over, the bottle was small, like a tiny foetus in her mind, possible to ignore for short periods, but as the day aged, so it grew inch by inch, until it dominated every corner of her conscious thought. There could only be one relief. The exchange of the concept for reality, the bringing out of the bottle from the bag, the feel of the cool glass in her hand, the fire of the amber liquid on her tongue, the peace of oblivion in her mind.

While the image remained small, she told herself she still had a choice, but as the hours passed and the need increased, the excuses began. What harm was she doing? She had no child to hurt, no husband to placate. She never - hardly ever - drank during the day. It helped her to sleep. She was a nicer person

227

with a drink in her. In the end, she always managed to convince herself that alcohol was not just harmless but beneficial. With brandy in her there were no memories, no guilt, no shadows. Like now. All round her the darkness grouped into ghosts, familiar faces of her family of which she was the last living representative.

When Malcy came in, she saw them shift as quietly as petals falling from a flower, but they did not go away.

'The logs are finished,' she told him petulantly. 'It's getting cold.'

He opened the coal scuttle, put on a canvas glove and began to make up the dying fire.

'You know I detest coal,' she said, ashamed of the whine in her voice.

'Dinner is ready;' he said, ignoring her peevishness. He removed the glove and hooked up the fire-guard.

'I'm not hungry.'

It was her ritual complaint, and it was true. Hunger had long ago given way to thirst.

'Come along, Miss Heather,' he said patiently. 'You have to eat.'

'Christ,' she exclaimed, 'how cold it is.' She wrapped her arms round her shoulders and shivered. 'Is the heating on?'

'It's warm in the dining room.'

'What a wretched bully you are.'

She was aware of her childishness, of his patience with her, but, restless and irritable, she could not hold her tongue. 'Where's Bella? I thought she was coming back today.'

'I don't think,' he replied without expression, 'we'll be seeing much more of Bella.'

'Why on earth not?'

He moved to the door waiting for her to precede him.

'I'm sure I don't know, if you don't, Miss Heather,' he replied implying somehow that she was to blame.

228

Immediately she felt guilty, as she walked ahead of him out of the room. She noticed at once that the table was set for two. 'Oh Lord,' she complained, 'who's coming for dinner?'

Malcy was at the hot plate ladling out the soup. 'Someone has to make sure you eat,' he answered, bringing her bowl and setting it down on the tablemate in front of her. Then he fetched one for himself. After waiting for her to be seated, he sat down and unfolded his napkin.

She was shocked. Her reaction was instant and instinctive inherited from generations of masters who did not sit down to eat with their servants. She was also annoyed.

'I don't believe I asked you to dine,' she said, hearing her grandmother's inflection of disapproval in her voice.

He spread his napkin over his knees, then he looked at her. 'You ask me to do a lot of things you don't remember.'

Colour flooded her face as she recalled scenes she preferred to forget. She was also bewildered. However efficient, however necessary, however occasionally above himself, Malcy had always been to her no more than a servant. She knew she would never, even in her drunkest moments, have invited him to dine with her. Seeing him seated at her table confused her perception of him, changed her perspective, so that she no longer recognised him in relationship to herself. She could not bring herself to ask him to go, nor could she eat with him. Her reasons were complicated. Partly she would not know what to say to Malcy as a dinner companion, but most of all it excused her from having to eat at all. It brought the bottle nearer.

Summoning the shreds of her dignity, she rose and walked to the door. Turning once before she closed it, she looked him full in the face, 'Good night, Malcolm.'

He did not rise. Instead he returned her look and smiled a little. 'Good night, Miss Heather.'

Hurrying upstairs she was aware of nothing except the need for a drink. Inside her room, she crossed to the wardrobe and groped for the bottle. As soon as she touched it, she knew it was empty - and she had been so certain. She had gone to the

229

cellar that afternoon. At least she was almost certain it had been today. Maybe it was yesterday. Her mind darted about looking for sign-posts but she could remember nothing. Not that it mattered. There were plenty of bottles in the cellar.

She did not like to go down to the basement at night - she hated the cellar even by day - but now she had no choice. As she hurried downstairs, crossed the pillared hall, she was once again aware of ghostly hands, the gleam of ghostly eyes. All her old familiar fears of the dark returned.

The cellar door was locked. She groped for the key on the lintel where recently she had found it again quite by surprise after months of searching. Nothing there.

Malcolm. A gust of anger swept her up from the basement back to the dining room. Flinging open the door, she demanded, 'Where is the cellar key?'

He was eating the salmon mousse. He looked up at her and then down, meaningfully at the table. Following the direction of his gaze, she saw the key lying on her unused side plate

'How dare you remove it!' she cried, striding across the room. 'What right had you to take it?' but what she also meant was how dare you presume to sit down at my table without permission.

As she reached down to take the key, he grasped her wrist and held it between his crooked and steely fingers.

'Get down on your knees and beg.'

Her thighs weakened with shock. For a moment she defied him, eye to eye, but hers were the first to shift as the pressure on her wrist and in her mind increased. Awkwardly she sank to the floor.

Strangely enough, with the key in her hand, she felt better. It was not just that the punishment seemed to excuse the subsequent act of drinking, but rather that Malcy had again assumed perspective. The uneasy transition was over. He had moved from being a servant, part of the background of her sober hours, to the dominant foreground of her whole existence. As she submitted to his will, she realised that the battle had been a long, exhausting war that had lasted most of her adult life. Now that the worst had happened, she could only feel relief.

'Drink yourself to death for all I care,' he said contemptuously.

She did care. It suddenly seemed important to appease him. Meekly she sat down in her place and took a mouthful of the now cold consommé.

Bella

Bella's train had been delayed. Travelling from Glasgow that morning after settling Mrs B with her sister in the bungalow at Largs had tired her. It was a two-mile walk from the station to the gates of Nightingales and another half mile up the drive. Rain soaked her wool beret and seeped through the shoulders of her duffle coat. Her case dragged on her arm and the trees in the long avenue dripped with cold heavy drops. She could sense no welcome in their leafless outreach, no recognition of her spoken greeting. Guided by the gleam of the terrace lights, she had no wish to return to the looming house. She would have preferred to shut herself up in one of the greenhouses and spend the night with her plants.

'You're as daft as a cross-eyed monkey,' she told herself, as, purposefully, she crunched over the gravel round the side of the house and let herself in the back door.

As she closed the door behind her, she sighed. The weight of stone and silence was oppressive. She still missed the pawing and scuffle of the dogs. Miss Heather should get a puppy, a golden lab that would grow big and take her out of herself. Cheered by the thought, she changed out of her damp clothing.

She found them in the dining room.

'So you're back,' said Malcy from the table. 'You took your time.'

But it should have been Miss Heather to speak first to ask why she was so late, and what was Malcy doing sitting at his meat in the dining-room?

'Where's the great Curly-locks then?' Malcy continued. 'Ditched you, did he? Thought you'd come back with a ring on your finger and the banns to be called? Thought you could walk right back as if nothing had happened?'

Kitchen talk in the dining-room? Now she knew there was something wrong.

Miss Heather spoke then, but not until she had looked at Malcy first, and her voice was nervous.

'I'm glad you're back, Bella. You must be tired. Come and have something to eat.' She glanced at Malcy again.

'You're learning,' he told her, his voice edged with sarcasm.

Bella ignored him. 'I'll take my meat in the kitchen, if it's all the same to you, Miss Heather,' she said firmly.

'Suit yourself,' Malcy replied but he followed her out of the room.

Down in the kitchen, she shifted the kettle to the hot plate.

'What's going on?' she asked sharply.

He sat down at the table and pushed his chair back. 'Things have changed around here since you took yourself off. You'd better get used to it.'

She took some cold ham out of the fridge and cut herself a slice of bread. 'If you mean sitting down to a bowl of brown water and yon finicky cold fish at this hour of night, count me out.'

'She begged me on bended knee,' he lied unconvincingly.

'As if. You took advantage.'

'Shut up! Listen.' He held his finger to his mouth. From beyond the unclosed door, they both heard footsteps.

'That's her. Down to the cellar for more booze. She's no' fit to have a place like this. If it weren't for me it'd go to wrack and ruin. She cares for it aboot as much as she cared for her bairn. Not one bleeding jot. She's an effing wash-out. Let her kill herself. See if I care.'

Bella looked across at him from the Esse. He reminded her of a thorny thrusting thistle, Miss Heather as the threatened wilting

232

lily. She, Bella, was the gardener, bound to tend the flower, yet at that moment it was the weed she pitied.

'I ken what you do for her, what you do for this place. More than anybody has the right to expect, but she's still the one who pays the wages, she's the boss and the house is hers. Nothing can change that.'

He grinned at her suddenly. 'Don't you bet on it, hen.'

Angela

On the first day of March, 1965, Angela Macbride woke from a bad dream. Two ravens sat on a telegraph pole watching the antics of an unsuspecting rabbit. She had observed their unhurried gloat from behind plate glass, unable to warn the rabbit and awakened with forebodings. The star column in the *Express* warned her of bad news so that when, later that morning, the postman delivered one letter, she knew what to expect.

The notepaper was headed Nightingales, the contents typed and duplicated, but her name had been handwritten and the signature was Malcolm's.

Dear Angela, she read,

Mrs Percy-Drake has asked me to inform you that owing to illness she will not be opening Nightingales to the public as from April 17 (Easter Saturday). Therefore it is with regret that I have to inform you that your valued services will not be required for the forthcoming season. She apologises for any inconvenience this may cause and thanks you for your assistance in the past. Naturally this is a disappointment to us all and we must hope for better times next year.
Yours faithfully, Malcolm Gould

Angela's instant reaction was disbelief. Never during her occasional visits to Nightingales over the winter had she suspected that Heather might not be well. Everyone knew she

233

drank, but maybe it was worse than that. Maybe she had cancer. Poor woman. At the same time, disappointment swept over her. Apart from her enjoyment of the work, she had hoped to put aside enough for a deposit on a Mini. What would she do now with her herb pillows and lavender sachets that she had been making all winter, the pots of mint jelly and blackberry jam?

Yet, when she thought about it, she could not pretend to be wholly surprised. Although she had not seen Heather for nearly four weeks owing to the bad weather and a bronchitic cough, she had from time to time wondered how she would be able to cope with the public. Like everyone else, she had assumed that Malcolm would take charge as he had done last year, and virtually every year since the Major's death. Poor dear Heather's drinking must be out of control.

The news was received with more than disappointment by the villagers. Some depended on the work to supplement pensions. Others had financial commitments that relied on the extra income. An extraordinary meeting of all concerned was held in the church hall.

'Get hold of Gould,' said the disappointed car-park attendant, ex-Sergeant Wootton, who regimented the visitors with relish. 'Make him see sense.'

'I wouldn't mind,' said one of the women coarsely making others laugh.

Eventually it was decided that the vicar should head a deputation in the hope that it might still be possible to change Mrs P-D's mind. The following day, therefore, Angela, on behalf of the indoor staff, Sergeant Wootton for the outdoor workers and the vicar representing the village, called at Nightingales at the pre-arranged hour of 3 pm.

Malcolm, immaculate in fawn dust jacket and dark pressed trousers, opened the door and ushered them into the breakfast room. A log fire burned in the grate and two large bowls of hyacinths scented the air. A fitful February sun switched on and off their faces.

'Is Mrs Percy-Drake in?' the vicar asked courteously. 'We have an appointment.'

'I'll see if she's well enough to come downstairs,' said Malcolm smoothly, offering cigarettes all round from a silver box before leaving the room.

They waited patiently. From time to time Angela buried her nose in the flowers. 'Aren't they superb,' she remarked, and, 'What a pleasant room this is.' She hoped that Heather would not be drunk. Her personality changed so. Last time she had seen her in that state was on the way back from the Midnight service. Heather had remarked on their way down the aisle that her - Angela's - charm bracelet tinkled like water in a chamber pot. Most embarrassing.

When eventually Malcolm returned alone with the news that Heather was too indisposed to see anyone, the vicar spoke for them all. 'Is there anything you can do to persuade Mrs Drake to change her mind about opening the house? So many of the villagers are dependent on the work.'

Malcolm shrugged and spread his hands in a gesture that implied understanding and hopelessness without having to commit himself to an actual answer.

'Perhaps if Mrs P-D were to have some treatment?' the vicar continued. 'I know of an excellent place.'

'I'm sure you're right, sir, but that would make no difference with regard to Nightingales. If Miss Heather were to be away, we should be obliged to close the house.'

'Poppycock,' said Sergeant Wootton. 'You could run the whole show standing on your head.'

Malcolm's quick glance conveyed both gratification and rebuke. 'It's hardly my place - ' he began.

'Of course not,' the vicar said patiently. 'No one expects you to shoulder all the responsibility. On the other hand, if Mrs Drake were to have some treatment now, she might be well enough to reconsider her decision in a few months time.'

'I agree, sir. Everything you say is right. It's not me that needs to be convinced. I do my best.'

The vicar stood up. 'Perhaps if I were to have a word, it might help.'

'Of course, sir. I was hoping you'd say that. Perhaps tomorrow?'

'I was thinking that now might be the right time.'

'I don't think - ' Malcolm began, moving to the door.

'I know the way, 'said the vicar striding ahead of him and closing the door firmly behind him.

Malcolm's expression did not change. Angela looked up at him. 'Malcolm, I was thinking,' she coaxed, 'if the grounds could be open, that is the gardens, the tea-room and the park, we could move the shop out of the house to the tea-room and most of the jobs would be saved.'

'Now there's an idea! Good old British compromise,' said Sergeant Wootton heartily.

'I'll certainly put it to Miss Heather,' said Malcolm smoothly.

'Put it to yourself, Gould,' said the sergeant bluntly. 'We all know that you run the show.'

Malcolm turned to him with candid eyes, neither denying or agreeing. 'It has to be Miss Heather's decision. You'll need to excuse me if I put her wishes first. She's my concern, just as the village is yours.'

'We know that, Malcolm, and we admire you for it, but there would be no harm in making the suggestion, would there?' Angela coaxed.

At that moment the vicar returned. 'Mrs Drake is not in her room. I couldn't find her,' he said apologetically.

A log exploded in the fire showering the grate with sparks. Malcolm moved at once to remove them. With his back to the vicar, he said. 'Nightingales is a big place, sir.'

'Surely you must have some idea of where she is?'

'I couldn't begin to guess, sir.'

'I should have thought she would have had the common courtesy to keep an appointment,' said the sergeant shortly.

Malcolm looked at him in silent reproach.

236

'She's probably just forgotten,' said Angela, peaceably. 'I think we'd better go.'

'Can I offer you some refreshment?' Malcy offered politely. 'Tea or perhaps some sherry?'

When they refused he saw them to the door.

'What a waste of an afternoon,' said the sergeant disgustedly as they descended the terrace steps. 'That chap's as close as the Sealed Knot.'

'All I can say is that she's lucky to have a servant like that,' Angela said, climbing into the back of the Vicar's Ford Popular.

'Possibly,' said the vicar, switching on the engine.

'What do you mean "possibly",' Angela demanded. 'It's obvious he adores her.'

'It occurs to me that he is perhaps a little over-protective.'

'But surely that's his job. Look what she's been through. The Major's tragic death, that great house to run, and then the child. She once told me that she lost her parents when she was four years old. Malcolm and Bella have been family servants most of their lives. We surely should be thankful that she has such a reliable pair to depend on.'

'All I'm saying,' said the vicar mildly, 'is that it might be better for her in the long run if she had to stand on her own feet. I'm not altogether convinced that Malcolm has the right approach.'

'I don't know how you can be so critical,' Angela cried. 'I think he's wonderful.'

'One thing's obvious,' said the sergeant, interrupting the argument, 'neither of them cares a hoot for the village.'

Heather

Heather watched the car crawl down the drive. Gradually her taut nerves loosened.

'I won't see them,' she had said to Malcy, panicking when he had told her about the deputation. 'Don't make me.'

Surprisingly he had given in.

237

He had been so thoughtful lately sending out all those letters, answering all the calls. It had even been his idea to close Nightingales for the season. She had thought about it but hadn't liked to suggest it, knowing how much it meant to the village and, so she believed, to him. There was also the financial aspect.

'Can we afford it?' she had asked anxiously.

'You'll not go short of the needful, if that's what's bothering you,' he had answered, making it plain that he was not just talking about cash.

Though she tried to deny to herself that brandy had been uppermost in her mind, she knew, shamefully, that it was always close to the surface.

'How about the villagers? They depend on the work.'

'There's justice,' he had said edgily. 'You think of the village while I'm thinking of you; but who thinks about me? All you have to do is sit back and act Lady Muck. Have you any idea of the work involved?'

Her eyes instantly filled with tears, never far from the surface these days.

'I'm sorry, Malcy. I didn't think.'

That's your trouble. You never think. Besides,' he added contemptuously, 'who wants all that riff-raff and scum treading dirt into the carpets, poking their noses in where they're not wanted.'

'The Major always believed it was our duty to share what we have with the public,' she said tentatively.

'Balls. He did it for the money.'

Though she winced at his crudeness, she knew there was some truth in what he said. Not the whole truth, though.

'Why do you always put the worst interpretation on my motives?'

'You're a fucking fake, that's why.'

'Malcy!' His language shocked her, sober. When she was drunk it made her giggle.

'This time, you'll have to choose. Me or the village.'

238

That was no choice at all. Like brandy, Malcy was necessary. Just as alcohol obliterated her guilt and her memories, so Malcy had taken over the management of her social life. Brandy and Malcolm had become the walls of her existence. The more she remained enclosed, the harder it was to break free. The truth was that she no longer wanted to escape. Fear of her life without the security of walls and ceiling was only part of the reason. Shame was the floor. The more Malcy controlled her, the less able she became, mentally, to face the world and the more brandy she drank the less able she was, physically, to manage her life. Together with shame came the need for punishment. Malcy had also become her scourge. Part of her welcomed his crude language, the private taunts and contempt. So long as she was punished, she could sin.

When she heard the vicar's knock on her door and polite query, her first instinct was to hide. She fled like a scared rabbit through the communicating door to Miles' old room and waited half concealed by the curtain, watching from the window until the deputation had gone.

It was not until the car had disappeared that she registered the changes around her.

Astonished, she stared at the room. Gone were the sepia-tinted school and army photographs, family groups and cricket teams that had covered the drab walls, to be replaced by white paint, unadorned. The high narrow bed was no longer dressed in the sun-bleached patchwork quilt - Eva's handiwork - but with an imitation leopard skin counterpane. One or two good pieces of furniture remained but the marble wash-stand had gone to be replaced by a full length cheval looking-glass which had come from one of the spare rooms. The faded Indian carpet had been exchanged for blue wall-to-wall Axminster of the same quality as the new stair carpeting. The Wisden cricket almanacs and back copies of *Sporting Life* that had once littered the bedside cabinet had also gone. Only one book remained. Because of the bible, she knew this was now Malcy's room.

Her first instinct was despair. What would Miles have thought? Tears filled her eyes as she stared around the transformed room. She was overwhelmed with shame and longing and loneliness. The removal of his possessions without a word, the obliteration of his personality, made her angry. How could Malcy have been so insensitive, so presumptuous. He had gone too far.

As always, she could not sustain her anger. As she thrashed around in her mind for someone to blame, she settled as usual on herself. She should have thought to offer him a better room. She surely had been the insensitive one expecting him to live like a tweeny in the garret. It was when she turned to go back to her own room. that she noticed the key had gone.

She knew, had always known what he really wanted, although, up till now, she had refused to recognise that knowledge. Repulsed and attracted at the same time, the old familiar sensations of fear mixed with sexual excitement that had always existed in her relationship with Malcy, returned. Why had she not got rid of him years ago? It was too late now.

I need a drink, she thought.

That night she dressed for dinner.

She was aware that Malcy, as he sounded the gong in the well of the hall, was watching her descend the rich red-carpeted stairs. In black velvet with a narrow ribbon around her throat she knew she looked good. She was feeling good. Teetering on the edge of drunkenness, she tripped on the bottom stair.

'Malcy,' she said clutching his arm as she tried to regain her footing. 'I've been thinking.'

'That makes a change,' he said dryly.

'About you,' she added coyly.

'Changes all round,' he said sarcastically, but, for the first time in weeks, he drew back her chair in the dining room to let her sit down.

'Seriously.' She leaned towards him, but she did not feel serious. She felt unashamedly frivolous. 'I want to tell you something.'

'No one's stopping you.'

'Don't interrupt. I want to tell you how much I appreciate everything you do for me. Look,' she said spreading a sliver of toast with pate, 'I'm eating. That shows you how serious I am.'

'What's brought this on all of a sudden?'

She could tell he was suspicious, not sure of her in this mood. She touched his hand reassuringly, and, at the same time, wondered at the strange light-hearted, flirtatious person she became with a little brandy in her. 'All I wanted to say was thank you for getting rid of those three ogres this afternoon. I appreciated that. Were they very difficult?'

'I handled it.'

'Of course you did "Your Malcolm is such a charmer!" That's what Angela Macbride always says. "I hope you appreciate him, Heather".'

'Appreciation costs nothing,' he said shortly.

'That's why I want to give you a little pressie. What would you like, I wonder?'

As he lifted the pate plates and took them to the sideboard, he said nothing. When, she wondered, had she - or anyone else for that matter - ever given him more than useful things at Christmas like an umbrella or a suitcase, a new shirt, perhaps for his birthday. Presents so often came with strings attached. She had more than once rejected his.

He served the chicken casserole from the hot plate. When she had eaten a small forkful, she looked up.

'I mean it, Malcy. I want to give you something special. Something I think you've wanted for a long time.'

He poured himself some water. She knew she was flirting with him, that he knew what was on offer. 'You know what I want,' he said crudely. Her body flared suddenly with a surge of excitement. 'On the King's bed,' he told her roughly.

241

They left the dining-room, the food uneaten on their plates and went upstairs, she slightly ahead, he on her heels, but they did not touch. The effect of the pre-dinner brandy was wearing off fast. She knew she could not go through with it sober.

'I won't be a minute,' she said pausing at the first floor landing outside her room but he caught her arm.

'Not on your nelly.' He knew exactly what she had intended. 'You can tank up afterwards.'

The great ornate King's Chamber was shrouded in dustsheets. Almost sober now and shivering, she wondered how she had managed to get herself into such a ridiculous position. Brandy had done it. Without brandy, this was a crass and ugly mistake. She looked at him hoping for a reprieve.

His face was white and his eyes blazed. He held his hands clenched at his side in a gesture that so reminded her of Will in a tantrum that her focus shifted and she saw him no longer as Malcolm, the servant who dominated her life, but as the child who had once watched her from behind the dining-room blinds, the boy from the orphanage who had been as deprived of love as her son had been deprived of oxygen, damaged. She was filled with a sudden anguish that moved the very muscles of her womb, a yearning, agonising ache. First she thought there must be tenderness. She put her arms around him. Taller by two inches in her heels, she drew his head against her breast and held it close. His golden hair was thinning just a little on top. She kissed his head. His body lifted in a long shuddering sigh.

'Malcy,' she said with a sudden flash of humour, 'you're going bald.'

'Is it any wonder with you on my plate.' he replied, his voice muffled against her dress.

But tenderness was not enough. The feel of his body in her arms, the touch of his head on her breast awakened other stronger urges that had lain suppressed by grief and alcohol, dormant since Will and Miles' death. Kicking off her shoes, she lifted his head and pressed her mouth to his lips. Lust loosened every muscle in her body. She remembered how she had loved to kiss.

He did nothing, neither put his arms around her nor opened his mouth to hers. She wondered if he were a virgin. She had never known him to have a girl friend. For all his domineering assertive ways, he seemed uncertain now. That excited her. For once she was in control.

After a while she drew back from him and began to un-knot his tie…

His upper body was child-like, smooth and hairless, unblemished, very thin. Running her hands over the smooth skin of his back she felt his flesh stipple with goose pimples under her touch. Impatient now she shrugged out of her dress. He stared at her body, but not with pleasure, not even with lust. There was a twist to his mouth that might have been pain, a bleakness in his eye that had nothing to do with love.

But she had gone too far. There was no going back for her, so she rejected the evidence of her eyes and with both hands drew him down with her on to the bed and entwined his body in her limbs. He began to struggle, pushing her off him. 'Bitch,' he hissed at her, 'You stink of booze.' Then suddenly without warning he lowered his head and sank his teeth into her left breast.

When she screamed, he raised his head and looked down at her. In spite of the pain she became still. In his eyes she saw into his soul, and, suddenly completely sober, she shivered.

He moved first, lifting himself off her body, and, with a final expletive, picked up his shirt and left the room. At the door he turned. 'Don't get blood on that coverlet. It's priceless,' he told her.

Looking down she saw that her breast was bleeding. She rose painfully from the bed. With one hand she staunched the blood - there wasn't much - with her silk underskirt, and with the other she drew the folds of her dress around her shoulders to cover her nakedness.

Back in her room, she examined the wound. The bite was not that deep but it was extremely painful. She needed a doctor, but how could she face the family quack with a wound like this. Who could she face? There was only Bella. With difficulty she drew on a nightgown that buttoned down the front, and, wrapping a mohair shawl around her shoulders crept down to the basement.

Bella was alone in the kitchen watching television. It was just after nine.

'What's up?' she asked, seeing Heather's face.

With trembling hands, Heather removed the shawl and took away the pad of cotton wool that she had put there to staunch the blood. The skin around the bite marks had already begun to discolour. Fresh blood oozed between her fingers. 'It hurts,' she said, trying to lighten her voice, but overcome with tears.

'Tchk tchk!' Bella clicked her tongue. 'What happened?'

Heather shook her head, unable to speak. She was shivering.

Bella switched off the television. She drew a chair near to the Esse, opened the oven door wide and made Heather sit close to the heat.

'It'll be fine,' she said shortly and left the kitchen

For a moment Heather thought she had gone to fetch Malcy and tried to call her back. Presently she returned alone with the First Aid box that was always kept handy in the office in case of accidents to the tourists.

'Did you ken that Malcy was born with teeth?' she asked as she washed the wound. 'I mind him at Big Lizzie's breast, frantic for milk, he was. She was never the one to indulge a bairn, as mebbe you know, so she took her time. When at last he caught her with his wee mouth, he bit her. He did nae mean it. It was just that she tantalised him when he was hungry.'

Heather remembered herself at dinner, primed with alcohol, playing the whore. She remembered other times when she was drunk tantalising him deliberately, nor was her behaviour recent. It had started when she had let him watch her from behind the blinds. All her life, it seemed, she had played with

244

his feelings and rejected his gifts. She had only wanted him because she was drunk.

'And that excuses him.' The sentence was both a statement and a question. She did not really know.

'Malcy's no' like other men,' Bella said, fixing a pad to the wound with strips of sticky tape. 'He lives in the wilderness.'

Then Bella made her a cup of tea and gave her two tablets from the medicine box to dull the pain.

'It was my fault,' Heather said. 'I'm not good for him,' and then to herself under her breath. 'He'll have to go.'

Having made the decision, she felt better. Her mind expanded with plans. Nightingales would go on the market at once. That would give the villagers something to talk about. Bella had made no secret of the fact that she would like to return to the Lodge. She would give Malcy a good reference. He could get another job easily enough. She herself could travel. She had always wanted to motor across Europe.

Later, in bed, in less pain, she felt fragile, but full of hope like an invalid on the mend. When sleep finally weighted her eyes, she realised she had done it all without a drink.

Bella

When Bella had settled Miss Heather in her room, She went straight to Malcy's door.

She had not approved of his move from the attic, gigglingly reported to her by Rose, one of the village girls who came in five mornings a week to do the housework.

'Suits me fine,' she added, 'one room less to clean can't be bad. How am I supposed to clear up after him if he keeps his door locked?'

Bella did not knock. She tried the handle and it turned. Malcy was not there. The room, considering Malcy's standards of tidiness, was surprisingly unkempt. His good suit lay discarded and crumpled on the bed, his shoes and socks were scattered on the carpet. An empty coat-hanger poked from the open wardrobe door. Automatically she began to pick up his things. She hung up his suit, slotted his shoes into the rack, folded his socks and put away his shirt. She did these things for him out of an abiding pity not founded on the excuses she had offered Miss Heather, but because she believed that Malcy could no more shed his nature than a nettle its sting.

The shabby bible by his bed looked incongruous in the now tidy room. Its presence surprised her for Malcy, as far as she knew, had never darkened the door of a church. Curiously she picked it up. The clasp was closed but not locked so she opened it.

The cavity was filled with post office saving books and bank accounts, all in different names. She shook them all out on the bed and glanced through them. So much money! Where had it all come from? A newspaper cutting neatly folded, clung to the bottom of the space. She took it out, smoothed it open and read it through. Carefully she re-folded it and put it back with the account books in the bible and closed the clasp. Then she went to bed.

At ten minutes to two she was still awake when Malcy returned, tip-toeing past her basement door.

She did not sleep at all that night.

Heather

Heather rose at nine, dressed with some difficulty in cord jeans with a loose smock top. The pain had dulled but her shoulder and arm had stiffened. Downstairs in the breakfast room, Rose had lit a fire which burned brightly in the grate.

'Good morning, Rose,' she said quietly. 'Would you bring me some coffee, please.'

When the girl had gone after a brief glance at her mistress who did not usually appear till lunch-time, she sat down at the telephone and rang her solicitor.

'John,' she said. 'I think I've come to my senses at last. I've decided to sell up. When can you come down?'

246

He made an appointment for the following day.

Her hands were shaking when she put down the receiver. Brandy flashed a golden message across her mind as she waited on a knife-edge for the coffee. Malcy brought it in.

She had already formulated how she would act in the face of his contrition. She would be magnanimous. The news that she was selling up would be punishment enough for she knew that he cared for the place. When she saw him, however, she was disconcerted. He looked vigorous and well. There was no evidence or expression that he was either sorry or ashamed. For a moment she began to wonder if the whole of last evening had been a ghastly drunken dream.

'Good morning, Miss Heather,' he said blandly. 'Looks like you had a good night.'

His effrontery astonished her. She supposed she ought to say something pertinent but what was the point? His attitude made her task easier.

'There you are, Malcolm,' she began quietly. 'I was hoping you would look in. I've just been in touch with John Spencer. I think you should be the first to know my plans. I've decided to put Nightingales on the market more or less immediately.'

Now that she had started she did not know how to stop. She could hear a rising note in her voice and her speech quickened. 'I'm sorry in so many ways, but in view of all that has happened, I think it will be for the best. It means of course that you and Bella too, will have to make other arrangements. Your reference should get you a post in a far better place than this and you'll find me not ungenerous...please ask Mrs Bushy to get a brace of pheasants from the deep freeze. We shall be feeding Mr Spencer tomorrow...' As long as she kept talking she could postpone the storm. Finally the words died out.

He never took his eyes from her face. She braced herself for his reaction.

Again he took her by surprise. Coming so close to her that her aching breast winced, he said in an even voice, 'I want Nightingales. I'll make you an offer you can't refuse.' She was

247

too stunned to speak. 'Think it over, Miss Heather. It may be the best offer you'll get.'

He turned and walked away. At the door, he paused and flashed her a radiant smile. 'I'll be back.'

Before she could collect her wits, he had gone.

Bella

That morning Bella pruned the roses in the parterre under a cloudless March sky. Though she kept close to the house she did not once look up at the windows nor did she return to the kitchen for her lunch.

At noon she joined Copperwheat in the tool-shed. They made the usual cup of tea on the paraffin stove and sugared it generously. She drank a cup thirstily and accepted one of Arthur's Marmite sandwiches. He told he that there was bacterial canker in one of the cherry trees in the orchard. She agreed to take a look at it.

The tree was known to her for last summer small sickly holes had appeared in the leaves of several branches. These had been removed and burned and the branches treated with a bitumous dressing but now she could see the canker clearly in the bark, that tell-tale exudation of resinous gum.

Above her, the clusters of buds enticed by a warming sun were beginning to open as purely and delicately as butterfly wings against the sky, yet she knew sadly that they would never mature into sweet red fruit.

'What do you think?' Arthur asked, as awed as she by the fragile beauty of the buds.

She wanted to say, 'Let it be. Let it bloom and flourish for as long as it can. Try Stockholm tar,' but instead she shook her head. The disease was incurable and it was infectious and there were the other trees to consider.

'It'll have to go.'

She stood staring up at the branches long after Arthur had gone.

Heather

After lunch, Heather thought about going out. The sun in warm shafts lanced through the windows dimming the fire, catching the winter dust in dizzy spirals.

Outside, the snowdrops had given way to daffodils on the drive. Nightingales was at its best. Yet the sun depressed her. Spring, that great burgeoning of the earth contrasted cruelly with her own sterility. She seemed to be sliding backwards into darkness while the world around her thrust forwards into light. She closed one of the curtains against the strident beams.

At first the thought of selling had been like a beacon illuminating her future with hope which Malcy's extraordinary proposal had extinguished.. He must be mad. Last night's behaviour and now this. All morning her mind had swung uneasily from incredulity to prejudice - he was the last person she wanted to own Nightingales; from guilt to fear - what more could he do to her? With the fear had returned the dry-mouthed, shivering need to drink.

Several times she rose to go down to the cellar and changed her mind. Once she thought of ringing Angela but the effort was too great. She tried to think ahead, to make a list of what she should say to her solicitor, but her thoughts disintegrated before she could put them down on paper. All the confidence she had felt that morning was draining fast.

When Malcy came in, she was still sitting at her desk in front of an empty pad. Instead of tea, he carried a bottle of Courvoisier and an envelope file.

'Sitting in the dark? We can't have that,' he said moving across the room to draw the curtains.

'Leave them alone,' she said sharply.

The sight of the alcohol warmed her body, filled her mouth with saliva, restored some of her confidence. She could wait a little longer.

He opened the drinks cabinet and took out two brandy glasses. 'Well, Miss Heather? Do we celebrate?'

She wished she had the strength to dismiss him, to tell him to take the bottle away but she knew she did not possess that sort of courage. Instead she asked nervously, 'Celebrate?'

He put down the bottle. 'I'm disappointed in you, Miss Heather. I understood you were putting the house on the market. I was hoping you had thought over my offer.'

Though his voice was light and controlled, she was aware of his inner excitement. It shone out of his pale blue eyes. Her heart began to beat in thick heavy strokes.

'I'm afraid I didn't take you seriously.' She laughed nervously. 'Did you win the pools or something?'

He held out the file, jabbing it impatiently at her, forcing her to take it into her hands.

'Read this. It'll show you how serious I am.'

'What is it?' she asked without opening the buff cover. Her mouth was dry and she was breathing from her throat.

'Open it. I guarantee you'll find it interesting.'

He hovered as she drew out a sheaf of papers including a grey-backed stockbroker's portfolio with the name of a well-known firm on the front.

'What is all this?' She rifled through the pages of figures but she read nothing, aware only of his closeness. Her breast had begun to throb. She wanted to cry out, 'Get away from me. Leave me alone,' but she did not dare.

'Proof,' he declared with triumph, 'that my money's as good as yours any day.' His voice had hardened and coarsened. 'Oh I know you think me trash, not posh enough to be lord of the manor, just a jumped-up servant with ideas above his station. Did you ever stop to ask yourself who it was kept Nightingales from rotting under your feet? Who slaved day and night to make it pay? Who turned it into a show place fit for royalty? It was me, hen, me, on my bloody tod. You owe me Mrs Percy-hyphen-Drake. You owe me big time.'

She cringed from his bitterness, but, at the same time, knew that there was some truth in all he said.

'What do you want me to do?' she asked faintly.

He seized the folder from her, flicked through the papers, till he found the one he wanted. He laid it on the desk in front of her. 'I want your name on this piece of paper promising me first refusal when you sell. I want it ready to show your poncy lawyer in the morning.' His voice changed again; menace gave way to craftiness, 'Go on , Miss Heather. What harm can it do?'

She mistrusted him completely. 'It won't be binding,' she said hearing the tremor in her voice. 'Not in law.'

He took a pen out of his breast pocket and held it out to her. 'You bet your life it'll be binding. It'll stick like glue.'

'And if I refuse to sign?' she whispered. She could not look at him or touch his pen.

He came so close that she could feel the heat of his breath. 'I think you will.'

Since the previous night her fear of him had changed from wariness to physical terror. Her body began to tremble, her muscles slackened and she could not move.

'Where?' she whispered, staring, without seeing the paper.

He pointed with his thin bent forefinger forcing her to look at the typed words at the top of the foolscap sheet.

I, Heather Percy-Drake of Nightingales, by Selworth, Hants, promise to give Malcolm Gould of the same address, first refusal in the purchase of the said house for a sum to be arranged by mutual agreement.

At the foot of the page there was a line of dots for her signature.

This was ridiculous, ludicrous. The ill-designed sheet with the naively expressed statement betrayed his ignorance. There was something so pathetic about it that she knew John Spencer would make mincemeat of it. She picked up another pen from the desk and sprawled her signature across the bottom of the page. He took it, folded it in a long manilla envelope and made her write *To Mr John Spencer* on the outside.

'Now,' he said triumphantly as he put the envelope into his file, 'you can celebrate to your heart's content. Make the most of it, hen.'

He did not stay for the toast.

Malcy

Mrs Bushy took off her apron.

'That's me finished for the day. The casserole's in the oven and there's a cold sweet in the fridge. Tell the boss I'll be in good and early in the morning to see to the pheasants. Did she say who's coming for lunch?'

Malcy was reading the *Mirror*, his face concealed by the opened sheets of paper.

'Did you hear a word I said, Mister Gould?'

He did not lift his eyes from the newspaper. 'You going now, Mrs B?' he asked pleasantly.

'What's that you're saying?' She had heard him perfectly well but she was annoyed with him. He did not reply. In a mood, was he? Well, two could play at that game. 'I've better things to do that to run after you,' she said loudly. If she didn't get a move on, she'd miss *Coronation Street*.

She opened the kitchen door and reached for her coat from the peg in the passage. At the same time Bella came in the back door.

'Bella Gould! It's about time,' she declared, following her back into the kitchen. 'Your lunch's still in the fridge   Where have you been all day?'

Bella ignored her. She had eyes only for her brother. What a pair.

'You'll get nothing out of him,' she told her with a sniff. Neither of them was listening to her. 'Might as well speak to a brick wall,' she grumbled. 'Well I'll be for the off, then. Tattie bye.'

Neither of them said goodnight.

As soon as she'd gone, Bella said, 'You're sick.'

252

He crushed the paper and stuffed it down the side of the chair. 'Who, me?' he asked innocently. 'Never felt better in my life.' He grinned at her and stretched back in his chair. 'Wait till I tell you the good news.'

'The only news I'm waiting to hear is why you hurt Miss Heather?'

He frowned. 'None of your business, poky nose.' Then he added, 'Believe you me, she can count herself lucky.'

The lid of the closed well opened a fraction for a moment before it slammed shut. She knew what he was talking about.

'Malcy,' she said in a different tone. 'I've been thinking. Let's you and me go back to Ladymuir. You can't expect Miss Heather to keep you now.'

He laughed. 'You're 'way behind the times, Crawface. Nightingales is up for sale. We've got the sack, you and me both.'

Relief weakened her legs. She sat down at the table.

'Only,' he added, grinning. 'We're no' going. She's the one for off, so don't you go upsetting yourself.'

She shook her head. 'I'll not let you touch her. You've done enough.'

'What are you havering on about? Did you not hear me right? She's selling. I'm buying. I always told you Nightingales would be mine one day. Did I not tell you?'

She remembered the account books in the bible.

'Where did you get all that money?'

He grinned at her again. 'Ask no questions and you'll get told no lies.'

'It's you that's lying. Do you think I rode up the creek on a bicycle?'

That needled him. He reached for the buff file under the chair and pushed it across the table. 'Take a look inside. That'll tell you who's lying.'

She glanced at the papers. 'What's all this, then?'

'That's power that is. That's negotiable property. That'll keep me in Nightingales like a lord.'

253

Heaviness weighted her world. 'Miss Heather'll never sell to the likes of you.'

'Little you ken,' he sneered, seizing the file from her and finding the relevant paper. 'It's here in black and white. Listen to this.' He read her the signed statement. 'First refusal means I get to buy. She signed it herself. All it needs is your name at the bottom as a witness.

'I'm signing nothing. You can't make me.'

He seized her wrist. ' I can make you do anything I like, Crawface. I'm the Magician. No one stands in my way, not you, nor the polis, nor the Queen of England herself. You'd better believe it.'

'Then get someone else to do your dirty work. I'm no' putting my name to yon rubbish.'

His manner changed. He cocked his head craftily and offered to bargain. 'Tell you what I'll do. When I get Nightingales I'll let you stay. I'll need a gardener. I might even up your pay. How about an extra fiver a week?'

She shook her head stubbornly. 'Not for fifty.'

Surprisingly he did not press her. 'Suit yourself,' he said slipping the paper back into the file. 'See if I care. You'll be the one to regret it.' He stood up and moved to the door. 'I'm off. Work to do.'

'What about Miss Heather's dinner?'

He grinned and made a drinking gesture with his hand. 'She's got all she needs.'

When he had gone Bella reached for the *Mirror* which Malcy had pushed down the side of his chair. It was folded to a central spread.

Victim Number Four? the half-inch capitals queried in bold. Underneath was a professional photograph of a middle-aged woman, well dressed, wearing a string of pearls and a Mona Lisa smile, against the backdrop of a studio curtain.

The column continued *This is the woman who died when a brutal murderer struck yesterday evening at 10 15 approximately. Marjorie Parkes, 44, ex-wife of cake-mix tycoon,*

254

Roger Parkes, 48, and mother of two, was walking her dog in the woods near Chidingfold when she was raped and strangled. Mrs Parkes, charity worker and fund-raiser for the RSPCA is thought by police to be another victim of the Christmas strangler who struck down Mrs Emma Coleman, 38, a mile from her home near Salisbury on Christmas Eve three months ago. The hunt is on for a brutal and elusive murderer who has evaded arrest too long.

The Christmas Strangler's chilling death role began on January 25 1965 with the savage murder of Mrs Peggy Garson, 45, found mutilated and raped in the back garden of her 18th century cottage in Oxfordshire, but another woman was to die before the police established the killer's horrific trademark, savage mutilation prior to strangling. Singer, Michelle Boot, 39, slaughtered behind her garage on the banks of the River Alne near Stratford-upon-Avon was the killer's second known victim. Mrs Boot, mother of three, professional singer, was struck down while her husband slept in their secluded bungalow only yards away.

Under photographs of the three victims, the column continued.

What is it that links the four women in the mind of the killer? Is there any significance in the fact that all were middle-aged, all country-dwellers living in remote areas, all the mother of sons? Detective Inspector Joe Slater in charge of the Emma Coleman case and now called to the incident room at Chidingfold isn't telling. Known to be a relentless cop, dedicated to hunting down this monster, 'I'm confident we'll catch him,' was all he would say at this stage.

Bella laid the paper down She stared unseeingly at her two hands upturned in her lap for a timeless period. She had read it all before in the cuttings inside the bible

Heather

Heather was not drunk. In spite of several brandies she was for the moment lucid, sane and unutterably depressed. She saw

255

herself as weak, degraded, worthless, despised by her servants no less than she despised herself. 'Count your blessings,' Nanny used to sing in a tremulous soprano. She was ashamed to try. There had been so many squandered and discarded.

Looking back on her life she could find nothing accomplished or completed. Time stretched behind her, a wilderness of lost opportunities. Worse than the man who had buried his talent in the ground, she had thrown hers away. She could find no redeeming feature in her past. Her mind, like a bee on the honey trail, darted from one event to another without finding a single sweet memory on which to rest. She would be better dead. Who would care? Maudlin tears of self-pity sprang to her eyes as she visualised the family tomb opened, Bella and Malcolm dry-eyed at her grave.

The thought of death was not new to her, but never had it seemed so attractive. A few more drinks would fix it, but this time she did not want to move out of the pit of depression. Opening the bottom drawer of her bureau, she took out the appropriate keys.

The gun-room was in the west wing. She unlocked three doors, passing fearlessly through metres of passages. Inside, she locked the door behind her.

She knew about guns. Lady Mowbray had been a good shot before arthritis had crippled her hands. She had believed it important that her grand-daughter should be able to handle a gun. Later, Miles and she had spent several September holidays in the Highlands where she had stalked and shot her first red deer. There were plenty of guns to choose from including some valuable ancient weapons displayed in cases on the wall, an armoury of appropriate sporting pieces, and, locked in a drawer, what she was really looking for. The Walther PPK which Miles had acquired during the war was in mint condition. Opening the magazine, she slipped in one of the three remaining cartridges. As far as she could remember, it contained seven rounds.

Back in the sitting room, she poured herself another dram, placed the gun in front of her on the desk and pulled out a sheet of notepaper. Slowly in her neatest writing she addressed it to the coroner.

She sat there for a long time reviewing her life, probing old wounds. When it came to words, she could think of nothing to write.

Malcolm

Malcy had no such difficulty. With the help of a printed form he was writing a will. He read it over several times, crossed out a superfluous word, added an extra phrase until he was satisfied. Then he laid out the sheet of paper that Heather had signed, and, taking a ruler from the pigeon hole in the office desk, carefully drew a line under the short statement. Neatly he cut it off, tore up the top into small pieces and put them in the waste paper basket.

Silly cow, he thought. Fancy being taken in by a trick like that. Women! Whoever gave them the vote?

Smiling to himself, he inserted the sheet with the signature into the office typewriter. There was room enough for the new paragraph. The next bit was trickier. Under Miss Heather's signature, he typed out the words, *First Witness* with space beneath for *Occupation* and *Address*. Adjacent he wrote *Second Witness* and under it the same requirement. Then he reached for an old Visitor's Book, opened it at a page dated two years back and lifted his pen. He had already practiced the signatures he had chosen. One had an address in Australia. The other, he happened to know, was dead.

At the bottom of the page he added a date. It would have been Will's eighth birthday. The first one Billy-boy had missed.

Folding the document in three, he slipped it into the envelope that Heather had addressed to her solicitor. Then he glanced at his watch. 9.30. She should be pie-eyed and raving by now. One sharp push from the top of the stairs and Nightingales would be his.

Heather

As soon as he opened the door, Heather realised she had been waiting for him. He saw the gun in her hand, and, momentarily, she caught the whites of his eyes.

He was talking fast. 'You be careful where you point that thing. It's dangerous, so it is. We don't want any nasty accidents now, do we?'

With a sickly excitement she saw he was scared.

'Come along, Miss Heather. You give it to me. You'll only hurt yourself.'

Slowly she lifted the gun, released the safety catch and pointed it at him. Her hand was shaking from the alcohol, no other reason.

'Not me, hen,' he said coming nearer with his hand out, then added under his breath, 'it's you who's for the chop, one way or another.'

She shot him in the knee.

Jesus Christ!' he cried, collapsing in agony. Blood spurted over his hands where he held his leg. She was terrified. Her teeth chattered. The gun stuck to her hand, her finger on the trigger moved of its own accord, and the shots went wild. One shattered a bowl of tulips and lodged in the earth.

Bella

A moment sooner and Bella would never have heard the shots. She had gone to Malcy's office to say what must be said and found it empty. She had looked around the tidy little room with the neat rows of ledgers, filing cabinets and pigeon holes and thought of Lizzie. 'A place for everything and everything in its place,' as she used to say. He was like his mother there.

The buff-coloured folder was on his desk. On top of it lay the envelope addressed in Miss Heather's hand to her solicitor. She looked at it without moving for a while. Then she picked it up and tore it into two pieces and put them in her pocket.

258

She was crossing the hall when she heard three shots. The first might have been a coal exploding on the hearth. The second and third were unmistakeable. 'Who's shooting rooks at this hour?' was her first thought, but instinct sent her straight to Miss Heather's living room...

Malcy clung to Bella as she bound a handkerchief round his lower thigh to stem the bleeding.

'Keep that crazy bitch away,' he whispered. 'She'll kill me, so she will.'

The pain was excruciating, hammering at his knee, shooting knives through his whole body. Outrage kept him conscious. 'I'll have the law on her. I'll sue her for every penny.'

Heather was near hysteria. 'Oh God what have I done?' She moaned repeatedly. 'I'm sorry. I'm so sorry. Will he be all right? Ring for an ambulance, Bella.'

'Later,' said Bella firmly. 'First, you'll help me take him down the stair.' She was firmly in control.

'We can't,' Heather cried, 'Just look at him!'

'There's no such word.'

As soon as they tried to raise him, he screamed, but Bella persisted. 'I want him down by me,' she insisted.

Mercifully he lost consciousness as they put their arms round his waist and half lifted, half dragged him down the basement stairs nor he did not recover his senses until he was stretched out on Bella's bed.

'We must get the doctor,' Heather said weakly. 'There was blood on her clothes and on her hands where she had held him. The sob of hysteria lifted her voice.

'And just what will you say to him?' Bella demanded. 'That you deliberately shot him? You just leave the doctor and the talking to me.'

'I can't let you take the responsibility,' she began weakly already sounding doubtful.

'Och, away to your bed, Miss Heather. You're doing no good here.' she answered sharply.

'Well, if you're sure you can manage…' If she did not have a drink she would collapse.

'Aye, hen, I'm sure,' Bella said gently.

Heather paused at the door. 'You love him, don't you.' It was a statement, not a question. 'I was never sure.'

Bella stared at her, black eyes impenetrable. 'What has love to do with it? You just do what's needed.'

As the door closed she turned back to the man on her bed. Staring down at his face, pallid from loss of blood, sweaty with pain, she could find no clue, no indication, no sign of the monster she believed him to be. She could not fear him, hate him or feel the repugnance that his deeds deserved. Cruel and wicked though she knew him to be, she was aware only of pity. Perhaps if she had ever really loved him she could have hated him now.

He stirred. His head turned sharply on the pillow and suddenly she thought of the fairmer's line ferret.

He opened his eyes. His features contorted with pain. 'Did you get the doctor? Did you ring the polis?

'Oh Malcy,' she said sadly, shaking her head,' you don't want the polis. Not you.'

His expression changed. His eyes shifted. He knew very well what she meant. His voice regressed to a childish whine that she remembered so well from the old days.

'You're no' to tell.'

Bella sat down beside him on the bed. With her rough palm she stroked a streak of hair from his brow. Uncharacteristically he closed his eyes to her touch and right up through the balls of her fingers she could feel his sickness which was not just the pain from his knee. She was filled with such tenderness that she wanted to lift him in her arms and hide him inside her; feelings that were so new to her that she did not know how to sustain them. She would have wept if she'd remembered how.

Part of that flood of pity flowed through her touch into his skin. With both hands he reached up to cover hers, pressing them hard against his brow as if she could heal him by her touch.

'Jesus, Crawface,'he moaned, 'my leg hurts,'

'I'll get you something for the pain.'

She ran upstairs to Miss Heather's bathroom. The cupboard was full of half consumed medications, paracetamol, aspirin, valium etc and there at the back eight mogadons in a bottle cleared labelled which had first been prescribed for Miss Heather when the Major was killed. She crushed them all into a cup of tea and sugared it liberally to disguise the taste. She lifted his head to help him drink.

'Yon's disgusting,' he murmured but under her coaxing fingers he drank every drop.

When he was drowsy she took a look at his knee. With gentle fingers she untied the tourniquet. After a very short while the blood cease to flow.

Four days later at 8 am on a chilly March morning, Curly swung round the drive in his van to the back of the house. Bella was ready, dressed in her best coat with a shopping bag containing sandwiches and a flask. Her luggage stood waiting by the back door.

'You're early,' she said approvingly as she let him in. 'The breakfast's made.'

'Great,' he said, rubbing his cold hands together. 'Lead me to it.'

He pulled up a chair, drenched the porridge in sugar and milk and picked up his spoon.

'You'll need all of that inside you if you're to shift they cases,' she told him, pouring out his tea. 'I'm away to say goodbye to the boss.'

Heather was awake. For the second morning in a row she had awoken without a hangover.

'I thought I heard the lorry. Has Curly arrived?'

'Aye. He's taking his breakfast in the kitchen. Yours is all set.'

261

'So you're really going, Bella?' she asked, conjuring regret into her voice, but she could only feel relief. 'Will I ever be able to replace you?'

'Arthur and Ted Copperwheat 'll manage just fine.'

'But they don't have your green fingers.'

'It's for the best,' said Bella evenly.

'And Malcy?' she asked. 'Did you ring the hospital last night?'

'He's coming too.'

'You're picking him up on the way, then?' Though she knew the arrangements, she needed to make sure.

'I told you, Miss Heather. He'll no' be bothering you again.'

Heather writhed inwardly with guilt. Perhaps she should have sent flowers, written to apologise to him, but Bella had been so cagey, not telling her where he had been taken, protective, she suspected, of them both.

'Will his knee recover properly, do you think?'

'His knee's just fine.'

The truth was that Heather had not wanted to see Malcy, preferred to forget he existed. She remembered exactly why she had taken the gun but was confused as to how she had come to shoot him. She must have been dreadfully drunk.

'What about his things?'

'All packed. He'll no' be coming back, Miss Heather. We'll neither of us be coming back.'

Heather closed her eyes, shaking her head from side to side. 'I don't know what to say. It's been so long.'

In the silence that followed, both of them thought, how will the other manage on her own? But where Heather's feelings were full of guilt that she could so easily part with the two of them, Bella thought, 'it's high time I was away.'

'Maybe I'll come and visit you at the Lodge one day.'

'You'll always be welcome,' said Bella, moving to the door.

'Before you go,' said Heather, 'there are a couple of envelopes on the dressing table, one for each of you.' She had written them both substantial cheques partly out of genuine gratitude and partly out of guilt.

Bella shook her head.

'Please, Bella. It would make me feel much better. I'm sure Malcy won't say no.'

But Bella was stubborn. 'I'm needing nothing and nor is he.'

Heather put on her slippers. 'I'm coming down to see you off.'

'You stay put,' said Bella firmly. 'It's a cold morning.'

'It's the least I can do.' She reached for her dressing gown.

Downstairs, Mrs Bushy had arrived with gifts; a framed verse illuminated with pink and gold roses entitled *Friendship* for Bella and a wallet for Malcy with his initials on the corner.

'He's a bit close with his cash,' she joked. 'See and tell him I said so.'

She had been told that he had fallen down the basement stairs, concussed himself and cut open his head which accounted for all the blood.

Bella put the gifts in her bag and shook the cook's hand. 'Come here,' said Mrs Bushy, put her arms round her and hugged her close. 'I'll miss you both and that's God's truth.' She shed some tears, but Bella's eyes were dry. There was a vast empty wilderness in her head with no flowers.

Curly stowed away three bulging suitcases and then dragged out a roped wooden chest. 'Cripes, what have you got in here,' he joked, 'the crown jewels?'

Heather watched him manoeuvre it into the back of his van. She recognised one of the Indian lead-lined boxes that had first belonged to Miles' grandfather who had been in the Indian army. What had induced Bella to choose that? When she had asked her if she might borrow a chest from the attic for her possessions, Heather had envisaged something smaller, but the thought was fleeting as she stood on the back doorstep hugging her arms round her body. Curly engaged gear. Bella looked back once, her black eyes large and blank.

Heather

'Queer folk, the Scots,' said Mrs Bushy waving vigorously. 'She never turned a hair after all these years, and, as for Malcolm, who'd have thought he'd ever go? I bet you he'll be back one of these days.'

Heather was silent. With that critical inner eye so quick to condemn her own motives, she perceived the truth. She knew why Bella had taken the lead-lined chest. There had been no ambulance in the night, no hospitalisation. Malcy had died of his wound and Bella was taking the responsibility. As long as she, Heather, remained in Nightingales, his ghost would stay to accuse her, to haunt her nights, to burden her days.

It occurred to her briefly that she herself should go to the police, but she dismissed the idea as soon as it was born, reasoning that Bella would then be implicated, but that was only an excuse. She would not go to the police on her own account.

On her way back to her room she called in at the cellar, and, after a moment of hesitation, she took Miles' last bottle of special Napoleon. John Spencer's visit, postponed from earlier in the week, had been re-arranged for that afternoon. She would save it for then, probably. Celebrate.

Suddenly she was crying. Tears poured from her eyes, scalded her throat, soaked her pillow as she flung herself face down on her bed, left her sobbing and gasping.

Not a celebration then: a wake.

Epilogue

It was a mild night, 45 degrees Fahrenheit, and the earth nicely friable, perfect planting conditions. The sky was cloudy, with only a few stars visible and it was dark in the garden for the street lamps of Ladymuir did not penetrate so far.

Bella dug for two and a half hours by torchlight, then she took the wheelbarrow to the back door...

After she had burned all her bedding in the bonfire site behind the gardens at Nightingales she had washed and sewn Malcy carefully into one of Miss Heather's good damask tablecloths and then tied him in two black plastic refuse sacks, but now, as she wheeled him down the garden path, it occurred to her that the plastic would delay decay, so she took them off. The linen shroud gleamed faintly in the near-dark. She no longer needed the torch. Her eyes had grown accustomed to the night.

Then she dropped in the bible, or rather its empty shell. The contents she had burned in the open grate in the sitting room the previous evening.

Lastly, she covered him. There was earth left over so she spread it across the rest of the plot she had dug over the day before and raked it level. As she finished, it began to rain. The rake tracks would be obliterated by daylight.

When she had finished she stood by the grave. No one would know he was there. Poor wee Malcy was safe.

As she scraped the mud off the rake and wiped her boots on the frayed mat outside the back door of the Lodge, she thought about planting sweet peas, a fragrant hedge of singing pastel blooms. Miss Heather's favourite flower. If she called at the Lodge in the late summer she could get a bunch.

After a cup of tea she went to bed and slept the clock round.